LETHAL WELCOME

There was no way I was leaving this house until we'd searched it. I ran the license plate from our thug's car. Before it came back, Rocky had organized his entry team and they were heading to the front door with two other uniformed officers.

"Gillespie," the first officer called out to me, holding up his radio. "Dispatch is calling you."

I was standing by the garage and had paused to hear what the dispatcher was saying. Rocky and the officers took a position at the front door, their guns drawn. The dispatcher repeated the plate of the goon's car and continued with, ". . . comes back stolen out of San Francisco."

I wondered if Rocky had heard. He knocked on the door, then called out, "Police! We have a warrant." Standard procedure even though we were pretty certain the place was unoccupied. He turned the knob, then jiggled it. "Locked," he said. "I'm going to kick it in."

I hugged the wall at the bottom of the steps.

Rocky moved back a few feet.

He took aim, kicked at the door.

And the whole damn thing exploded in a flash of fire.

ROBIN BURCELL

DEADLY LEGACY

AVON BOOKS
An Imprint of HarperCollinsPublishers

This is a work of fiction. Names, characters, places, and incidents are products of the author's imagination or are used fictitiously and are not to be construed as real. Any resemblance to actual events, locales, organizations, or persons, living or dead, is entirely coincidental.

AVON BOOKS
An Imprint of HarperCollins*Publishers*
10 East 53rd Street
New York, New York 10022-5299

Copyright © 2003 by Robin Burcell
ISBN: 0-06-105787-8
www.avonmystery.com

First Avon Books paperback printing: February 2003

Avon Trademark Reg. U.S. Pat. Off. and in Other Countries, Marca Registrada, Hecho en U.S.A.
HarperCollins ® is a trademark of HarperCollins Publishers Inc.

Printed in the U.S.A.

10 9 8 7 6 5 4 3 2 1

To my husband, Gary, for always believing in me. (Now if I can just get him to believe that the time I spend napping on the couch is how I create scenes for my books, I'll have it made.)

A portion of the author's royalties will be donated to COPS (Concerns of Police Survivors), in memory of the men and women who have given their lives in the line of duty. COPS provides resources to assist in rebuilding the lives of surviving families of law enforcement officers killed in the line of duty.

DEADLY
LEGACY

1

Another Saturday night, and I was home alone. In my line of work, I knew better than to make any plans. If I did someone was murdered. If I didn't someone was murdered. It was easier not to make plans. I tried to overlook that it was a hell of a lot lonelier, too.

Sometimes it made me wonder what had possessed me to become a cop.

But that's what I was. Homicide inspector. San Francisco PD. And for all the glory it brought me, if you could call it glory, I still thought about what would have happened if I'd chosen a different career. Some nine-to-five thing, where I wasn't waiting for the call that told me to put my life on hold because someone had lost theirs. I glanced at the TV news, watched the smiling face of Senator Harver, who was announcing his intention to run for Governor, and wondered if he'd ever regretted his career choice.

I switched the channels, pausing on the latest incarnation of *Star Trek*. What I really wanted was a beer, but I was on call, and right about the time I was actually concerned about *Star Trek*'s plot, the phone rang.

I stared at it, not sure if I wanted to answer it, and knowing full well that my pager and cell phone would both start up if it was work. Then again, maybe it *was* a normal call. At eleven P.M.? Right.

I answered on the fourth ring, just as my pager went off. "Hello?"

"Kate?" My partner, Rocky Markowski.

"Rocky," I said, forcing a lightness to my voice. "Any chance you were lonely and just needing company?"

"Yeah. Me and the two dead people sitting in a car in the So Ma area," he said.

Great. I took down the location and told him to give me a half hour. I dressed in jeans, a turtleneck, and a hooded sweatshirt, then brushed my shoulder-length brown hair into a ponytail. Ten minutes later, holstered gun and badge tucked safely on my belt, I was heading down my stairs and knocking on my landlord's kitchen door, because his car was blocking mine in the driveway.

It was chilly out, maybe in the low fifties, typical Bay Area conditions for early summer nights, and as I drove down the street, I cranked up the stereo. Much to my chagrin I heard Cat Stevens belting out, *"Another Saturday night and I ain't got nobody . . ."* I wasn't sure what bothered me more. That he seemed to be singing my life on the radio, or that I was old enough to know who he was. I quickly found another channel, a little more modern pop. Traffic on University Avenue wasn't too bad, and 880 even lighter. I zipped across the Bay Bridge in the Fast Trak lane and made it to the city in twenty minutes flat. Driving like that left no time to contemplate what one couldn't have—like a life that didn't involve leaving home in the middle of the night to go look at dead people.

I took the first exit which took me into the So Ma area, which was what the locals called everything located south of Market Street. It was the home to some killer deals on clothes during the day (the original designer outlets before outlet malls became all the rage).

The street dead-ended beneath the on ramp to the Bay Bridge, and at night, with the columns and expanses of freeway overhead, gave true meaning to the term concrete jungle. This one happened to be lit with flashing red, blue, and amber three-sixties from the radio cars at the perimeter. A uniformed officer waved me through after seeing my gold star, which I held to the window. I parked just a short way past him, popped my trunk, and got out a pair of latex gloves, my notebook, pen, and Stinger flashlight. I wrote down my time of arrival, 11:28 P.M.

Rocky stood about fifteen yards ahead, speaking to a number of uniformed officers. Beyond them was a small two-door sedan, looked like a white Mercedes, lit up by two radio car spotlights. A crime scene investigator in dark blue coveralls was snapping photos of the exterior of the car, another was taking photos of the surroundings, their flashes going off one after the other like giant fireflies bobbing beneath the freeway. Rocky saw me and walked over. He was a short man, stocky, with a flattop haircut and a round face. Tonight he wore a rumpled khaki raincoat, apparently going for the stereotypical detective look.

"Yo, Gillespie," he said.

"Yo back. What are we looking at?"

"Two as-of-yet unidentified bodies in a brand spanking new Mercedes. Driver male, passenger female. Both thirty-something. Vehicle's registered to a Genevieve E. Harrington. Got a radio car watching her house for us."

As he spoke, I gave my name and badge number to the uniformed officer who kept the crime scene log. Rocky did the same, then lifted the yellow tape that was strung several feet around the car as an inner perimeter to keep the curious from getting too close. This late at night not too many ventured out, but there was always a chance.

"Who's the RP?" I asked.

"Couple teens looking for a place to neck. Isn't that what everybody does on Saturday nights?"

"I wouldn't know," I said, wondering what was up with this Saturday night thing. I was feeling older by the minute. "What'd they report?"

"Driving down the street, figuring the couple in the car were doing what they were thinking about doing, until they realized they're dead. Kid called on his cell phone. Got 'em back at the Hall," he said, referring to our all-inclusive building that housed everything City Hall could need, including San Francisco's finest. "Got 'em in separate interview rooms. Called their parents. They're both sixteen."

Too young to be seeing this sort of thing—not that there was a right age. "Any chance someone in the car is this Harrington?"

"Don't know yet. Ran a 10-27 on both, but so far no match on driver's licenses."

"Speculation?" I asked as we stepped up to the driver's door.

"Looks like a murder-suicide."

"Let's keep our fingers crossed that we find a note." Not to be macabre, but one could only hope. A murder-suicide was a closed case. It meant there wasn't a killer on the loose. Time was not of the essence.

I looked into the window, seeing two figures shrouded in shadows cast from the police spotlights behind them.

The driver, a white male, was slumped across the center console, his left arm hung down at his side, his fingertips extended toward the floorboard, where I saw a black semi-auto and below that a square of white paper, the note, I hoped. The back of the man's head seemed oddly shaped, as though someone had taken a club and caved in his skull. A fifteen-thousand-candlepower light beam from my Stinger told me I was looking at the exit wound. "Jesus," I said, aiming the flashlight upward. Bits of flesh, hair, and skull were spattered on the headrest and headliner of the car.

It didn't matter how long I worked Homicide, each time I saw a body ravaged by violence, I was always besieged with a helpless feeling, wondering what would have happened if a patrol car had taken a right instead of a left. What if they'd shone their spotlight down a particular street, seen the car parked . . . what if . . .

No use going there, I thought, as I turned my attention to the female. From where I stood, I couldn't see her face, and I walked to the other side of the car and peered in, and saw the dark bloodstain on the chest of her lavender sweater—from the looks of it, expensive cashmere.

As I aimed my flashlight, my gaze followed the light beam up to her blood-spattered face to her full lips with a coating of bright pink lipstick, her blond hair, and then her brown eyes, wide open in an unseeing stare. A myriad of emotions swept through me. My pulse seemed to slow in my veins. "Oh my God," I whispered.

"What's wrong?" Rocky asked.

I took a step back as I made the connection between the woman and the name of the registered owner of the car. "I know her."

"You do?"

I nodded, swallowed past a lump in my throat. "I, um, haven't seen her in a couple of years . . ." Even now her face brought back a lot of memories, and with it hurt, bewilderment . . . how could I have been so wrong?

"Who is it?"

Little Miss Perfect. The name came unbidden and I felt a stab of guilt at even thinking it at a moment like this. Aloud I said, "Eve Tremayne. She . . . was a college friend. Genevieve is her grandmother, I believe." I knew her simply as "Gran."

Rocky was quiet a moment, then said, "I'm sorry."

"We weren't close," I lied. To remember otherwise hurt

too much, and I forced myself back to the interior of the car, looking for missed clues, anything that would explain this tragedy. It didn't matter what I felt about her, what our relationship was—that we had been best friends. What mattered was that she had been murdered, and for the time being, I was responsible for her. I was a cop. What had happened was in the past and I could deal with it . . . my gaze caught on a square of white on Eve's lap beneath her right hand. I bent down to get a better view, wondering if it was a suicide note.

"Find something?"

"Maybe." On closer inspection I realized it was only a facial tissue with the perfect lip impression in bright pink, her favorite color. The box of tissues it had come from was wedged beneath the driver's body in the center console. And that's when it struck me how odd this was. "If someone's going to blow you away," I said, thinking of Eve and our last parting—my anger and hurt—her nonchalance while she applied her lipstick as she stared at me over her makeup mirror . . . "I'd think the tensions would be a little too high to worry about appearances."

"Your point being?"

"Would she take the time to apply lipstick if she was about to be killed?"

"Well, I wouldn't," Rocky said, aiming his flashlight at her lips, "but only because that shade doesn't go with my outfit."

I smiled, knowing he was trying to cheer me in the only way he knew how. "Yeah," I said, nodding at the front of his coat. "It's hard to find a color that goes with aged mustard."

"That's chartreuse to you." He looked down, smoothing out his lapel. "What the hell color's chartreuse anyways?"

"About the same color as crawdad guts."

"That'll teach me to use words I can't spell," he said as we worked our way around the car again, trying to see if there was anything we'd overlooked. The light moment didn't last, however, because I couldn't stop the unbidden memory of the last time I'd seen Eve—not something I wanted to replay. And with that thought came my father's constant words: "Why can't you be more like her?"

I hated that he had compared me to Eve. Everyone idolized her. She fed the homeless, helped out at the shelters, gave to her church.

To my father—and everyone else—Eve had been perfect, and what they didn't know wouldn't hurt them. But I knew . . .

Rocky cocked his head, eyeing me. "Earth to Kate . . . ?"

"What?" I asked, drawing my thoughts back to the present.

"I asked if you think that's a note by the gun or more lipstick prints?"

"Sorry," I said. "Thinking about something else." I looked at the white square on the floorboard near the male victim's fingertips. "Could be a note. Definitely not tissue."

"Any idea who her friend is?"

"Not a clue. Like I said, I haven't seen her in a few years."

"Tremayne. Where have I heard that name?"

"Her father ran for District Supervisor a few years back."

"That's where I heard it. Wasn't he the front-runner, dropped out all of a sudden because of bad health or something?"

"That's him."

"So what was the real scoop?" he asked, as we strolled over to where one of the crime scene techs was doling out coffee from a thermos.

"The real scoop?"

"Yeah. Why'd he really drop out? Someone got something on him, right?" he asked, handing me a Styrofoam cup.

"I wouldn't know," I said, hoping he'd leave it at that. I sipped at the too-strong brew, trying not to grimace over the taste, and was grateful when one of the CSIs called out that it was a suicide note on the floorboard by the gun. Rocky immediately went over to see, and I followed.

Once it was photographed at every angle, the CSI lifted it out with gloved hands to let us have a look, and Rocky read it aloud. " 'Sorry it had to end this way.' Signed, 'Josh.' " He shrugged. "That makes it nice and tidy. Or it will once the ME confirms it."

"You have doubts?" the CSI asked.

"You know what they say. It ain't over—" Rocky stopped, looked at me, apparently noticed I was a million miles away, and put his arm around my shoulder. "What are you thinking about?" he asked me as I stared at the steam rising from my cup.

"Making the notifications." I hadn't seen the Tremaynes in years. They'd be devastated and I wasn't sure if I wanted to be the one to tell them. I didn't want them to ask why I had suddenly dropped from Eve's life—I didn't want anyone to ask—and wondered if I could be taken off the case. But I knew my duty. "We should probably contact her parents first," I said.

Several minutes later Rocky dropped off his car at the Hall and I picked him up there before heading out to the Tremaynes, worried about how Eve's mother would receive me. I'd always felt that she barely tolerated my presence, that I was not the sort she wanted for her daughter's friend. Eve's father was a different story, however, making me feel welcome. He'd always called me his "other daughter"—not that it mattered now. I had cut off all ties to the Tremaynes, and to my relief, Eve's parents weren't home.

"The grandmother's?" Rocky asked.

I looked at my watch. Almost two A.M., which translated

to oh-dark-thirty in cop talk—anytime after midnight. "That's about our only alternative," I said.

Our drive took about five minutes, a time any commuter would kill for during daylight hours. A patrol car was blacked out and parked about a half block down the hill, the officers having kept an eye on the place from the initial call and finding the vehicle with the bodies. Rocky turned off his headlights as we pulled up beside the officers' car and identified ourselves.

"Nothing moving since we got here," the driver said. His face was shadowed in the confines of the patrol car so that it appeared I was talking to a silhouette.

"What time was that?" I asked.

"Maybe around twenty-three-thirty hours?" he said, turning to his partner, who nodded.

I wrote down the time for our report. "You mind coming up while we check on the premises?" Not that I expected any trouble from Mrs. Harrington, but I didn't want to be mistaken for a prowler. People tended to panic at night, bring out the heavy artillery if they don't see a uniform.

"Not a problem."

We parked about two buildings down and walked up with the younger officer, P. Worth, according to his name tag, and a rookie according to his face. He looked barely old enough to drive. His partner, an older white-haired man, followed, and I quickly went over the situation with the officers as we approached, at the same time contemplating how to tell Mrs. Harrington that her granddaughter was the victim of a murder-suicide. It was not an easy thing to do with someone you didn't know very well. My past with Eve made it more difficult. Perhaps for selfish reasons I didn't want anything dredged up, questions as to why I had cut myself off from Eve so suddenly all those years ago. If I was lucky, I told myself, Mrs. Harrington wouldn't be home either.

I'd been to her house before, two stories that from the architecture and smooth plastered siding appeared to have been constructed in the 1920s or '30s. A hedge of boxwood surrounded a sundial amid a bed of flowers, giving the place the illusion of having a front yard.

I'd shared Thanksgiving dinner here and recalled how sweet Mrs. Harrington had been, which made me realize that I didn't want to appear at her door with what must surely look like an army of cops. I asked Ramirez, the older officer, to wait outside by the garage with Rocky while Worth accompanied me. We stood on either side of the door, a practice ingrained on us from day one, basic officer safety. I rang the bell just as I had all those years ago, when Eve had invited me on a whim to stop by on my lunch hour because I was on duty that Thanksgiving.

Hearing nothing, I pressed the doorbell again and waited, almost anxiously, wishing that Shipley and Zimmerman had been on call this week instead of me.

"Maybe it's out of order," Worth said.

"Maybe," I said, rapping sharply on the wood panel. The first knock caused the door to push slightly open, bringing with it the sound of the TV droning on in the background.

Definitely not a good sign.

I'd been to enough murder-suicides to know that there was a good chance there might be more victims.

"You think we should go in?" Worth asked.

Rookies. "We need to do a welfare check."

I radioed Dispatch that we were making entry, looked over, and got a thumbs-up from Rocky that he and Ramirez had heard my radio traffic. My flashlight in one hand, my gun in the other, I waited until Worth was ready. When he gave me a nod, I pushed the door open the rest of the way and shouted, "Police!"

We waited a split second, then entered, the beams of our

flashlights flicking over couches, tables, empty doorways, and knickknacks centered on little crocheted doilies. The rooms were large and we cleared each, along with every closet, and came up with nothing. So far, other than the front door being unlocked and the TV being left on, everything appeared undisturbed, and I was somewhat relieved. Now all that was left was the garage, accessed by a set of steps that led down. The door was locked from the inside, a good sign, but no guarantee that all was well.

I nodded to Officer Worth. We aimed our weapons and flashlights, unlocked and opened the door, burst through. And came face to face with Eve's grandmother, Mrs. Harrington, crying in the middle of the garage.

2

We made sure the room was clear, then rushed forward.

"What happened?" I asked as we helped Mrs. Harrington to her feet. She was so small and frail, and I didn't remember her having hair that white, or being that old—in her eighties, I guessed.

"I-I don't know," she answered, pulling a tissue from the pocket of her blue terrycloth robe. She dabbed at her eyes, then stopped when her gaze focused on me. "Kate? Is that you?"

"Yes, Mrs. Harrington."

"What on earth are you doing here?"

"We found your car and were worried about you," I said, not wanting to give her any more than what I thought she could handle right then.

"My car . . . ?" Tears rolled down her wrinkled cheeks and I wondered if she was beginning to understand the nature of our presence.

I glanced at Officer Worth. "Do me a favor. Go sit with her while I bring my partner up to speed."

"Will do." He took her arm and helped her up the steps and into the house while I opened the garage door, then closed it after Rocky and the other patrol officer stepped in.

"I take it you found something?" Rocky asked.

"Mrs. Harrington."

"Who's in her Mercedes?"

"We haven't gotten the full story yet." I called in a Code 4 on the radio, then gave them a quick rundown.

When we walked into the house, Mrs. Harrington was fiddling with her portable stereo. Officer Worth stood to one side, shrugging his shoulders at my questioning look. "She seems to think it's broken," he said.

"Mrs. Harrington—"

"I don't think they took anything," she said, opening the CD player. "They were burglars, weren't they?"

"I don't know," I said gently. "Can you tell us what happened?"

"It was dark. Someone hit me on my head and I was locked out, and I didn't know if they were outside waiting . . . I-I stayed in the garage. I couldn't find my glasses."

They were hanging from a chain around her neck and I tapped at them. "You probably couldn't see them in the dark."

"Oh dear. I do that all the time."

"Are you hurt? Do you need an ambulance?"

"No. I'm more worried about my stereo. Do you think they tried to take it and something happened? I can't get it to work. The classical music Eve brought over won't play. Well, I think it's classical. She's taking violin lessons."

In all the years I knew Eve, I'd never heard her play, and wondered if she carried her violin case around like a prop. But it was not my place to disillusion her grandmother. I had come here to make a notification, but she looked so fragile, pale . . .

"Mrs. Harrington. I know this isn't easy right now, but about what happened here tonight—"

"I-I can't . . . can we finish tomorrow? I'm really very tired."

People in shock tend to act in odd ways, and she was certainly exhibiting signs. "Does Eve live here with you?" I asked. I knew Eve had talked about moving closer to her grandmother, but that had been a long time ago.

"No, no. My grandson, Lucas, stays here. Do you remember him? Eve's cousin?"

I had only a vague recollection of a scrawny blond kid just out of high school. "I think so."

"He's all grown up now and just moved in with me. Such a nice young man. He's out to dinner with some friends. And Eve lives next door now. It's so nice to have my grandchildren near. And I have a handyman who is in and out. He takes care of the apartment building behind us."

"Did your grandson take your car?"

"Lucas? He has his own car. One of those little Volkswagens."

"Do you know who has your car?"

Her eyes welled with tears at the question, and my heart went out to her. Maybe she knew why we were here. Even so, I was afraid to tell her. She didn't look well.

"Are you sure you wouldn't like to sit down?"

She nodded and I helped her to the couch just as someone opened the front door with a key.

I glanced up to see a rather handsome sandy-haired man, late twenties, early thirties, wearing blue jeans and a gray wool sweater, a small pizza box in his hands. There was a definite resemblance to Eve and I assumed he was her cousin Lucas, definitely grown up. He stood in the doorway, eyeing the two uniformed officers standing in the living room.

"Gran?" he asked, looking from her to each one of us in turn. "What's wrong?"

"Can I talk to you a second?" I said.

"About what?" he asked. "Who are you?"

"Inspector Gillespie. I'm . . . looking for information on your grandmother's car," I said.

He glanced at his grandmother, then nodded at me, holding his hand out toward the kitchen, apparently sensing there was more wrong than what I was telling him.

I followed him in and he set the pizza box on the counter. "What is going on?" he asked.

"Eve is dead—"

"What?"

"We found her and an unknown man in your grandmother's car, both shot. Her parents weren't home and we came here, found your grandmother in the garage, crying. Someone came in the house and locked her in there. She said she wasn't hurt."

"Oh my God." He leaned against the counter, looking up to the ceiling as though composing himself. After several seconds, he said, "Are you saying that Eve's killer came here?"

"I have no idea."

"Gran doesn't know, does she? About Eve?"

"I haven't told her yet."

He closed his eyes, took a breath, then looked at me. "She has a bad heart. We can't tell her. Not tonight. Not after she was attacked," he said, then looked into the living room and saw that she was crying.

He rushed to her side and put his arms around her, holding her to him.

"Tell me you're not hurt, Gran?" he asked as I walked into the room.

"I'm fine," she said, wiping her eyes on the sleeve of her robe. "I heard a noise in the garage and went to check. Someone hit me on my head. And they . . ." Her mouth started trembling, but she took a breath, squared her shoulders, and seemed to force a smile to her face. "But I'm okay. I don't think anything was stolen."

I asked, "Did they say anything to you?"

"Well, yes. One of them said they had the wrong house and then they left. But I was locked out and I couldn't get back in . . ."

"How long ago was that?"

She looked over at the clock. "An hour, maybe?"

"Gran? Why wasn't Eve here? She was supposed to stay with you while I was gone."

She looked up at him, her hand covering her mouth. "Oh dear. I forgot to feed the cat. Bruno must be starved. I've got to go look for him. He's probably snuck right into her house again."

"Mrs. Harrington. Do you know where Eve went?"

Mrs. Harrington shook her head. "She left in my car."

"Gran. You can't mean she took off in *your* car. She has her own."

"That's exactly what I mean," she said. "Why do you think I went into the garage? They've been gone for hours and I thought they were finally home. They went to go visit *her*. My housekeeper's daughter."

"They?" I said, figuring we finally had some possible names for our unknown male. I pulled out my notebook and pen.

"Marguerite O'Dell, and—"

"No, Gran," Lucas said. "She means, who took off in your car?"

"Oh. Eve and my handyman," she said.

"And what's your handyman's name?" I asked.

"Joshua Redding," she said.

"Do you have an address for him?"

"In my phonebook."

"I'll get it for you, Gran," Lucas said, walking into the

kitchen. He returned a moment later with the phonebook in hand.

I copied Joshua's address into my notes. "You said Eve lives next door?"

"Yes."

"And when you were attacked, you heard one of the men say that they had the wrong house?"

She nodded.

"We'll need to check her residence."

Without asking, Lucas walked over to a small table by the door, opened the drawer, and pulled out a key chain with a pewter cat hanging from it. "This is to her house," he said. "It's the gray house on that side." He pointed to the east.

"Just to be safe," I told Lucas as he handed me the key, "we need you both to stay here, and keep the doors locked."

"Of course." He put his arm around his grandmother and we headed out the door.

Once we were out of earshot, Rocky asked, "What the hell's going on here? We did just leave an open-shut murder-suicide, didn't we?"

"I don't know."

"You think someone knew that Eve was murdered? Or is this just some sort of weird coincidence?"

"Hard to imagine it's coincidence," I said as we came up on Eve's place. Her house was similar in structure to her grandmother's. The front door was locked and there didn't appear to be any sign of forced entry. I wasn't about to enter, however, until I had checked the entire perimeter, and so I assigned Worth to watch the front. Once he found a place of concealment, Rocky, Officer Ramirez, and I moved to the side yard. A wrought-iron gate was closed, and Rocky reached in and lifted the latch, swinging it open.

As we passed through, I stepped on something hard. I looked down and saw a padlock gleaming in the dim light from the street lamp. I checked closer, saw it had been cut, and pointed it out to Rocky, then Ramirez. They both nodded. This was not good.

We traversed the length of the house, ducking beneath windows. When we reached the end of the house, we stopped. The backyard was small, neat, consisting of a grassy area and a brick walkway that led to a moonlit bench near the ivy-covered back wall. To our left, three wooden steps led up to a porch, painted gray to match the house. Two French doors faced out to the backyard, and even where I stood at the base of the porch stairs, it wasn't hard to see the splintered wood near the lock.

I called in an "open door" and the dispatcher ordered our channel cleared for emergency traffic only. Officer Ramirez took a position at the back of the house. Rocky and I stood on either side of the doors, held our weapons at the ready. Chances were good that the suspects had left by now. Enough time had passed. Most burglars were in and out in a matter of minutes.

But then, most burglars didn't hit houses belonging to possible homicide victims.

3

I opened the door and a large gray tabby flew out, startling us. I took a calming breath and waited for Rocky to signal he was ready. When he nodded, I aimed my gun toward the door. "Police Department!" I shouted. "Come out or we'll send in the dog."

It was a ruse for the stupider crooks. Amazed me every time it worked. We gave it a few seconds, heard nothing, and entered.

Rocky followed me, our flashlight beams flickering over the expensive furnishings. No matter how softly we walked, our footsteps echoed across the hardwood floor—an eerie sound, as though the house knew its mistress was never returning. I only hoped our suspect, if he was in here, couldn't hear it.

To our right was the kitchen, and we cleared that next. I pointed down the hall to the first door on the left. I stood to one side, turned the knob, then waited for Rocky's ready signal. I wouldn't move until he gave it. I had to depend on him being behind me, to cover me should anything happen.

I felt his tap on my shoulder, heard him whisper, "Go!"

At his signal I opened the door far enough to see two wingback chairs, a sofa, a music stand and violin. Everything picture-perfect, just like the Eve I knew. The door swung to the right, so I moved to the left. Rocky came in on my heels, the beams from our flashlights sweeping the room. It was clear. We immediately moved to the next door down the hall.

Rocky gave the tap, whispered, "Go!"

We entered a bedroom. I cleared the right and front, Rocky the left. There was a silver brush-and-mirror set, and next to it, a tray with jewelry on it. I took the mirror, pointed toward the four-poster bed. Rocky nodded. Paused a few feet away with his weapon and flashlight aimed beneath the bed. I was about to use the mirror to peer beneath it when I heard something in the hall. I glanced toward the door, caught a movement.

And saw the profile of a man wearing black.

I aimed. "Police!"

He bolted.

Rocky and I flew after him as I called out on the radio. We burst into the living room. He ran out the front door, fled down the walkway. Worth jumped from the bushes, tried to tackle him. Missed. Something flew from the suspect's pocket as he slipped past Worth. We chased after him and a dark-colored sedan pulled out from the curb. The suspect got in. The car sped off, its tires screeching.

"Son of a bitch."

Ramirez came running around from the back. "Gone?" he asked.

I nodded, angry and frustrated. "Don't suppose anyone got a plate number?"

"Too fast," Rocky said, trying to catch his breath.

"Got a CD," Worth said, pointing to the ground where he'd jumped on the suspect.

"There's a big haul," I said, eyeing the CD. The Beatles' *A Hard Day's Night*.

"So maybe the suspect likes oldies," Rocky said.

I called in what little vehicle description we had, then we

went back in—not that we expected to find anyone. We cleared the house again, making our way to the room we hadn't yet reached, and I remembered thinking that I wanted Eve's house to be different. Everything seemed so . . . normal.

And then we came to that last door. The room where the suspect undoubtedly had been when we entered.

Apparently it had been secured by a deadbolt lock, and judging by the shattered doorframe, kicked in. I pushed open the door, saw a set of stairs leading up and another door ajar. We ascended, pushed open the door at the top, and stopped in our tracks.

"Holy shit," Rocky said.

I simply stared in shock. Even after all this time her betrayal hurt, and I tried to get past it. I had wanted to be wrong about her.

Rocky stepped into the room. "Guess Miss Tremayne did a lot more than play violin. I'd say she was playing kinky."

I didn't know what to say and I followed him into the room, wanting to detach myself from what I knew about her so that I could look at everything with the cold eye of an investigator. There were whips and chains on the walls, an assortment of sex toys lined up neatly on a table, bonds of leather and spiked metal, much of it designed to elicit pain. The ceiling was mirrored, as was one entire wall—the wall that would have had a window on it, and the remaining walls were paneled in dark wood. I suspected the room was heavily insulated, since the square footage seemed less than what the size of the house would have indicated, and the window was undoubtedly covered to keep anyone on the outside from hearing what went on within.

I was sick to my stomach. I didn't want to be here seeing this, but I continued on, opening a door that led into a closet filled with leather clothes, cuffs, and collars. "Must be the costume room," Rocky said, holstering his weapon and lifting a black leather bustier.

I holstered my weapon, had the presence of mind to call in that we were Code 4 to prevent them sending anyone in to look for us, then found it.

The photo album Eve had told me about.

It was large, leather-bound. I carefully opened it, forcing myself to look at every picture, four per page, each in its own plastic sleeve. They were all photographs of Eve next to various men. They were more suggestive than explicit—a good thing, I supposed—but I knew the truth behind them. Some of the men I recognized, some I didn't. Politicians, businessmen, fathers, husbands, sons. I figured the album spanned the last ten or so years. I scanned them quickly, praying I had been wrong.

And came across the one photo that told me otherwise.

My gut twisted. I glanced up at Rocky. He was busy searching through a closet. I took a breath, unable to believe I was even contemplating this. I was about to do something that went against everything I believed in as a police officer at a crime scene, and my hand shook as I reached for the page. I slipped the photo from the plastic. Slid it into my pocket.

Rocky looked up at that precise moment. "What's that?" he asked, strolling over. "Her big book of conquests?"

I cringed inwardly at his words, but managed to remain calm on the outside.

"Who knows?" I said, casually flipping past the page where I'd taken the photo, then continuing toward the back of the album—only to land on a page with a photo of my ex-husband's face staring up at me. Eve's hand rested on his thigh in a manner that exuded intimacy. All semblance of calm fled and more anger and hurt surfaced. "Damn you, Reid," I said.

Rocky whistled. "Definitely not a good thing when you

discover your ex-husband's photo in a dead lady's apartment. What do you suppose it's doing here?"

I didn't answer. The pictures seemed sequential, which meant this had been taken in the last couple of years. Reid was seated next to Eve, his arm around her protectively, and I recognized the tie he was wearing in the photo. Red and blue paisley. I'd given him that tie the Christmas after we were married—and taken it to the Goodwill the month after he'd left me.

"Maybe the photo was taken after your divorce?" Rocky suggested.

I didn't answer.

"You want I should take him out for ya?" Rocky asked in his best *Godfather* imitation.

I appreciated his levity, the break it gave me, and I forced a smile. "Not worth the cost of the ammunition," I said, moving away from the book, hating that she still had this power to hurt me. "We better get back to the Harringtons'. Let them know what's going on, get some CSIs out here."

"There's a photo missing."

I froze at his words.

"You think the burglar took it?" he asked. "It seems odd that one's missing from right smack in the middle of this page."

I made myself look at the photo album, realized he was on the second to the last page—not the beginning, from where I had taken the photo in my pocket.

He was right. There was *another* photo missing.

He would have thought it strange if I didn't comment, so I said, "We'll have to make sure the CSIs dust the book."

We started down the steps. "Sorta makes you wonder whose photo it was," he said.

"Doesn't it?" Yet all I could think was that I wasn't sure if I wanted to know.

"Probably too much to hope that this was your basic cat burglar?"

"At this point," I said, trying to keep my mind strictly on the crime at hand, "I'm wondering if it's too much to hope that our murder-suicide is really a murder-suicide. Why would someone come breaking into this house right after Eve was killed?"

"Because they liked sex toys and Beatles music?"

"Funny," I said. We exited the house and I posted Ramirez at the door to wait until the CSIs arrived, then told Worth to accompany us back to the Harrington house. The gray tabby sat on the sidewalk, watching us, its eyes glowing.

"That the cat we almost shot?" Rocky asked.

"Looks like it." I made a kissing noise. "Here, Bruno. Here, kitty."

The cat dignified me with a meow, but didn't move. I strolled over to it, calling softly, and then leaned down and picked it up. It started purring as I scratched its head and I carried it to the house. Rocky knocked on the door and Lucas Harrington opened it.

"Lucas?" his grandmother called as we stepped into the entryway. "Is everything okay?"

He turned, startled that his grandmother had come up behind him. "Gran."

She looked at the cat in my arms. "Thank goodness. Eve would be heartbroken if anything happened to him."

Her words struck me, and I wanted to insulate her from what I knew. That her granddaughter was dead. "Mrs. Harrington . . ."

She looked up at me and I saw tears through her eyeglasses. She pulled them off, letting them dangle from their chain like a necklace. "Something's happened to Eve, hasn't it?"

I wasn't sure what to say, or rather, how to say it.

She shook her head. "Of course something happened to her. How silly of me to think you'd be here if it hadn't. A car accident, right? You said you found my car. And she was in it, wasn't she?"

"Gran—" Lucas moved toward her.

"No. Eve is coming back. She was just going to run Josh to see that girl. She's coming back—right?"

No one answered. No one could, and she turned away, wiping the perspiration from her brow. "Is it hot in here?"

"You should sit down, Gran."

"We were going to the ball together," she said. "Eve was going to take me to the Black and White Ball. She wanted to hear the violinists in the symphony. It's all Josh's fault. If he hadn't—"

"Gran, don't do this."

"Stop it!" she said. "I'm tired of all this secrecy about the O'Dells. Just stop it, stop it, stop—" Her hand clutched her chest. "Oh dear," she said.

And then she sank to the ground.

4

Rocky and I broke Mrs. Harrington's fall. "Oh my God!" Lucas said. "She has a bad heart."

"We need paramedics," I told the rookie officer, his face paling fast.

He nodded, looking around in a panic.

"What are you doing?" Rocky asked him.

"I need a phone to call nine-one-one."

The rookie's partner tapped his radio, mouthing, "You are nine-one-one."

The kid pulled up his mike, his voice high, and called out, "We need paramedics at our location, Code Three. Possible heart attack."

"Ten-four," the dispatcher replied in a much calmer tone. "Medical emergency."

"Gran? Gran?" he said, patting her cheek, trying to rouse her. "Oh, God. Gran?"

I reached over, put my fingers on her carotid, felt a steady but fast pulse. She was breathing, and all we could do was monitor her, make her more comfortable, until the paramedics got there.

It seemed forever, but they finally arrived. Both Lucas and the rookie officer looked panicked as they wheeled her on the gurney out the door. "You're going to be okay," Lucas said, following them.

They transported Mrs. Harrington to the hospital, Lucas riding with her in the ambulance.

After that, we called for CSIs so that we could turn over both crime scenes for processing. It was while we were waiting that I saw a framed snapshot of Eve standing in front of a cabin, her arms held up as though she'd just conquered the world. She'd shown me that photograph the summer after we'd graduated from college, excited because she'd spent several weeks working at a retreat filled with nothing but politicians, who, as she'd said, "oozed power like it was testosterone." And, I realized as Rocky and I walked out the door, that was the beginning of the end of our friendship. I had not seen the signs earlier, and wondered if things might be different if I had . . .

We stopped at a mini-market before heading back to the Hall. I was dumping extra packets of fake cream into my coffee, Rocky adding extra fake sugar to his.

"I'm thinking we can forget about the murder-suicide theory?" he said, as he swirled the granules into the coffee with a red plastic stir stick.

"Pretty safe bet," I said. Which meant I'd removed property from a crime scene related to a homicide, and wrestled with my conscience over the act. Granted, the photo wasn't a piece of evidence that would exonerate someone from murder, but if discovered . . .

How had I let my emotions get the better of me? I shouldn't have removed it, but it was too late now, and I knew I'd have to tell my lieutenant—then pray I didn't get busted down to patrol.

I refused to think about it and we walked out of the store, standing on the sidewalk in the cool night air. "We stay out here long enough," I said, "we can watch the sunrise."

"Yeah. I always liked this time of night when I worked graves. Peaceful."

We stood like that for a few seconds, just staring out into the starry sky. Then out of the blue, he asked, "You hear anything from Torrance?"

His question caught me off guard. Lieutenant Mike Torrance headed up Management Control, SFPD's version of Internal Affairs.

"Officially or unofficially?" I asked. Officially would mean I was in the midst of some IA investigation, not something I'd care to think about. Unofficially was a different story. We'd almost been an item, but neither of us could seem to get it together at the right time—that being the easiest and least painful way to put it.

"Just wondering if you'd talked to him lately. Nice guy."

My ass, I thought as I got in the car. I wasn't sure what was up, but I let the topic of Mike Torrance die a quick death. I was too tired to think about him, and too tired to care. I wanted to go home and put the whole night from me, but knew we needed to ID our male victim. "Let's run by this Josh Redding's house. See if it's him in that car."

The address the Harringtons had given us for Josh Redding was to a one-story house bordering Daly City, and as expected, when we got there, all was dark except the porch light. Rocky rapped sharply on the door, then rang the doorbell once. After about a minute, we saw the mini-blinds separate slightly, then heard a woman's voice calling out, "Who's there?"

"Police," I said, holding up my star for her inspection.

"Oh, um, did you want something?"

No, we always knock on people's doors at oh-dark-thirty, I thought, tired and emotionally drained by everything we'd been through tonight. "Can we talk to you?"

"About what?" She remained where she was, peeking through the blinds.

"Josh Redding?"

"Okay."

She didn't move.

"Maybe not through the window?" I asked her.

"Oh. Hold on," she said, then let the blinds close. A moment later the door opened, revealing a slightly overweight woman in her fifties, her red hair pulled up in curlers on top of her head. "There's no Josh Redding here."

"And you are?"

"His mother, Vera Redding."

"Does he live here?"

"Here?"

I nodded.

"He, um, stays here now and—*who* did you say you were?"

I identified myself, then Rocky, finishing with, "We work Homicide."

"Oh, well, Josh isn't here right now," she said, as though we were the neighbor kids just coming over to play. She tied the sash of her green robe, but didn't move from the doorway.

"Would you mind if we came in for a moment?" I asked, as Rocky shifted beside me, undoubtedly losing patience fast.

"In?" Vera Redding said. "You mean now?"

"Now would be good."

She stood aside, a bland smile fixed on her face as she led us into her kitchen, then asked to see our IDs. After inspecting them closely, she asked, "Has something happened?"

"We're not sure, but we think Josh may have—"

"I don't think I want to hear this," she said, sinking into a chair at the table. "I don't want to hear that my boy is in trouble."

I swept right past that statement. "When did you last see him?"

"Earlier this evening . . . just before dinner. He stopped by after working all day at the apartments that Genevieve Harrington owns. He was driving her car. A white Mercedes."

"Anyone with him?" Rocky asked.

"Genevieve's granddaughter, Eve. She's such a sweet girl. We've known them for years."

I reached into my pocket, pulling out my little notebook, my fingers brushing the photo I'd taken from Eve's room, and I wondered if anyone really knew her at all. "Does he know someone named . . ." I flipped to the page I was looking for. "O'Dell?"

"Marguerite O'Dell?" Her gaze narrowed. "If I never see her again it'll be too soon. She tried to pass off that little brat of hers as Josh's kid, not that he'd listen to me. Well, maybe now he might—" She looked from Rocky to me and said, "Why are you asking me all these questions?"

"There's been . . . an accident. We found the car belonging to Eve's grandmother . . ."

"Oh, dear God."

"We haven't been able to identify the male who was driving."

She buried her face in her hands, shaking her head. "This can't be. I just talked to him. He told me—" She looked up, her eyes glistening. "When did you find him?"

"We don't yet know if it's—"

"When?"

"Between ten-thirty and eleven P.M."

A tear slid down her cheek as she glanced at the clock on the kitchen wall, shaking her head. "It didn't happen. It didn't."

"Mrs. Redding . . ."

"I'm sorry." She brushed at her tears and smiled at me. "Was there something else?"

Shock, I figured. "We need your help."

"My help?"

"For an identification," I said quietly.

"You mean to see if there's a mistake?" she asked, her voice rising in pitch. "That it might not be my son?"

I didn't want to give her false hope, nor did I want to add to her pain, so I didn't answer her question.

She shook her head. "No. I don't have a car. I can't. I—"

"We can give you a ride," Rocky said.

"No, that won't do at all. I'll call my neighbor. That is okay, isn't it? I need to take out my curlers and get dressed. I—" She stood and crossed the room to the counter, picking up the phone, then punched in a number, her neighbor's, I assumed. "Carter? It's me, Vera. Something's happened and I need you to come over. The police are here now." She nodded, said, "Okay," then hung up. "My next-door neighbor is coming over. He'll take me."

"Are you sure?" I asked. "We'd be glad to give you both a ride . . ."

"I think I just want to be with my friend. He'll only be few minutes. I'll-I'll go get dressed."

She walked through the dining area into the living room and then down the hall, leaving us alone.

"Sounds like it's probably him in the car," Rocky said.

"Most likely," I said, jotting down the last of my notes on her statement as someone knocked on the door.

I glanced up as Rocky parted the kitchen blinds. A bald-headed man in a dark gray bathrobe stood on the porch. Rocky let him in and took his personal information for our report, then Vera came out, still in her night clothes. "I really need to eat something first," she said. "I have low blood sugar. Is that okay?"

"It shouldn't be a problem," I said. "If you can just give us an approximate time, that would help."

"Carter?" she asked, looking at her neighbor.

"Don't worry about me," he said. "Just tell me where and when."

"Ten—fifteen minutes?" she asked us. "And then we'll drive straight there?"

"That will be fine," I said.

I gave them each a business card before we left. In the car, Rocky said, "Not bad. If we're lucky, we'll get our second victim identified, and be in bed by lunchtime."

"That's lucky?"

"It is if you want to get out of bed before the game starts this afternoon."

It was close to five in the morning when we returned to the Hall, our plan to finish up some preliminary paperwork, and wait for Vera Redding to show. I was typing a list of witnesses contacted so far and must have dozed off, because I saw Eve staring at me over her compact, applying her lipstick, bright pink. "It's all about power," she said. "And there's nothing you can do about it, so take the photo. Because they're his handcuffs around my wrists, his bed . . . and I have the negatives."

The negatives. I'd forgotten about the negatives . . .

I woke with a start.

"What the hell?" I said. My computer screen was filled completely with *N*s.

"Good morning, Merry Sunshine." Rocky sat at his desk, grinning, his Polaroid camera in hand. He waved a not quite developed photo at me, then dropped it into his top desk drawer and locked it tight.

I didn't have the energy to worry where that picture was going to end up. I'd done something terribly wrong and all for nothing, because I didn't know where the goddamn negatives were. "What time is it?"

"After seven."

Think about the case, I told myself. "Vera Redding?"

"Called to say she was going to be late. That was twenty ago. She should be here any minute. Figured I'd wake you and we can go wait at the morgue. I called the desk downstairs to let them know where to send her."

I got up, stretched out my stiff limbs, and grabbed my jacket. "Radio car have any luck at the Tremaynes'?"

"Still not home," he said, slipping into his raincoat.

We left the office, and our footsteps echoed down the empty hallway as we walked to the elevator, the upper floors deserted this early on a Sunday. "How's Mrs. Harrington doing?" I asked.

"Okay. Panic attack. The doc says he doesn't want her excited in any way. Lucas is still with her."

"We did send a radio car out there to sit on her place, didn't we?" I was beginning to fade fast and couldn't remember.

"We did."

The morgue was adjacent to the Hall, entered off a breezeway from the north terrace. We entered the lobby, walked past the front counter into the viewing area.

We stood around, chatted a few minutes, talked about current cases, told a few dead body jokes. All in a day's work. About seven-twenty, I started worrying. "She did tell you she was on her way, right?"

"That's what I heard," Rocky said, looking at his watch. "Maybe they got caught up in traffic."

"On a Sunday?"

"Okay, maybe she got the times mixed up. She was a little batty, wouldn't you say?"

I thought back to all the nuances of the case and our stilted interview with Vera Redding. I telephoned her house. No answer. "I'm going to send a unit by, see if the neighbor picked her up."

A few minutes after eight, a dispatcher called back. I listened, trying not to swear at her for something that wasn't her fault. "Thanks," I said, hanging up, attempting to remain calm. That lasted about a millisecond. "Son of a bitch."

"What's up?" Rocky asked.

"She's gone. A patrol officer checked with the neighbor. He gave her a ride, all right. To the goddamned airport. Said she caught an eight o'clock flight to Mexico."

5

The unexpected departure of Vera Redding when her son might be in the morgue was puzzling, to say the least, and I was beginning to wonder if anyone involved in this case so far was normal.

"Why would Joshua Redding's mother flee to Mexico if her son was possibly a victim in the morgue?" I asked, thinking aloud.

"She's flakier than we thought and got a good deal on a flight?" Rocky suggested. "So what's next on your agenda?"

"See if we can get our male victim ID'd, for starters," I said, not really having an answer.

"No return on the prints?" Rocky asked the Coroner's investigator.

"None yet," he said. "Not too unusual on the weekend, especially with the problems the computer's been having."

Great. "Let me know when we get something back," I said. "In the meantime I'm thinking we have no choice but to work this as a double murder."

"There goes the game," Rocky said when we were back in our office.

"You'll be home in time."

"This from the girl who already got a nap. I'd like to be home and awake. It helps when you want to see the score."

"Tape it."

"Funny. Where we off to, now?"

"See if either of our victims ever made it by Marguerite O'Dell's place last night." We ran the name in the computer, found an address, and after downing copious amounts of coffee, we drove out there.

The O'Dells lived in a row house, no lawn, and not much different from those around it, except the white daisies in the window box. At last a sign of normalcy, I thought. There was no parking directly in front, typical for the city even on a Sunday morning, and we had to look for a space around the corner. "Keep your fingers crossed," I told him as we made our way down the hill, then up the three steps to her front door.

I rang the bell, and a moment later heard a shuffling just before the door opened as far as the security chain would allow. A young girl with short dark hair peered up at me through the space, her brown eyes alive with curiosity. I put her around six.

"Well, hello there," I said.

"Hello."

"What's your name?"

"I'm not supposed to talk to strangers."

"Very smart." I pulled my star from my belt and showed it to her, then handed her one of my cards. "We're the police."

"You don't look like the police. I don't see a police car or any police clothes."

"You're right," I said, ignoring Rocky's smirk. "Is your mom home?"

"No."

"Is anyone home?"

"Well, *I* am."

Rocky's grin grew wider.

"Anyone else?"

"My grandmother," she whispered. "But I'm not sure we're related. I think she's an alien, maybe stolen by aliens."

"Really?"

"What's a devil's spawn?"

Talk about your loaded question. "It's an expression some people use. Why?"

"Is it when you're related to someone you shouldn't be?"

"*Bonnie!* Get away from that door!" came a voice from within.

"It's the police," the girl called out. To me she said, "I have to go," then shut the door on us.

"Well, what do you make of that?" I asked Rocky.

"Spunky little thing."

I knocked again. This time the door was opened by a woman in her early forties with short brown hair, flecked with gray. Despite her lack of makeup, and her severely plain gray dress, she was very pretty, probably model material in her younger days. She regarded me with narrowed blue eyes and a disapproving stare. "May I help you?" she asked.

"Inspector Gillespie, Homicide detail. This is my partner, Rocky Markowski. We're looking for Marguerite O'Dell."

She stood there.

"May we come in?"

"Very well."

She held the door open, allowing us to enter into the living room. Just out of earshot, Rocky whispered, "Definitely aliens."

I ignored him.

The woman closed the door and turned toward us. "Please, sit down," she said, sounding anything but welcoming.

Markowski and I sat on matching armchairs, dusty-rose colored with tiny flowers imprinted on the fabric. She took a seat on the couch, her movements stiff and precise. To our left was a fireplace, painted white, and over it a single gold cross. Nothing else adorned the white walls. Not a single photograph, book, or magazine, not even a TV. The only thing to read that I saw was a white leather-bound Bible on the coffee table.

"Are you Marguerite's mother?" I asked.

"Yes. Lillian O'Dell."

"What can you tell us about her?"

She sat ramrod straight and looked me directly in the eye. "Marguerite hasn't lived here in over six years and I don't even know her address. There's really not much I can say about her."

"And yet her daughter is here?" It was a guess on my part.

"I have no idea why she brought that child here. She said it was an emergency. She didn't say what."

"Just out of the blue?"

"Yes."

"When was this?"

"Late last night." She looked at her watch. "I happened to be on my way to church when you arrived. Will this take long?"

"I hope not. Was she alone?"

"With her daughter. No one else."

"May I ask why you haven't seen her in six years?"

"What does this have to do with your presence?"

"We're conducting a homicide investigation and any background information will help."

She hesitated, looking down the hallway, catching sight of the girl, who quickly ducked back into whatever room she'd been in. "Marguerite left," she said, her voice turning icy, "because she refused to follow the rules I had set forth."

I translated that to mean she got pregnant and mom didn't approve. Clearing my throat, I glanced at Rocky, who said, "Is it okay if I use your bathroom, Ms. O'Dell?"

"Just down the hall, first door to your left."

"Thanks," he said.

I immediately asked, "What explanation did Marguerite give last night for her sudden reappearance?"

"None," she said, watching Rocky as he headed down the hall.

"Do you know the Reddings? Josh or his mother, Vera?"

She looked at me, her lips pressed together as though she were suddenly displeased. "I have never met the mother. Josh works for the same woman that I do. Mrs. Harrington. My daughter met him there, which I suppose is my fault."

"Why is that?"

"Because I wanted Marguerite to be more like Mrs. Harrington's granddaughter, Eve, so I took her over there whenever I had a chance over the years that I worked there. Marguerite was flighty, irresponsible. Eve was always so . . . well, she put everyone's needs ahead of her own, something Marguerite had a difficult time learning. I . . . wanted them to be friends, and they did for a while—become friends, that is."

The photo was burning a hole in my pocket, and, all guilt for taking it aside, I wanted to pull it out, wave it in front of her face, and prove that Eve wasn't a saint. Instead, I asked, "And what happened to their friendship?"

"Around the time my daughter became pregnant, it ended."

"Do you know who the father is?"

"I suspect Josh Redding."

"Any reason why Josh Redding or Eve Tremayne might have been coming to visit Marguerite last night?"

Once again her glance strayed down the hall before she answered and I wondered if she was worried that the child would overhear. "None whatsoever. Marguerite has assured me that she has repented that part of her life. Why are you asking these questions now?"

I kept my voice low so that I wouldn't be overheard. "We're investigating a homicide. Genevieve Harrington said that Josh and Eve might have come to visit Marguerite last night."

"Josh?" she asked, looking momentarily surprised. "Here? I can't believe that. Eve wouldn't do that. She promised—"

"Promised what?" I asked when she cut herself off.

"That Marguerite wouldn't see him. It was imperative that she *not* see him."

"Why?"

"He tempted her like the devil. Eve understood. She consoled me after Marguerite left. She told me that if Marguerite ever came back, she would keep them apart. Eve, you see, wasn't tempted by the same things. She was different . . ."

To say the least, I thought, as Lillian O'Dell closed her eyes and clasped her hands, saying nothing for several seconds. I wondered if she was praying, when suddenly she said, "I am late for church and my granddaughter is here. Is there anything else?"

I wondered if that was given in order of importance to her. "Any information I can get will be a great help in solving this case and possibly identifying the deceased—which is why I need to speak with your daughter."

She looked at her watch. "I expect her, I'm hoping, after church. If you like, I'll call you when she returns."

"I'd appreciate it," I said, standing, as Rocky came back into the room.

I gave her my card and we left. Markowski and I headed back up the hill and around the corner to where we were parked. I called for a team to sit on her house, watch her if she left or if anyone showed up. I wasn't taking any chances, and without any sleep, Rocky and I were in no condition to watch her ourselves.

"Talk to the kid?" I asked when I was finished with my call.

"Yeah. Cute thing. Doesn't know much, other than her Mom dropped her off here, because she got mad after she found out the pretty lady visited. Don't ask me what that means. But up until yesterday, the kid had never even met her grandmother."

"You get an address on her?"

"Yeah, right. She wouldn't even give me her last name. Said she wasn't allowed to give it out to strange old men."

"She called that one right," I said with a laugh as I unlocked the car. "What'd the rest of the house look like?"

"Like a friggin' nunnery. Nothing on any of the walls, not even a photo."

I started the car, signaled, and pulled out, then parked where we could watch the O'Dell house until the officers arrived. "I'd think the woman would have at least one photo of Marguerite, even if she did leave home in disgrace."

"I'm guessing Marguerite was a little too impure for her mother's tastes. Especially if she was hanging out with Eve Tremayne in her little room of toys and ended up pregnant."

"Try telling that to her mother," I said. "She seems to think that Eve's ready for sainthood."

"Are you sure you're not the one who's prejudiced? Just because someone's into kinky sex doesn't mean they're bad."

Rocky's words echoed in my head long after we'd returned to the Hall, and I sat at my desk, wondering.

"You okay to drive home?" he asked, getting ready to leave himself.

"Yeah. I'll just down some more coffee before I head out."

"See you tomorrow."

"See you."

But I didn't get up after he left. I waited until I heard the door shut after him, then several minutes beyond that, just to make sure he wouldn't walk in on me.

Was I prejudiced? And if so, could I investigate this case with a clear mind, despite my background with Eve?

I pulled out the photo I'd taken from Eve's room, stared at it, and knew without a doubt.

I *was* prejudiced.

I had to be, because right now, even though she was dead, I hated Eve. I hated what she had done, drawn me into her life once more. And I hated that I would have to ask for the case to be reassigned.

Because that meant that I would have to reveal the truth about the face I saw next to hers.

The face of my father.

6

I sealed the photo in an envelope, locked it in my desk, and made a determined effort not to think about it. I didn't succeed. By the time I made it home, I was wired from the excess of coffee, yet mentally exhausted. I turned on the TV, figuring I'd watch something just to wind down and get Eve and my father off my mind, if even for a moment. The next thing I remembered was the phone ringing. I answered it and forced a pleasant "Yeah" from my parched throat.

"Figured you'd need a wake-up call." It was Rocky.

"What time is it?"

"Seven-thirty. My wife said if I was this hard to wake up, you'd probably still be asleep."

I sat up, eyeing the TV. The morning traffic report showed a view of the Bay Bridge. Typical bumper-to-bumper trouble. We were expected early on Mondays. Case load meetings, the lieutenant's way of staying abreast of what we were working on—like I'd want to bring up Eve's case in front of the entire Homicide detail. It was bad enough I'd dreamed about it all night. At least I think, I did.

"Make the requisite excuses," I said. "I'll be there as soon as I can." I dragged myself into the bathroom, turned on the shower, then grimaced at my reflection. There were five diagonal red stripes embedded in my right cheek, marks from the pattern of my couch pillow. Classy.

An hour and a half later I was stepping off the fourth floor elevator. When I walked into the office, Gypsy, the Homicide detail secretary, handed me a file folder. "The responding patrol officer's report on your weekend homicides," she said. "Just now came in."

"Thanks," I said, opening the file to read it.

I slipped past the lieutenant's door to my desk. Rocky wasn't in the office. Ed Zimmerman and his partner, Felix Shipley, were. Zim was about fifty, slightly paunchy, with gray hair and a ruddy face. The top button of his pale blue shirt was undone, his yellow tie loosened.

When he saw me, he grinned and covered the mouthpiece of the phone he'd been speaking into. "Nice cheek marks, Gillespie. We're not keeping you up or anything, are we?"

I gave him a sarcastic smile but didn't comment, since Zimmerman made it his goal in life to irritate me. I used to be concerned with why, until one day it occurred to me that maybe he was a jerk for no reason other than that it was in his genes.

I set the open file folder on my desk, then slipped out of my tan blazer, hanging it on the rack next to Shipley's blue sport coat. "Where's Markowski?" I asked him.

Shipley looked up from a report he was reading. He was younger than Zim, mid-forties, with salt-and-pepper hair. He was also the senior Homicide inspector, having been in the detail for the last ten years. "He called from the corp yard. Apparently someone broke into the car from your weekend homicide. Stole the stereo."

Great. Like there wasn't enough baggage to deal with in this case. Last I heard, the Fencing detail was going to set up a sting on what they thought was an inside job by a city employee. "Haven't they caught that guy yet?"

"They're thinking it's slightly bigger than just the one

worker. Rumor has it that Management Control is looking into it."

"Really," I said, surprised. Management Control, AKA Internal Affairs, was strictly a police watchdog—Lieutenant Mike Torrance's turf. If that was the case, they suspected a cop's involvement.

Before I had a chance to ponder that, Lieutenant Andrews stepped out of his office, loosening his red tie. I did a double take at the sight of him. When I last saw him on Friday, he'd had a full head of very short, very curly black hair. Now there was nothing but dark skin.

"Gillespie?" he said, his voice stern. "You want to play catch-up since you missed this morning's meeting?"

Before I could answer, he turned back into his office.

I glanced at Shipley. "What's with the hair?"

"I'm guessing a midlife crisis thing."

"His wife left him," Zim said, looking up from his report. "Heard it from one of the guys down at Murphy's Law. She's been having an affair with some rich real estate guy."

"Well, that explains his bad mood," Shipley said. "So I wouldn't go rocking his world any when you go in there."

Great. Nothing like adding to his burden. I grabbed the file folders that contained my updates on my active cases, as well as the report from Eve's homicide, but purposefully left my father's photo locked up in my desk. I wasn't sure how or when to broach the subject of taking the photo, but now was obviously not a good time. Maybe if I started off slow, just asked to be removed from the case.

When I entered Andrews's office, he was staring at one of his college football trophies. He'd chosen police work over professional football—our gain, NFL's loss—because his mother had told him it was better to be an unsung hero than a flash in the pan. Every now and then I think it got to him, the wondering what-if, the money he might have made, and now was apparently one of those times.

"You wanted to go over those cases?" I asked.

He looked over at me as I sat. "Markowski told me about your double homicide. He said you knew one of the victims."

"I did. Which is why I need to be taken off the case."

"That part he didn't mention."

"I didn't tell him."

Andrews leaned back in his chair. "You mind telling me?"

"The female is Eve Tremayne. We were . . . friends."

He said nothing, merely waited for me to continue. Suddenly I didn't know what to say, ignoring that the truth might be best.

"We, um, had a disagreement, a falling out of sorts."

"And this is preventing you from investigating her murder because . . . ?"

"I don't think I can be fair or impartial."

"She's dead. What's there to be fair or impartial about?"

Now or never, I thought. "Her relationship with my father."

Andrews steepled his fingers, stared down at his desk for a moment, then looked right at me. His eyelids seemed puffy, his face tired. "You don't think your father's the first man who fell for a girl the same age as his daughter?"

"Of course not. It's just . . ." I didn't know how to say it, or even how much to say.

"He's been dead a long time, Kate. I think you're taking this too personally."

Personally? Of course I am, I wanted to say, because that room we'd found in Eve's house only told a small part of the story . . . but I couldn't bring myself to tell him everything, not when he had his own set of problems to deal with, so I simply said, "If you'd known her like I did, you'd know what I meant."

"I appreciate your concern," he said. "And I can imagine it hasn't been easy stirring up old memories."

"It hasn't," I said, relieved he saw it my way.

"Despite this, I have every confidence that you'll investigate this fairly and impartially."

I stared for a full second, hoping I hadn't heard right. "But I'm *asking* to be taken off."

"And I'm saying no."

"But—"

"Our resources are stretched thin enough as it is. Zim may be a good contact. He knows the Tremayne family well."

I didn't comment. Including Zim in this investigation was not something I looked forward to. Hell, working this case wasn't something I looked forward to, and I wondered if it was too late to request a transfer to working midnights on patrol.

"And Gillespie—do me a favor? We've had enough bad press, and I've got a lot more on my plate than I want, so let's keep this whole thing low key."

"Yes, sir."

I left Andrews's office, wondering what to do. Just keep quiet and pretend nothing happened? That there was no past? But I knew I couldn't. If there were negatives in Eve's home, and they were ever found, developed . . . before I could go there, Rocky walked in.

"You're never gonna guess what's going on at the corp yard," he said. "They wanted to know if I was sure there was a CD player in the Mercedes when we had it towed in."

"You tell them we have a side business on stereos with brain matter on them?"

"Go for big bucks on the Internet," Shipley said.

"I told them I'm thinking we mighta noticed a gaping hole in the dash," Rocky said. "Especially with all them wires hanging out. Like I wasn't gonna document that tiny detail in the midst of a goddamn double homicide investigation."

Shipley got up and walked to the coffeepot. "What the hell sort of operation they have out there?"

"Who knows?" Rocky said, shrugging out of his jacket. "I mean, how many stereos gotta get stolen from that place before they figure out it's an inside job?"

"A lot," I said as my phone started ringing. "Shipley told me he heard IA's checking into it."

"No shit?" Rocky asked, looking at Shipley. "No wonder they gave me the third degree."

I answered the phone. "Gillespie, Homicide."

"Kate? It's me. Hold on a sec."

Typical, I thought. My ex-husband calls me, only to put me on hold. Reid was an investigator with the District Attorney's office, which meant I had to deal with him more often than I liked whenever any of our investigations coincided. This investigation was definitely going to coincide in ways I had yet to understand, and I was curious as to why he was calling.

He came back on the line about sixty seconds later. "Sorry about that," he said.

"Don't mention it. You need something?"

"I ran into one of the guys working graves last night. Said that you had a double homicide this weekend."

"That's right."

"I heard Eve Tremayne was one of your victims. I know you were friends in college. You okay?"

"I'm fine, Reid. How about you?"

"Pardon?"

"I thought you knew her."

There was a second of silence, then, "Well, yes, a little. Just wondering if there's anything I can do for you."

Oh, I don't know. Maybe tell me why there's a photo of

you dating someone else while we were still married?
"Thanks, Reid," I said, then hung up.

Rocky gave me an odd look, something he usually did when he heard Reid's name. "What'd he want?"

"Sending his condolences about Eve."

"You gonna tell him you saw his picture in Eve's book?"

I smiled. "That'd go over real well, don't you think?"

"Too bad you didn't have it before your divorce. You coulda used it for a little leverage for alimony. Gotten more from him."

"More what? He still owes me the money he borrowed just for attorney fees."

Rocky gave an exaggerated sigh. "Next time you might wanna marry rich."

"I'll keep that in mind," I said. "But with this job, I don't exactly find them lining up outside my door for a date, rich or not."

"He into that stuff we saw up in her room?"

"Reid? If he is, he never let on."

The conversation went downhill from there, and I decided to get a fresh jolt of caffeine before I started on a search warrant for Eve's place. I stopped by Gypsy's desk. When you had a good secretary, it was wise to cater to her needs. She opted for a cranberry muffin and a mocha.

Ten minutes later, I was standing in line at Starbucks, wondering if I should have mentioned to Andrews that Eve and my ex were involved as well. Maybe that would have gotten me off the case. I overlooked that the truth in all its stark reality would have gotten me off the case damn quick. Not a pleasant thought. Which is why I drank my latte there. I wanted a few minutes to myself before getting back to a case I didn't want to investigate. A case I shouldn't be investigating, because my past was about to collide with the present.

And I had the feeling that I wasn't going to be the only victim.

Fifteen minutes later I picked up Gypsy's order and, mocha and cranberry muffin in hand, I headed back to the Hall. My pager went off in the elevator and I stuck the muffin bag in my teeth in order to free up a hand to read it. At that precise moment, the elevator stopped and the door opened. In stepped Lieutenant Mike Torrance and Kent Mathis, a sergeant also from IA.

I felt my face turn red as I stood there, bag clenched between my teeth, holding out my pager to read it. Of all the times to run into Torrance, he had to walk in on me now?

It didn't help that Mathis was here to witness this. They were polar opposites, these two. Where Torrance was tall, slim, hair and eyes about as dark as a raven, Mathis had the stockier build of a professional body builder, not to mention blond hair, blue eyes, and a grin that widened significantly when he saw the look on my face as I stood there.

"Never a dull moment around you, Gillespie," Mathis said.

Feeling like a complete dolt, I smiled, replaced the pager, and as gracefully as I could, removed said bag from my mouth. The message was from Rocky, saying that IA was en route to talk to us about the stolen stereo.

Timing was everything.

"Latte?" Torrance asked me, I guess to be polite, since it had been awhile since we'd last seen each other.

"Mocha," I said, trying to be cool and casual.

When the elevator stopped on my floor, Mathis held it open with his hand, allowing me and then Torrance to step off.

"Well," Torrance said. "Is it?"

"Is it what?" I asked.

"Still better than sex?"

His question caught me off guard, and I tried to think of a snappy comeback. He was referring to a bit of conversation we'd had coming home from a case in Lake Tahoe several months ago—my stupid remark about my first-ever taste of a mocha he'd bought. Just like a man to remember the stuff you'd sooner forget. And just like a man to make your first conversation in several months about sex.

With that, I smiled nonchalantly and said, "I wouldn't know. The mocha's for Gypsy."

"Too bad," he whispered, and all nonchalance fled as I tried to ignore the wicked sparkle in his eye.

Before I could delve into what that meant, we reached Homicide. Lieutenant Andrews was standing in the hallway outside his office door, apparently just leaving. He looked up, saw the three of us, and said, "Something going on that I should know about?"

"Don't worry," I said. "We're clean this time."

"A miracle in itself," Andrews said.

"Seriously, they're looking into a series of thefts at the corp yard." I looked at Torrance. "That *is* why you're here, isn't it?"

"At the moment," he said in his annoyingly cryptic IA way. "Mind if we use your office? You're welcome to sit in," he said to Andrews.

"I was on my way out, but it can wait," Andrews replied. "It's always an experience to see IA in action."

"Depending on which side of the investigation you're on," I added in a low voice—apparently not low enough. Torrance glanced at me, clearly amused, considering I'd been on the receiving end of a number of his investigations.

I ignored him and gave Gypsy her mocha and muffin before following them into Andrews's office. We took a seat, Andrews sitting behind his desk. Rocky joined us a minute later. Torrance pulled a small spiral notebook from the inside breast pocket of his suit, along with a gold pen. He eyed me and said, "Markowski informed you of the missing stereo from your homicide vehicle?"

"He mentioned it, yes."

"I know he's been asked, but I'll need to ask you as well. You're sure the stereo was there last night before the car was towed? It wasn't checked on the inventory," Torrance said.

Before I could answer, Rocky said, "Like I told Sergeant Mathis this morning, it was a simple oversight. I woulda noticed if it was missing beforehand, if it was *really* missing."

"What's up with the third degree on this?" Andrews asked. "You're not saying my people took the damn thing, are you?"

"No," Torrance said. "We suspected a corp yard employee, until we got an anonymous tip the other night that a line officer was involved. Helping the guy fence the stolen stereos, apparently. We'd of course appreciate it if you kept this quiet until we finish the investigation." Then to Rocky, he asked, "Do you even know what it was? Tape player? CD player?"

"Sorry," Rocky said. "I guess it never occurred to me that someone would be so hard up to steal a brain-spattered stereo."

"Do you have any idea?" Torrance asked me.

"The CSIs will have photos of the dash along with the rest of the interior shots they took," I said. "You want me to forward copies of the photos so the CSIs won't be wondering why you're looking into it?"

"If you can, yes," Torrance said, jotting something down in his notebook.

Andrews said, "You'd think they'd put up some better cameras in that place."

"Or do some sort of sting," I said, standing. "I have a search warrant to write. So if there's nothing else?"

"Actually," Torrance said, "there is something . . . if you have a minute?"

"Sure," I said, hesitating at the door.

I was surprised to see Rocky shift in his seat, tugging at his tie as though it had suddenly grown too tight.

I was even more surprised when Torrance stood and said, "We can talk in the hallway." A fact made more curious when you considered that other than our brief conversation a few minutes before in the elevator, we hadn't spoken three words to each other in several months. Fool that I was way back then, I'd pretty much told him to go to hell, and he, being the man he was, took me literally.

We headed down the hall to a private corner where we wouldn't be overheard, and I stood there thinking that if we were talking in the hallway, it meant this wasn't official business—always a good sign when one was dealing with IA. Yet when I met his gaze, his dark eyes so intense, I was suddenly taken aback.

I decided to be direct. "What's going on?"

He shoved his hands into his pants pockets, looking suddenly uncomfortable. "I wanted to tell you in person, not on the phone, and truthfully, not like this."

Warning bells went off. "This isn't one of those 'I'm-getting-married' speeches, is it?" It was a stupid thing to say, but I couldn't get over the "not on the phone—not like this" bit.

He smiled and shook his head. "It's the 'I'm-leaving' speech."

"Leaving?"

"The PD. I wanted to let you know before a background investigator showed up knocking on your door."

"Background? For who?"

"FBI."

I felt my mouth drop open, snapped it shut and hoped he

didn't notice. I couldn't believe he was leaving. And then I wondered if it was my fault or if I should even flatter myself. "The FBI?"

He nodded. "It's something I've wanted to do."

Just like that. Hit me with a ton of bricks in the midst of a double homicide. I crossed my arms and smiled, amazed I could be so cool, calm, and collected on the outside, when I was anything but on the inside. "So when do you leave for Quantico?" I asked casually.

"Assuming I pass the background, in about a month." He glanced out the window at the traffic below. "I guess this is where I give you the 'Just-be-happy-for-me' speech?"

"I am. Really. I'm just . . . surprised." And then I thought of Rocky, his cryptic *"Have you talked to Torrance?"* on the way back from our homicide, and then the way he'd seemed suddenly uncomfortable just now when he'd seen Torrance had wanted to talk to me. Determined to concentrate on the fact that Torrance and I had never gotten past first, maybe second base—so what was the big deal?—I tried to ignore the fact that I was hurt that Rocky knew about this FBI thing before I did.

I pulled out my pager, made a pretense of reading an old page as though I'd just received it, then said, "Well, I have to go. I hope things really work out for you."

The way he looked at me, the several heartbeats of silence, spoke volumes. But all he said was, "See you around, Kate."

And I realized that once again I had missed an opportunity to right things between us. But all I could think to say was, "See you."

I walked toward my office, feeling his gaze at my back. When I entered, I turned and saw him still there at the end of the hall, watching me. All my instincts told me to go back, talk to him. Hash out this thing before he left, before it was too late. But before these thoughts truly registered, Gypsy called out to me.

"Visitors, Kate."

I looked up to see Rich Pierce from Missing Persons standing beside Gypsy's desk. He was taller than average, about six-four, black hair flecked with gray, late forties. He wore brown slacks, white shirt, and a brown shoulder holster that had his initials worked into the leather.

"Gillespie," he said. "Got a minute?"

"Lots of minutes," I said. Just none to myself.

"This is Daisy," he said, stepping to the side to introduce a young woman seated in the waiting area near Gypsy's desk. "She, uh, wants to know the progress of the missing person's report she made on her husband. Joshua Redding."

7

Daisy Redding reminded me of a new-age wood sprite. She had short blond hair, the top gelled into little spikes; numerous piercings in her ears and one in her nose, was all of five-one or five-two, maybe ninety pounds, and wore a swirling ankle-length paisley skirt.

"Why don't we go into an interview room?" I said, indicating a door at the far end of the office.

"Is Josh okay?" she asked, turning to Inspector Pierce. Her eyes widened. "Oh, my God. It said Homicide on the door. That's why you brought me here, isn't it? Where's Josh?" she demanded, then turned to me. "What happened to him?"

I led her into the interview room, grabbing a box of tissues from my desk. The entire office turned silent, the other inspectors' expressions somber, each having faced similar situations on numerous occasions. It didn't matter how long you did this, it never got easier. As I turned to close the door behind me, I saw Rocky walk in from Andrews's office. His gaze took in the woman, then met mine just before I shut the door.

Daisy Redding immediately sat, and I handed her the tissues. She took one, twisting it in her hand. "Who—who would do this to him?"

What was I supposed to say? She looked so innocent, so

naïve, especially with the little jeweled bobby pins in her hair. But then, I knew better than to be deceived by appearances. Eve had had a way of looking innocent, too. She'd done it her entire adult life.

I kept my voice even, matter-of-fact. "When did you last see Josh?"

"Saturday night. Maybe around seven . . . he was going to help an old friend." Though she had yet to shed a tear, she grabbed a second tissue and began shredding it as well. "He said she was having some problems and needed his help. He didn't think he'd be gone more than, um, more than a couple of hours." She looked away, at the bare wall, for several seconds. "Only he didn't come back. I figured, you know, he maybe got to drinking, something like that." She closed her eyes and covered her mouth with her hand. "I don't know what I thought. I mean, he doesn't really drink, but—"

"This friend, Mrs. Redding. Any idea who it is?"

"Eve. Eve Tremayne. He works for her grandmother."

"Is there anything else you can tell us about that night? Anything he might have said to indicate what she needed to talk to him about?"

"I wish I knew. I'm sorry. I—when did you find him?"

"Saturday night around eleven."

She closed her eyes as though to compose herself. When she opened them, they were glassy. "Can I see him? See if it's really him?"

"We can arrange that," I said, glad she'd asked. Getting positive ID on our John Doe would save time. First, however, I'd have to call the morgue to make sure the body was suitable for viewing. "It might take a few minutes . . ."

"Oh, well, I really need to be going." She stood suddenly, her face paling as though the thought of suddenly seeing a dead body might be too much to handle. The shredded tissue that had been in her lap fell to the floor unnoticed.

"But you just said you wanted to see him."

"I know, but . . . I've never seen a dead body before."

"I'll be right there with you." I was not about to let her walk out only to have her flee the country, as Joshua Redding's mother had. I wanted to know what the hell was going on. "Is that okay, Mrs. Redding?"

"Daisy. That's what everyone calls me."

"Daisy. Before we go, I need to get some personal information from you. Do you have a driver's license? ID card?"

She patted her pockets. "I think I left it at Josh's house."

Not *our* house. "How long did you say you and Josh were married?"

"Um, about two months now."

"Any reason you can think of why his mother would take off to Mexico?"

"Mexico?" She looked surprised. "No."

"Okay," I said, standing. "Ready?"

She nodded and I opened the door, allowing her to step out first. Markowski was leaning against the file cabinet, apparently waiting for me. "Ya got a sec?"

"Sure," I said. To Daisy, "You mind?"

"No." She seemed almost relieved. I imagined that I would be, too, if all I had to look forward to was viewing my deceased husband's remains.

Markowski and I stepped a few feet away, and he nodded toward Andrews's office. "You'll never guess who's bending the lieutenant's ear as we speak."

"Who?"

"The Tremaynes."

I glanced toward the office, but the door was closed, as were the blinds. Suddenly I thought of all the complications, the reasons I didn't want to see them. "I can hardly wait," I said, wondering if this case could get any worse.

"They asked for Zimwit personally. Said they heard

something may have happened to their daughter, and re-members him from doing such a great job somewhere along the line. This thing's turning into a friggin' can of worms."

If Zim started digging around and found those negatives, anything I'd hoped to keep private would no longer remain that way. "Can of snakes is more like it," I said.

"Yeah, well, maybe you'll get lucky and the LT will reas-sign it to Zim after all."

"Christ, that's all I need." My only saving grace was that I hadn't told the Tremaynes—or anyone else—why I'd ended my friendship with Eve. "They still in there?" I asked, not looking forward to seeing them.

"Yeah, but I thought you wanted off the case. What's up?"

"Nothing I can go into here," I said, eyeing Daisy, who looked at the exit and then at me, as though wondering whether she could make it out before I could stop her. "Right now I need to get her to the morgue before we do anything else. I'd like some sort of identification on our John Doe where someone actually goes and sees the body before they flee the country."

• "I'll call down there and make sure they're ready for you."

"Thanks." I waited until I saw him at the phone on his desk. When he gave me the nod, I led Daisy past the file cab-inets to the back door of our office and out to the hallway, thereby avoiding Gypsy's office as well as the lieutenant's. I wasn't ready to face the Tremaynes yet, and I needed to think about what I was going to do if Andrews did assign the case to Zim. Rocky I could handle. And Shipley, too. They could be trusted with my past. Zim, on the other hand, would hold it out for the world to see, just for the shock value.

I glanced at Daisy walking beside me, her hands clasped in front of her like a nun's, her knuckles turning white. I wanted to tell her it would be okay, but I knew better. She'd

come here to locate a missing person, we were leading her
to the morgue and, I didn't even know if I'd still be on the
case or where it was going. Silence was the best course of
action, and I kept it. Despite that, her nervousness increased
as the elevator descended.

We exited the lobby, crossed the north terrace. The high-
rise jail, something we called the glamour slammer, stood to
our left, the morgue to our right. Had I not guided her to the
morgue's public entrance, I had a feeling she would have
continued straight on through to the parking garage.

She balked at the door. "Are you sure we need to do this
now?"

"I wish there were some other way," I said.

"You'll be there for me?"

"I will," I said.

"The entire time?"

"I won't leave you," I said, assuming she was talking
about her time in the morgue. She seemed to accept that,
preceding me in, then pausing in the lobby.

Mac Flanders, a Coroner's investigator, was working at
his desk behind the counter. "This the one for the John
Doe?"

"Yes."

He stood towering over Daisy. She looked up at him, then
quickly away. He shrugged, then led the way to the viewing
room, where we waited for him to bring the body out.

Daisy watched, and when our John Doe's face came into
view, she said, "Oh, my God."

She covered her mouth with her hands, spun around, and
fled the room.

From the morgue lobby, I saw her through the window,
leaning on a post, vomiting into the ivy. "Do me a favor," I
told Flanders. "Let me know once the prints come back on
him."

"Will do," he said as I grabbed several tissues from the secretary's desk, then brought them out to Daisy.

She took them, wiping her mouth. "Thanks."

"I'm assuming you know him?"

She nodded, covering her mouth with her hands, the tears coming faster now.

"Who?" I asked.

"My husband."

"Josh?" I asked.

She said nothing for several seconds, then whispered, "Yes."

8

Once Daisy recovered, I escorted her back to my office, leaving her with Rocky, who was going to ask her for permission to search their home, thereby avoiding the trouble of getting a search warrant. *One down, the next to go,* I thought as I stood outside the lieutenant's office. I was about to knock when I heard them through the door. Eve's father was speaking. "What does this mean, 'no print verification'?"

"It means," Lieutenant Andrews said, "that there has only been a tentative ID, based on what Inspector Gillespie reported."

I heard an intake of breath, then a woman's voice saying, "Are you telling me that my daughter could be lying there dead and you don't even *know* it?"

"Of course they know," J. T. Tremayne told his wife. "The lieutenant said Ms. Gillespie identified her."

Ms. Gillespie. Not Kate. Not Inspector.

I tried to examine why this should bother me, and as I knocked, and Andrews called for me to enter, it occurred to me. The title J. T. Tremayne had applied to my name made it formally impersonal. Gone was the history, the past. I was now just Ms. Gillespie. Wasn't that what I wanted?

I supposed it could be worse, I thought, opening the door to see Andrews seated at his desk, looking none too pleased. Zim sat in the chair I had occupied earlier, leaning back, one leg crossed over his knee. Beside him sat Eve's mother, Faye, who looked up, her gaze widening a bit when she saw me. "Kate . . ."

My name hung on her lips, and in her eyes I saw a thousand questions she wanted answered. But she looked from me to her husband, who stood leaning on a cane, regarding me with narrowed brown eyes.

He seemed older than I remembered, grayer, and the cane was something new. He lifted it, pointing it at me. "*This* is the inspector you have assigned to the case?" he asked with a vehemence that stunned me. I'd expected it from his wife, not him.

"She is," Andrews said. "Inspector Gillespie."

"I think *not,*" Tremayne said, rapping the tip of his cane on the ground, startling his wife. "I insist that you take her off the case and reassign it to Inspector Zimmerman."

As long as it's anyone but Zim, I wanted to say, but Andrews had his own agenda. "With all due respect, Mr. Tremayne," he said. "Inspector Gillespie is one of our best—"

"Please!" Faye said, her tone desperate, reminding us all that there was a whole lot more at stake here than who the investigator would be. "I want to see Eve."

"Of course, Mrs. Tremayne," Andrews said. "Inspector Zimmerman?"

Zim stood, then held out his hand for the Tremaynes to precede him through the door.

Faye looked at her husband, then down at the ground, when he refused to meet her gaze—an interesting undercurrent, to say the least. I didn't have time to dwell on it, though, as they started out, and I intended to remain behind to ask Andrews to reassign it once again—to anyone but Zim. But before I could open my mouth, Faye Tremayne walked back into the office, alone.

"Kate," she said, holding her hand against her heart. "I . . . I just wanted to apologize for my husband. He's under a lot of pressure, is all. He seems to think the police are plotting against him. It's silly, I know, but Eve's death affected him in ways I can't begin to describe."

"I understand," I said, surprised by her demeanor toward me. And when it became apparent that she had something more to say, but seemed reluctant to say it, I added, "I'm sure you're both under a great deal of stress right now. And I'm truly sorry for your loss."

"Yes," she said, glancing out the door, then back at me, as though worried her husband might return. "Anyway, I—I wanted you to know that it would mean a great deal to me if you came to Eve's funeral."

I was stunned. Never in the time I'd known the Tremaynes had Faye ever treated me with anything more than a cold politeness—something that had always left me with the impression that my status in life was beneath her. Yet here she was, telling me how much she wanted me to attend. And I didn't know what to say.

"You will come, won't you?" she asked.

She had lost her daughter and nothing else should matter beyond that. "Yes," I said.

She gave a faltering smile, as though the effort were something she wasn't used to, and I wondered if I'd misjudged her all these years, if maybe it was just her personality and nothing to do with me at all. She left and I looked at Andrews, who gave a slight nod, indicating I should follow. Which meant he wasn't succumbing to any pressure to pull me from the case. Whether that was good or bad, I wasn't sure. Good that Zim wasn't getting it, bad that I still had it.

Even so, I wanted to know what Andrews expected. "About Zim—" I said.

"Just think of him as an ambassador."

"Meaning?"

"Ambassadors kiss ass very well, but have little power. You're still the lead on this case, Markowski's your partner, and Zimmerman's your ambassador to the Tremaynes. Royalty works like that, and I get the feeling that J. T. Tremayne has cornered the market on thrones."

His phone rang and he answered it, and I figured I could approach him later on this whole thing. I knew I was playing with fire, that I shouldn't be on this case, and that Zim was the last person I wanted to take it over. But what I needed was a few minutes of uninterrupted time to tell Andrews why—the real reason why—and with the Tremaynes waiting to see their daughter, this wasn't it. So off I went, dutifully following Zim and the Tremaynes to the elevator.

When we arrived at the morgue, Mac Flanders met us in the lobby.

"Flanders," Zim said, attempting to be cordial. "This is Mr. and Mrs. Tremayne. They're here to make an identification."

"Got a few to pick from," Flanders said, leading us to a viewing room away from the main part of the morgue. "Been a busy weekend." That was when I realized how perfect he was for the job. Death hit all walks of life, without discrimination, and like death, Flanders didn't discriminate. He treated everyone with the same dose of caustic humor.

Neither of the Tremaynes, however, seemed to notice his comment, and as we walked in, Mrs. Tremayne's nose wrinkled at the smell of antiseptic and death. It was a smell that stayed with you long after you left, and one you never forgot. The thought fled the second Flanders pulled out the body and Faye Tremayne saw it. Her chest seemed to cave in with a keening sound that only a mother could make.

"My baby. Eve . . ." She crumpled against her husband, who closed his eyes as she cried out, "No!" She hit him on

his chest, not with any real force, and in that space of time, it didn't matter that it was the Tremaynes I was dealing with. Two people had lost their daughter, and their grief was profound.

"I'm so sorry, Mrs. Tremayne," Zim said, clasping his hand on her shoulder. "I'm so sorry."

Zim walked them from the room and out to the lobby, while I remained behind. Flanders rolled his eyes, not because of Mrs. Tremayne's tears, but because he knew Zim—a man who, if he had a sympathetic bone in his body, kept it hidden for special occasions—the Tremaynes' presence being one of them.

"Zim can be so touching," Flanders said to me.

"Yeah. Tugs right at your heartstrings. What's with DOJ?"

"Your guess is as good as mine. We got five bodies in here, all waiting for fingerprint ID. Finally had to have a clerk drive out to Department of Justice, taking the print cards with him. Maybe we'll get something back in the next couple of hours."

"That would be nice."

"To say the least. You know what a pain it is to have only a visual ID?"

"Wouldn't know," I said, picking up the phone to call my office.

He laughed. "Yeah. Me neither. Makes you wonder what the *hell* they did before the advent of computers."

Something I'd rather not contemplate. I liked computers. Didn't know a thing about them, other than that they made my job a hell of a lot easier. At times.

"Gypsy," I said, when she picked up her extension, "can you start on a search warrant for Eve's place? I—we need to go back in there, and I have a feeling her father will rip us apart if we don't go by the book on this."

"I'll get started on it."

"The lieutenant there?" I asked, figuring I'd better make an appointment to see him and get this case reassigned, preferably before I got in too deep.

"Sorry, Kate. He just took off."

"How about Rocky? We need to get a statement from the Tremaynes." And I didn't want to take it.

"He left for a few minutes. Said something about doing a search later on Daisy's place?"

"Tell him not to leave when he gets in. That search can wait. We need to do Eve's place as soon as the Tremaynes leave."

I hung up, ignoring the feeling that this was going to be the case from the worst kind of hell, then headed out to the terrace. Zim and the Tremaynes had started toward the Hall as I pushed open the door. "Zim, hold up a minute."

He stopped to look back at me, the Tremaynes pausing at his side. "Yeah," he said, as though I were some minor annoyance he was forced to deal with. True to some extent, I supposed.

"We need to take a statement from the Tremaynes before they leave. Rocky should be back in a few to take it."

"I don't think this is a good time."

"Regardless," I said, keeping my tone level but firm. "We have a double homicide, their daughter is a victim, and Mrs. Tremayne's mother was an assault victim. Now, they either want to solve this case, or they don't."

"Let me talk to them a sec," he said.

I let the door fall shut between us to give them some privacy. Through the glass I saw Mrs. Tremayne dry her tears as she leaned into her husband. I'll admit to being perturbed that I'd had to use Zim as a go-between, but what the hell. I'd get over it. Soon Zim turned back to me, waving.

I exited, and he said, "They think they want to wait for their attorney."

"What?"

Zim sort of shrugged, looking slightly uncomfortable.

"Am I misunderstanding something here?" I asked.

Faye Tremayne wouldn't meet my gaze. J. T. Tremayne simply stared at me.

Anger swept through me and it had nothing to do with Eve or anything she'd ever done. To have a set of parents put their interests before that of finding their daughter's killer was beyond anything I could comprehend. I didn't even bother addressing Zim. I looked straight at Tremayne, knowing he was behind this, and again I thought of the strange role reversal, his vehemence, his wife's sudden empathic cooperation. "Your daughter is lying dead in our morgue. I'd think you'd be interested in finding out who murdered her, not worrying about incriminating yourselves—unless you *would* be incriminating yourself?"

J. T.'s gaze narrowed as he clasped the top of his cane with both hands and leaned forward slightly. "What are you trying to imply? That I killed my daughter?"

I took a breath, told myself to calm down and not to commit career suicide over the likes of the Tremaynes. That thought lasted all of two seconds, when he started to turn away with his wife.

I closed the distance between us. "You're going to just leave?"

They continued on.

"What is with you rich people?" Probably not the most diplomatic thing to say, but I wanted their attention.

Behind me I heard Zim clear his throat in warning.

I ignored him. "If that was my daughter in there and the police needed my help, I'd ask which hoop they wanted me to jump through and how high."

Mrs. Tremayne tugged on her husband's sleeve and they

stopped. Together, they exchanged a few quiet words, then faced me.

J. T. spoke, his voice filled with suppressed anger. "You want to talk? Then talk here, now. Both of us together. We're not suspects, and I refuse to allow you to treat us as suspects."

"Here?" I said in disbelief.

If there was ever a time for an ambassador, this was it, but when I looked over at Zim, he simply stood there, his arms crossed. I wondered if I could convince them to wait ten minutes for Rocky, but the look on Tremayne's face told me otherwise.

"Fine," I said, pulling my notebook and pen from my pocket. I'd take what I could get. "I'd like to find the person responsible for this murder and for the attack on your mother, Mrs. Tremayne, so if this is where you want to do it . . ."

J. T. bristled, but his wife said, "It's for mother and Eve," then dabbed at her nose with her handkerchief.

He pressed his lips together, then limped to the bench near the morgue door, his wife at his side. "Ask your questions now," he said, his voice cold and even. "Because after this, if you want to speak to me or anyone else in my family, it will be through our attorney. Do I make myself clear?"

"Exceedingly. Do you know who Eve was supposed to have seen that night? Where she went?"

"No," he said, the word coming out harsh.

His wife put her hand on his arm and said, "I'll do this. I am the one who last saw her." She looked down at her lap a moment, took a deep breath, then said, "When I last spoke with her that day, she was not planning on going anywhere. Her cousin Lucas was going out, and so she planned to stay with Mother."

"Do you know why she'd be in the company of Joshua Redding?"

Faye Tremayne looked up at me in shock, then burst into tears at the question.

"She *wouldn't* be in his company," J. T. said.

Faye shook her head. "That's what I don't understand. He's my mother's handyman. Why would Eve have *anything* to do with him? He didn't go to church. They had nothing in common."

Maybe he was into S&M? I wanted to say, but didn't. I had a little compassion in me and figured now wasn't the best time to bring up Eve's sex life. Not until I found out if it was related to the murder. "They weren't friends?" I asked instead.

"Not that I know of."

"Did she have any . . . unusual hobbies, anything that might put her in the path of someone violent?" A roundabout way of asking what they knew of her private life, I suppose.

The Tremaynes looked at each other, as though trying to contemplate what that might be. Mrs. Tremayne shook her head. "No. She played the violin and went to church. There were church activities . . . singing in the choir, fundraisers, the symphony, that sort of thing. Nothing else."

"Do you have any idea who could have killed her?"

"I do," J. T. said, causing his wife to look at him in surprise. "That's why I wanted our attorney. I'm not about to name names without knowing the consequences," he said, his wife pulling away from him as he spoke. He tried to bring her back into his embrace. "You're upset," he said.

"And I have every right to be. It's *my* daughter who's lying in there."

All is not well in paradise, I thought, then figured I'd better bring them back to the point. "This is only an investigation," I said. "We are not about to make an arrest based solely on your suspicions." Neither spoke, so I asked, "You have a name?"

"Joshua Redding," Tremayne said.

I paused. If that was the case, it strengthened the murder-suicide theory, but did nothing to explain why, or rather who, was behind the break-in of Eve's house. "What makes you think he's involved?" I asked.

"He sent me a blackmail letter. My attorney has it."

"Blackmail for what?"

"That's not something I'd like to go into now," he said, with a slight tilt of his head in his wife's direction.

I held out my hand, indicating he should follow me so we could speak in private. We stepped away a few feet. "You were saying, Mr. Tremayne?"

He glanced over at his wife, then back at me. "She knows of the blackmail, not of the reason. Right after I announced that I was going to run for District Supervisor, I received a note about a . . . past indiscretion. It was clearly intended to prevent me from running."

"You're talking about the election you dropped out of six years ago?"

"Yes. I mean, no. I'm talking about this election."

"And who was this discretion with?"

"That's not important."

"It could be."

"I'll leave that for my attorney to decide."

"Was the note signed?"

"No."

"Then how do you know Joshua Redding was the black-mailer?"

"Because right after he left the note, he was stupid enough to follow it up with a call to my cell phone and demand money in return for his silence. I happen to have Caller ID," he said, pulling out his cell phone. "It came back to Vera Redding. From there it was a pretty simple deduction, don't you think?"

He pressed a button on his phone, showing me the number with Vera Redding's name on it, dated two days before Eve was killed.

"I understand how this looks," I said. "But not why he would kill *Eve* if he was trying to blackmail *you*."

"It's simple. He told me that if I didn't pay, he'd make Eve pay. That's pretty clear, don't you think? Especially when she paid with her life."

"Anything else you can tell me?"

"No," he said curtly. We both returned to where his wife sat waiting, and I nodded to Zim, who guided them back to the Hall.

When I returned to my office, I found a note from Rocky saying that he and Shipley were en route to Eve's house to start the search. As soon as I read it, I headed out, not wanting to identify the true reason for my haste.

I was fearful that someone might turn up something on my father even more incriminating than the photo I'd taken. And with that knowledge came the realization that tomorrow, no matter what, I was going to have to come clean about taking the photo.

And then deal with the consequences that would surely follow.

9

We failed to find anything that appeared significant or remotely incriminating at Eve's, and I'll admit to toying with the idea of keeping the photo secret. What could it hurt?

But inside I knew I couldn't keep it to myself. Tomorrow was the day, and I'd have to deal with the punishment.

It was late by the time we left Eve's house, but not late enough to keep me from losing sleep over everything that could go wrong with this case because of that damn photo. If that wasn't enough to keep me up, there was always the little matter of Torrance leaving the department. I didn't like that his departure bothered me, especially after having spent the last few months convincing myself that he meant nothing to me.

Needless to say, I was tired the next morning when I got up and left a little earlier than normal, just to have some time to myself, maybe read the newspaper in peace, drink my latte while it was still hot.

All peace fled after I read an article on J. T. Tremayne, who made a formal announcement that in memory of his daughter, Eve, he was running for Board of Supervisors. It was, he said, the least he could do to make San Francisco a safer place for its citizens by "cleaning up the Police Department and eliminating the incompetent inspectors so that crime can be fought where it counts—in the streets."

There were plenty of other choice comments, and after reading several, I tossed the paper aside and sipped at my latte, which only reminded me of Torrance again, because of that damn comment I'd made about mochas being better than sex.

Depressed over that thought and disgusted over the article, I opened my desk drawer, then paused at the sight of the sealed envelope containing my father's picture. I took a breath and told myself this was the time to take care of it. I hated that it was there, a dirty secret to be hidden. Not just because of what my father had done, but because I had succumbed to the need to protect his reputation, just as Eve had told me I would . . .

"Yo, kid," Rocky said when he came in. "You look down in the dumps."

"Us incompetent inspectors get like that sometimes."

"I take it you read the article?"

I didn't answer. Guilt was weighing me down. I'd taken the photo, compromising a crime scene. Maybe J. T. Tremayne wasn't that far off in his assessment of the operation we were running . . .

"I wouldn't worry about it too much," Rocky said, misreading my silence. "You saw who he was running against, didn't you? Miles Standiford."

I tried to pay attention to what he was saying. Standiford was a current supervisor in the same district, ultraconservative and pro-cop.

"If we're lucky," he continued, "Standiford will trounce him, since it's obvious that Tremayne intends to use his daughter's murder as a rung in his political ladder."

Gypsy walked in just then, handing me a sheet of paper and a thick manila envelope. "Let's hope the voters see it that way," she said to Rocky. To me she said, "Here's your gun residue analysis and your crime scene photos."

"Thanks," I said, setting the photos on my desk to look at the gun residue analysis.

"Well?" Rocky asked.

Not what I would have expected. I held it up. "Bet you lunch you can't guess."

"You're on. It's negative. We both know it wasn't a murder-suicide."

"Wrong. It's positive." I gave him the paper.

"Josh Redding pulled the trigger? I have a hard time believing that."

"Same here. Except that last night, Tremayne said that Josh Redding was trying to blackmail him for some affair he had." I told him what Tremayne had said and how Josh had allegedly told him that Eve would pay.

"That sure as hell places more weight on the murder-suicide theory."

"Either that, or someone went to a lot of trouble to fire the weapon in our male victim's hand to make sure we thought it was murder-suicide."

"You're thinking that Tremayne lied to you about this blackmail thing?" Rocky asked, getting up to pour himself some coffee.

"I don't know. He was certainly being evasive over some of the issues. Like who he had the affair with," I said, picking up the crime scene photos of the car Eve was killed in. They were clear, precise close-ups. "Definitely a CD player there."

"Maybe now Torrance will believe us. You want me to take those to him?" he asked.

Before I could define the reason why, I stood suddenly and said, "Finish your coffee. I'll take them to IA."

Rocky gave me an odd look, but I ignored it and headed to Torrance's office, nodding to Mathis and the other IA inspectors as I entered Management Control. Torrance's door was open, and I saw several boxes stacked in front of his desk, all taped shut. I realized he already looked like an FBI agent, sitting at his desk in a crisp white shirt, blue and burgundy striped tie, and leather shoulder holster. He looked up from the report he was reading and saw me. "The photos?" he asked.

"As requested," I said, just as Sergeant Mathis stepped into the doorway.

"We need to get going, Mike," he said.

"Be right there." Torrance stood, put on his navy suit coat, then took the stack of photos from me, quickly going through them, pulling those that showed the CD player still in the car. "Any motive yet?" he asked.

"Possibly," I said, leaving it at that, since he was apparently in a hurry.

I didn't expect him to look up at me, waiting to hear my answer.

"What's wrong?" he asked.

"I'm fine. Why?"

"You've been avoiding me for weeks. You could have sent Rocky up with the photos. What's going on with this case?"

I hated that I was that transparent. I hated that he knew exactly what was going on with me before I did, because he was right. This case was different. Personal. I could have waited for Andrews, but I didn't, and here I was. I glanced at the photos on Torrance's desk, then looked at him, not sure what to say or where to start.

Apparently whatever he saw in my eyes told him this was bigger than a murder case with a few problems, because he moved past me to the door, leaned out, and told Mathis, "I'll catch up with you in a few." Then he shut the door, returning to sit on the edge of his desk.

Suddenly I wasn't so eager to share. "I don't want you to be late because of me."

He didn't move.

"I guess I came up here so when you started an IA on me, you'd know the background."

"On what?"

"I, um, found my father's picture in Eve Tremayne's room the night we searched her house. I took it out of a photo album when Rocky wasn't looking."

Several seconds of silence, then, "Not good, Kate."

"Tell me about it."

"Your only saving grace is that he can't be considered a suspect."

"I know."

"Can you?"

I looked at him, not sure I heard right. "You're asking me if I can be considered a suspect?"

"Yes."

"No," I said, taken aback at first until I realized he was simply making sure all the bases were covered.

"You're sure?"

I thought about it. Where was I that night? Home watching TV. "Not unless someone gave me a ride. My landlord's car was blocking mine in the driveway."

"Why, Kate?"

It seemed he was asking about so much more than the subject we were discussing. Questions like why things had never worked out with us. But I knew better than to read anything into his words, and I stuck with the subject at hand. "We were best friends, but sort of drifted apart after I became a cop. Then out of the blue, she starts taking an unusual interest in my father's life."

"Unusual how?"

"Making flimsy excuses to come see him at our house. Nothing specific, but I remember it just seemed . . . odd. I thought she was trying to blackmail him," I said, recalling

my unease that night all those years ago when I let myself
into my father's house. "I walked in on her while she was
emptying what appeared to be semen from a condom onto
her shirt, just before she tried to tear the shirt. When I con-
fronted her, she said I was wrong and that if I said anything
to anyone to ruin her reputation, she would ruin his. She said
she had pictures of him handcuffing her to the bed. Photos
of her in that same shirt that would literally ruin his life."

"And what did your father say?"

"I never told him," I said, picking up the crime scene photographs, staring at Eve's lifeless body. "He was a fifty-year-
old man who'd been abandoned by his wife once before and
who had given up on life after my brother died. Suddenly he
thinks a young woman finds him exciting and he's talking
about the future," I said, tossing the photos back on Torrance's desk, angry even after all these years. "He died of a
heart attack a few weeks later, never thinking anything was
amiss as far as I know."

"And you didn't report it?"

"To whom? She never went through with whatever it was
she planned. My father was dead. No victim, no crime. She
told me later that she knew I was walking in at that moment
and she'd set the whole thing up to twist a knife in my back.
Make me think ill of my father. She told me she liked to in-
flict pain. Physical . . . mental . . . ," I said, shoving my hands
in my pockets, looking away. "It all turned her on." And the
pain, to me, had been intense. She'd been my friend. I'd ad-
mired her. Shared my secrets with her. My dreams. Until
that summer she'd gone away to that camp to work and had
returned changed, hungry for power. And I wondered once
again if maybe it had always been there and I'd somehow
missed the signs . . .

"I'm sorry you had to go through that," he said quietly.

When I looked at him and saw his gaze was filled with

compassion, not censure, I knew why I'd come to him first.
It didn't matter that he was IA and that I had done something
wrong and he was obligated to act upon it. What mattered
was that I cared about what he thought and I wanted him to
know *why* I had done this before he found out from someone else in the course of his official duties. Even so, I
wanted to shrug it off, act like it was no big deal—self-
preservation, I suppose—so I said, "Thanks, but it was a
long time ago."

"And now?"

"Now? Now I think someone killed Eve because she was
at it again." I told him about the photo album, Reid's and the
other photos—and the missing photo.

"You mean there are *two* missing pictures?"

"Apparently. My father's, and a second photo, from the
back of the book. I think the photos were placed in the
album in chronological order."

"You think she was blackmailing them all?"

"I can only surmise that she was."

"In light of that missing photo, the one you didn't take, it
might be interesting to see who shows up at her funeral—"

"Or who doesn't," I said. "Because if she was blackmailing them all, that makes them each a suspect."

"If she was blackmailing them all," Torrance said, "that
makes your ex-husband a suspect. And each one of those
people will need to be contacted, but not by you."

I stared at the floor, knowing what was coming next.

"You'll have to be removed from the case," he said.

10

To say that Lieutenant Andrews was upset to have IA escorting one of his investigators into his office for such an impropriety was an understatement.

Here was a man who never swore, never raised his voice, and in the space of a few minutes had to have been tempted to do both. The one good thing about Andrews, though, was that you could easily gauge his anger by the volume of his voice. Soft was bad. At the moment, all he was doing was staring at the top of his desk, while I repeated to him what I had told to Torrance.

"What were you thinking?" he asked.

I could barely hear him—*not* a good sign. "Apparently I wasn't, sir."

He took a breath, stood, and stared out the window to the street below. "Where's the photo?" he asked, not looking at me.

"In my desk."

"Bring it here."

I stood, left the two of them in the office, and got the photo from my desk.

Rocky was there, watching me. "What's going on?"

"You don't want to know."

I returned to Andrews's office and shut the door. I put the

envelope on his desk. He took it, opened it up, looked in. "Who knows about this?" he asked.

"Just the three of us," I said.

He handed the envelope to Torrance. "What's your suggestion?"

"Lock it up in my safe, until we know if it is pertinent to the investigation or not. My guess is that it won't be. But if we let the DA know, he'll have to disclose it to the defense. He's already going to have to deal with the scandal of Reid's photo showing up in the album. If anything comes of it, we can bring the photo out."

"And an IA investigation?"

"I'll leave that up to you. She's your investigator."

Andrews nodded.

Torrance took the photo and left.

I waited for Andrews to say something. He let me sit there for several very long minutes. Finally he said, "You could have compromised the entire case."

"I'm sorry."

"Sorry isn't going to get it back on track. I expected better from you." He turned his back on me again, looking out the window. "Tell Rocky he's the lead. He'll have to work with Zim on this."

"Yes, sir."

"You can provide background if needed. You may help with surveillances. You will not take an active participation in any of the investigation. Is that clear?"

"Yes, sir."

"For the rest of the afternoon, you might consider working one of your other cases. In the field."

Translation: stay out of his way, if I knew what was good for me.

"Yes, sir."

I left, not wanting to tell Rocky who his new partner was going to be.

"Why don't I like the look on your face?" Rocky asked when I returned to my desk to gather some case files.

I glanced over at Zim, saw he was busy on the phone. "I'm being pulled from the case."

"Why?"

"I'd rather not go into it right now. You're going to be lead investigator."

"With who?"

I gave a nod in Zim's direction.

"Shit," Rocky said. "I have to go to Eve's funeral with Zim?"

"Andrews said I wasn't to do any investigating."

"What can you do?"

"Backgrounds and surveillances."

"What the hell'd you do?" he whispered.

"Trust me, you don't want to know."

"He gonna kill me if I go in there?"

"Put it this way. He told me to work the rest of the afternoon in the field. You might want to give him some time before you even *think* of mentioning my name," I said, then took my case files and left.

I spent the rest of the afternoon following up old leads on cold cases, things I could do by myself without a backup. By the time I got home that night, I had pretty much beat myself up over what I had done, taking that photo. Wondering why I felt it necessary to protect the reputation of a man long dead—I'm sure in part to keep his name from being bandied about the department in relation to a sex scandal. But was I selfishly trying to protect myself? *There's Kate Gillespie. You heard about her father, didn't you? Poor man. Victimized by a pro, didn't even know it,* I thought when my phone rang.

It was Rocky. "How ya doing?"

"Fine. Andrews cool off any?"

"By a degree, maybe. You want to tell me what's going on?"

"Not right now. Let's just say I made a stupid mistake and the people who need to know know."

He was quiet a moment. "Okay. I'll leave it at that. You up to going to Eve's funeral tomorrow?"

"You got Andrews to approve it?"

"I told him in a surveillance, you'd look a sight better on my arm playing a mourner than Zim would. He agreed, since Eve's mother apparently wanted you to go anyway."

"What time and where?"

"Ten at Starbucks."

"Why there?"

"Let's just say the LT's still not real happy with you, so I wouldn't suggest you show up at the Hall in the morning. Or the afternoon, for that matter."

The next morning, I dressed in black, then headed to Starbucks, where Zim and Rocky were going over autopsy reports and photos while having muffins and coffee.

I ordered a mocha and muffin and joined them.

"Look at this," Rocky said, pointing to a photo that showed three elongated bruises running horizontally across Eve's upper left arm. "Didn't our male victim have similar bruising on his right arm?"

Zim glanced over, looked at the photo, and said, "Sure as hell did. Wonder what made them?"

I sat there and watched them, feeling very much the outsider when Rocky said, "Let Kate see them, Zim. I want her opinion."

"I thought—" Whatever Zim had been about to say died at the expression Rocky gave him. He handed a manila folder to me. "John Doe" was crossed out on the tab and Joshua Redding's name had been written in above it.

I opened it, thumbing through several photos before I found the one he'd been talking about. There it was—similar, but not identical, elongated bruising. "Finger marks," I said.

"Could be," Zim said. "But maybe not."

Rocky rolled his eyes.

"Someone was holding them when they got shot," I said. "What's the trajectory of the entrance wounds?"

Rocky flipped through the autopsy reports on both subjects until he came to the info he was looking for. "Both appear to be angled from the driver's side of the car."

"So the guy holding Joshua's arm shoves the gun in Joshua's mouth, blows him away, then takes care of Eve while his accomplice is holding her arm from her side of the car?" I asked.

"That's sorta what it looks like. Execution."

"Except they leave the murder weapon behind. More like a hit, I'd say. Set up to appear like a murder-suicide."

"Maybe," Zim said, "it's more that someone doesn't like daddy's brand of politics? You two will have to keep an eye out for political bigwigs at the funeral. The type that would hire a hit."

I looked at the photos a few minutes longer, before tucking them back into the folder, then finished my poppyseed muffin. "If you were going to hire a hit, who would you go to?"

"One-eight-hundred Hit," Rocky said. "They're in the Yellow Pages."

"Funny. Remind me to check with organized crime," I said, then caught myself. "I mean, you might want to check with organized crime on that."

"I'll do that while you two are at the funeral," Zim said.

About five after eleven, we drove to the funeral home, intending to watch who arrived, perhaps jotting down a license plate number or two while we waited.

Rocky pulled into the funeral home lot, parked in the back, then grabbed a lunch bag from the floorboard by my feet. Rocky liked to pack snacks. "How's Scolari doing?" he said, taking a bite of a sandwich, corned beef on rye.

Scolari was my former partner. After his wife was murdered, he'd retired from the PD, immersed himself in his PI business, and pretty much withdrawn from the rest of the world. "Fine, I guess. Haven't seen him in a few weeks."

"I was thinking of giving him a call. See if he wanted to go to a game or two. He needs to get out," Rocky said, surveying his reflection in the rearview mirror and wiping a bit of mustard from the corner of his mouth. "Hey, check out the two goons getting out of the Caddy back there."

I adjusted the sideview mirror with the door control and saw a man standing near a black Cadillac, buttoning his suit coat as the wind whipped at it, revealing what looked like a shoulder holster but no badge of any sort, and a second man exiting from the driver's side. Both wore dark glasses. They looked around, apparently studying the lot, their gazes appearing to rest on our car.

"Maybe we'd better play the grieving couple," I said.

Rocky wrapped up the remainder of his sandwich, then handed me a couple of unused napkins. "In case you cry," he said.

We got out, and he put his arm around me while I pretended to wipe my nose with said napkin. It wasn't exactly the softest thing in the world, but the ruse worked. The two seemed to dismiss us to check out the other cars as we entered the funeral home.

Once inside, we took a seat in the very back and watched as everyone else entered, many speaking in hushed tones over the background music.

"Where's the two Secret Service types?" Rocky asked after a while.

I didn't see them in front, and so took out my lipstick case and a tube of lip gloss, using the mirror to check behind me. "One of them's standing at the door," I said, applying a thin coat to my lips.

"Why's a dead woman need bodyguards?"

I put away the lip gloss and case, curious myself, when I recalled the autopsy photos. "Maybe they're representatives from one-eight-hundred-hit?"

"Yeah. They look the type."

"Think I'll just go find the ladies' room," I said, standing and dabbing at my eyes with the napkin.

"Don't be too long," Rocky said, studiously reading the memorial folder. "Wouldn't want Andrews to accuse you of getting involved."

"Funny." I skirted my way out of the pews into the aisle. The "goon," as Rocky had called him, was standing on the side of the double doors that led to the lobby. He looked like a gangster from an old-time movie, the way he wore his hat low over his face, along with his dark glasses and narrow mustache. I moved toward him, giving a quiet "Excuse me" as I passed, along with my best apologetic and grieved smile. Several people were entering and I slipped in between them, brushing up against the man with my shoulder, as though by accident.

"Sorry," I said, then paused as though doing a double take. "You look familiar. You were a friend of Eve's?"

"The family's, actually," he said.

"I'm Kate," I said, holding out my hand and leaving him no choice but to snub me or take it.

He clasped mine and I noticed a small scar, of maybe a half-inch, on the knuckle of his thumb. "John Smith," he said.

"Nice to meet you." I shook hands, then continued on.

I could see his reflection in the glass of a large print on the wall opposite from where he stood. He never turned around.

Once in the ladies' room, I tossed the napkins, grabbed a few real tissues from a box on the counter, then waited about a minute before heading back out. When I came to the door he was still there. I gave a smile, then returned to my seat.

"Well?" Rocky said.

"He's definitely on the range a lot." I tapped a similar scar on my own right hand, something that came from the slide of a semi-auto. "Said his name is John Smith."

"There's an original name."

"Yeah."

A pastor entered from a side door, probably where the family was being seated—a side room with a view of the open casket, but out of view of the general mourners, and I thought of Eve's mother, sitting there, waiting . . . because when it was all over, she'd have nothing left but her memories. Memories and the occasional dream of what was. Not a lot of comfort. Which was why I tried to think of Eve before she'd changed. Before I'd learned that her many kindnesses to others were simply her way of befriending them in order to determine their value to her needs.

I looked at my watch, figuring it was nearly time for the funeral to start, when there was a commotion in the lobby. I turned, surprised to see Daisy Redding, still looking like a wood sprite, and at the moment hitting the hand of the goon, who had her firmly by her shoulder as he tried to remove her from the premises.

"Holy shit," Rocky said, mirroring my sentiments exactly as we took in the scene, noticing her eyes were red-rimmed, and not just from crying.

She was smashed.

"Leave me alone," Daisy said, staggering against the man. "I need to shay shomething."

He tried to escort her out as the crowd murmured their astonishment. And just as Rocky and I started that way, she kicked the stranger in the shin.

"He din't kill her," she said, attempting to enter the chapel, addressing the mourners. "You hear me? My huzbin's a good man."

"I don't know who that big guy is, but I'd feel a lot better if we got her the hell out of here," I told Rocky.

We hurried forward, stepping between the man and Daisy. "How about some air?" I told her, taking one arm while Rocky took the other. The goon at first didn't want to let her go, until Rocky flipped his coat open just enough to reveal the star on his belt. Suddenly the man couldn't release her fast enough, and I was torn between wanting to ID him and taking care of Daisy. The way she was swearing, she apparently didn't realize that he carried a gun.

Right about then, she looked at me, her gaze widening as she tried to focus on my face. "You. Thish is your fault."

"I know," I said, willingly taking the blame. Anything to get her out. Unfortunately, she wouldn't budge, and when she tried to kick at us, we stepped behind her, blocking the view of the mourners while we asserted a slight twist to her wrists, a bit of pain compliance usually reserved for arrestees, to get her moving. It worked immediately.

"You're hurting me," she said, once we were outside.

"You're drunk," Rocky said, as if that explained everything.

"How'd you get here?" I asked.

She nodded to a blue Nissan, mud-splattered as though she'd been joy riding on muddy country roads. It was parked partway on the sidewalk, inches from a fire hydrant. "Right there. Drofe it myself."

"I'll bet you did," Rocky replied.

"We'll call a cab to take you home," I said, pulling out my cell phone.

"You can't make me leaf."

"It's either that or a nice cozy jail cell."

"I'm staying at Joshua's mom's," she said as a black limousine pulled into the lot.

I assumed it was for the family and didn't pay any attention until Rocky said, "Check out who came for the show." He nodded at the limo, which had parked in front of the funeral home doors.

The limo driver exited and held the passenger door open for a man, late-forties, tall, slim, dark hair. I knew him well. I'd arrested him on more than one occasion, the last time on a money laundering charge—a charge of which he was later acquitted. Nick Paolini. Mob boss extraordinaire.

He looked up, saw me, and immediately approached, not paying any attention to either Rocky or Daisy Redding.

"Inspector Gillespie," he said, taking my hand as though it were the most natural thing in the world for him to do. "Forgive me if I seem a bit surprised by your presence at my dear friend's funeral."

11

Before I could utter anything that sounded remotely proper—after all, what does one say to a mob boss at his friend's funeral?—Daisy stumbled forward out of Rocky's grasp, right toward us.

"Y'know what?" she said to me, then glanced in surprise at Paolini, perhaps taken aback by his dark Mediterranean looks. Even if one didn't know what he did for a living, he commanded attention. "Oh, God," she said, trying to focus. "I think I'm going . . . to be . . ."

She leaned forward and hurled. Right on Paolini's polished Italian loafers.

There was a tense moment of silence as he looked down, assessed the damage. Took a step back.

Then he pulled out a silk handkerchief. "They were old," he said, wiping the toes of his shoes. I was relieved to see the damage was minimal. And almost as if Paolini had read my mind, he nodded at Rocky. "Your partner was not so lucky."

Rocky looked at his pants, saw the damage, and swore under his breath while pulling Daisy away. "Probably not the guy you want to get sick on too often," he muttered. "Trust me, he's—"

"Get the ETA for the cab," I told Rocky, giving him my sternest look.

"On it," he said, immediately drawing Daisy Redding out of our hearing and toward some more discreet bushes, should she hurl again.

Paolini strolled over to the trash can and dropped in his handkerchief. When he returned, he said, "I imagine you must be wondering why I'm here, Inspector."

Call me suspicious, but I'm wondering why you're volunteering information. Aloud, I said, "It crossed my mind."

"J. T. Tremayne is my attorney."

"I wasn't aware he'd switched from real estate to criminal cases."

"I have various properties he's handled over the years." Before I could digest that interesting tidbit, he smiled, his gaze narrowing slightly, then asked, "Why are *you* here, Inspector?"

"Eve's mother asked me."

"And she asked your partner?"

"No. He's here because there were some unanswered questions regarding Eve's death. You wouldn't happen to know anything about it?"

"Unfortunately not."

"Since she was your friend, and mine at one time, perhaps after her service, you can discuss the matter with my partner? It's his case."

He held my gaze for several seconds, as though trying to determine my intent—as if there were any question. "I'll talk to you, Inspector. No one else. Where would you like to meet—other than where we had our last private discussion?"

Couldn't blame him there—he'd been in custody at the time. "Oh, you know me, somewhere wide open and public." I too had my preferences.

"Her family is having a reception after the funeral. Since you're dressed for the occasion . . ."

I hadn't intended on going to the Tremayne home afterward, despite Eve's mother's invitation. But Eve's relationship to Paolini put a whole new twist on the fact she might have been a victim of a hit—a type of homicide that Paolini was well familiar with.

Which made me wonder . . . maybe it had nothing to do with her father's politics, and everything to do with her *godfather's* politics.

Regardless, I questioned Paolini's willingness to help me. That in itself was enough to keep me suspicious. And definitely enough to pique my interest.

I nodded toward Markowski. "Okay if I bring my date?"

Paolini smiled, something reminiscent of a devastatingly handsome crocodile. "By all means, Inspector. As long as he remains in the background."

He gave me the address, not that I needed it. When he entered the funeral home, I strode over to the bushes where Daisy was hurling her guts out. We needed to get her away from there before the service was over, before the goon saw us, and I was trying valiantly to hold my breath when a couple in their seventies came walking past, apparently late arrivals.

They stared, the older woman gasping as Daisy retched once again. I smiled at them as I patted Daisy's back. "Overcome by grief," I said. The woman nodded and the man hurried her past.

The moment they were out of sight, I said, "Screw the cab. Let's throw her in the backseat of her car. Since you already smell like vomit, you drive her in her car and I'll follow in yours."

Her keys were in the ignition, the purse on the floorboard. I held open the back door, Rocky assisted her, and she fell into the backseat like a rag doll. "He dint kill her."

"We're taking you home," I said.

"I'm shtaying at myfriendshouse." She slurred out the address. "Joshua's mom's."

Twenty minutes later, Daisy was safely at the Reddings', the key to the front door on the ring to the ignition key. As soon as we settled her on the couch, Rocky turned to leave, wasting a perfect opportunity, in my opinion. Unfortunately, it was no longer my case, so I figured a gentle reminder was in order. "Anything you want to ask her while we're here?"

"Good thinking," he said. Then he asked Daisy, "Do you know Marguerite O'Dell?"

She looked up at him, smiling. "Of coursh I do . . ." Her head fell to the couch cushion, she closed her eyes, and that was the last we heard. She was out cold.

"We could throw water on her," Rocky said.

Had I not made the appointment with Paolini, I would have attempted it. But Rocky needed to change, and keeping a mob boss waiting when he was doing one a favor generally wasn't a good idea. "We should get back," I said. "Paolini's sort of expecting us."

"What?"

"I asked him if he'd talk to you."

"And we both know the answer to that."

"He agreed to talk to me."

Rocky nodded. "Don't think Andrews could complain about that."

"My feelings exactly." Everybody knew Paolini had his preferences on who he dealt with.

"Besides," Rocky continued, "if you're sitting there looking pretty and I'm going out gathering info, Andrews can't fault you if Paolini walks up and bends your ear."

Not quite how I'd have put it, but apt.

We headed back to the car. Rocky got in, started it up, and immediately reached for the corned beef sandwich, apparently not noticing the odor of vomit he brought with him.

The thought of food after that was nauseating in itself, but then, I wasn't the one eating, so I rolled down my windows and made the not so subtle suggestion that he take us to his house first to change.

Rocky lived about five minutes away, and his wife was in the front yard, pulling weeds from a small flowerbed.

"Hi, Kate," she said, as we walked up the stairs.

"Hi, Susan. How's the knee?" She'd twisted it a week before, chasing after their youngest at the park.

"Just got back from the doctor's. Thinks it might need to be scoped."

"Thank God for insurance," Rocky said, kissing her on the cheek. "I need to change my clothes."

She waved her hand in front of her nose. "Guess so. What happened?"

"Overwrought widow crashed someone else's funeral," he said, moving past her into the house.

"Would you like to come in?" she asked me. "Have something to drink?"

"Actually, I wouldn't mind waiting out here. Too nice a day to spend it all inside," I said, taking a seat on the steps. The warm sun penetrated the black merino wool of my dress, the offshore breeze was light. All in all, not a bad day to sit on a front stoop with nothing better to do.

Susan smiled, then got back to her weeding. It was normal moments like these that made me wonder what it would be like to have traveled a different road. Taken up a more sedate career, gotten married—to someone other than Reid—had a kid or two. But then I thought of Daisy Redding. A lot of good it did her, even if she didn't have kids yet. And it still wouldn't erase my father's past, because I still would have gone to college and met Eve and brought her home and—

"How's your aunt, Kate?" Susan asked.

"Not bad," I said, glad she'd interrupted that train of thought. I closed my eyes and turned my face up into the sun, feeling blissfully catlike. "She's taking an art class this semester. Really enjoying it."

"And your nephew?"

"Doing better. Pulling his grades up."

"I knew he would," she said, then started tugging on weeds again.

A few minutes later, Rocky came out, dressed in a navy blue suit.

"Ready?" he said.

"Ready."

He kissed Susan good-bye, said he'd be home for dinner, then headed to the car.

The Tremaynes lived off of Sea Cliff in a posh area of the city that was home to a number of stars and other notables. Nick Paolini's limo was parked just past the Tremaynes' home as we arrived, and Rocky parked behind it. As we walked up the hill, his driver got out and opened the passenger door. Paolini sat inside, his eyes closed, listening to classical music, seemingly unaware of our presence for several seconds.

"*Scheherazade,*" he said, holding up his hand, indicating he would be but a minute longer. Finally the music ended. "This is one of my favorite pieces," he said as he exited the limo. It was strange to think of this man caring about anything, but here he was, clearly moved over a piece of music. "Wait for me here," Paolini told the driver.

We started down the hill, my walk made more difficult in black high heels, not my usual choice for a shoe. Other guests were arriving at the same time, and I admit to being curious as to who I might run into, what I might find as we entered the front door of the mansion, a place I hadn't been to in a number of years. But then I had to remind myself that it was Rocky's job to do the intelligence work, gather the information. I was there to sit pretty, listen to Paolini, and back up Rocky if necessary. I was not happy about the role, but I had no one to blame but myself.

We were shown into a salon that opened out to the backyard, where tables were set up beneath a canopy of trees across an emerald green lawn. Azalea bushes in full bloom surrounded the vast yard, a bright pink backdrop contrasting against the black of the gathering mourners. Funny, but all I could remember were the barbecues. Sitting back here on balmy summer nights, wine spritzers, the smell of burning charcoal and searing meat as Eve's father put the steaks on the grill.

"Refreshment?" Paolini asked, indicating the buffet set up beneath a white tent.

"Definitely," Rocky said, making a beeline for the food.

"No thanks," I said.

Paolini led the way to a table at the far end of the yard, and as he held out a chair for me and I sat, I noticed a heavyset man, dark hair, silver at the temples, watching us from several feet away. I recognized him as District Supervisor Miles Standiford, the man Tremayne had decided to run against. Apparently their political rivalry didn't extend to the realm of Eve's funeral, because he was talking to Eve's mother, Faye, who left him to come greet me.

"Kate," she said, clasping my hand in hers. "I'm so glad you could come."

"Thank you," I said, very much aware of Paolini at my side and wondering if I should introduce a mob boss to Faye Tremayne, even if her husband was allegedly his attorney.

I wasn't good at the etiquette stuff, but before I could decide whether to complete the introduction, she smiled, then looked at Paolini and said, "Would you mind if I spoke with Kate privately?"

He gave her a polite nod, looked at me, and said, "Perhaps a cup of coffee?"

"Actually, that sounds great."

"If you'll excuse me," he said, his manners, as always, impeccable, then walked toward the same tent where Rocky had disappeared.

Faye Tremayne waited until he was out of earshot and said, "They told me what you did, taking that horrid girl away."

"I'm only glad I could help," I said, wishing that Rocky was here instead of stuffing his face with food. To have Faye Tremayne out of the presence of her husband was big. Unfortunately, the main thing I wanted to know—who her husband had had his affair with, and anything else to do with Joshua Redding's blackmail—was probably not the thing to ask at her daughter's funeral. And that meant all I could do was give her a sympathetic smile of encouragement and hope she might tell me something I wanted to know anyway.

She was silent a moment, her eyes glistening with unshed tears, then, "I wanted to apologize again for my husband. I'm glad he didn't succeed in getting you removed from the case. He didn't realize how important it was to me that you investigate."

Not exactly what I wanted to hear, but I kept my expression neutral, waiting to see what she was leading up to.

"I can trust you," she said, and I tried to ignore the rising guilt. "Eve told me you knew about her illness."

"Illness?"

"That . . . sex thing." She stopped to take a breath, and I wondered if she was talking about the incident with my father. "You see," she said, "Eve couldn't help it. Having sex.

She was seeing a psychiatrist, and I was so worried it would get out, or that my husband would find out."

"He doesn't know?"

"No. I couldn't bear it if he did. God only knows I've spent every waking moment from the day I learned of it worrying about it. That's why I wanted you, Kate. You knew. You wouldn't let it get out where someone would misinterpret her behavior. That's why I know you'll do everything in your power to find Eve's killer. You will, won't you?"

Misinterpret her behavior? How did one misinterpret what Eve did to me or my father? But all I said was, "We're doing all we can."

"I—I didn't know how I was going to go on . . ." She gave me a tremulous smile as a tear slipped down her cheek. "I just . . . I need to know that you won't abandon her, Kate. That you'll find out who did this to her. Promise me . . ."

She held my gaze and I thought, how was I going to promise her something that I couldn't fulfill? It was no longer my case. And in the back of my mind, I wondered if I hadn't taken my father's photo, sabotaged my own standing, just to avoid this very moment. Maybe deep down I knew that she'd demand this of me. But I realized it wasn't her I'd expected to approach me. It had always been J. T. Tremayne I had pictured in this position.

"Please," she said, grasping my hands, her whispered plea reminding me that she had lost her daughter.

And I did the only thing I could think in this situation. "I promise."

"Thank you, Kate," she said. She smiled, brushed the tears from her eyes, and said again, "Thank you." And then she left.

She wasn't gone two seconds when Standiford approached as though he'd been awaiting that moment. "I'm Miles Standiford," he said, holding out his hand the way politicians do.

I shook it. "Kate Gillespie," I said, curious as to why he sought me out. I was sitting at a table in a veritable garden of who's who, and I was a relative nobody.

"Eve's mother told me you and Eve were friends. I thought perhaps we might have met at one of Eve's little parties," he said, his gaze dropping to my neckline. When he finally looked into my eyes once again, he smiled, his overly white teeth reminding me of something I might see on a vampire moments before his fangs magically appeared.

I hated vampires, but got past the feeling with the knowledge that this was a conversation worth cultivating. I thought of the only thing that Eve and I had in common anymore and leaned forward conspiratorially. "Eve and I had a mutual friend. Reid Bettencourt."

"Ah," he said, looking at me thoughtfully, then taking a seat at my table. "A member of her little club?"

" 'Club' seems so . . ."

"Inappropriate?" he said, his tone suggestive.

"Precisely." I wondered what the hell he was talking about, but offered up a devastating smile as though I knew. Immediately I thought of Reid's photo in her album, the way they held each other. The other photos . . . I tried not to think of my father's. "I can't imagine things will be the same, now that she's gone."

"Such a shame," he said, his gaze lingering on my neckline once more. "How is it that I overlooked you in that delightful Garden of Eden?"

"I couldn't say," I replied.

Standiford looked up, saw Paolini approaching, and immediately rose from his seat. "Well. I'll leave you to your conversation. Perhaps we'll meet again?"

"Indeed," I said.

Standiford went the opposite way, avoiding Paolini completely.

"Not quite a latte," Paolini said, handing me the cup.

I knew better than to be flattered that he recalled how I liked my coffee. "Thanks." He sat and I said, "Do you know him?"

"Standiford? A bit conservative for my voting tastes."

"Go figure," I said.

Paolini smiled and held up his cup as though for a toast. "No congratulations on my recent acquittal?"

"I thought of sending a card, but it seemed so . . . gauche."

"Touché," he said, then sipped his coffee. "What is it you think I can help you with?"

"For starters, *why* offer?"

"Perhaps our interests are the same."

"Somehow I doubt that."

"I take it you're out here because Eve's death was not the cut-and-dried murder-suicide that I was told of?" he asked.

"Murder-suicide? Where'd you hear that?"

"Around."

Interesting. I watched his face closely. "I'd say it appears to be more of a hit."

His gaze narrowed ever so slightly. "Why?" he asked, sipping from his porcelain cup.

"Call it instinct."

"And you trust your instincts?"

"Most of the time."

He didn't respond, just took another sip of coffee and looked over at the house, deep in thought. Suddenly he stood. "If you'll excuse me. I should pay my condolences to my attorney, perhaps head him off as he seems to be walking this way. He mentioned that he wasn't pleased by your being assigned to the case."

I glanced in that direction only to see J. T. Tremayne strolling across the lawn toward us, stopping occasionally to accept the condolences of various guests. "Of course."

Paolini left, and I admit I appreciated his effort. I decided to get up and find Rocky when I saw Eve's cousin, Lucas Harrington, standing near a group of older men and women.

I walked toward him, and when he looked up and saw me, he broke away from them, meeting me halfway.

He extended his hand. "Inspector Gillespie?"

I shook hands with him. "How is your grandmother?"

"Not bad, considering. She was crying because of the Black and White Ball this weekend. I don't know if you were aware of it, but she and Eve were on the planning committee. They flew to Paris a few weeks ago to get their gowns, and, well . . ." He looked away for a second as though composing himself. When he turned back, he smiled. "I'm sorry. You're not here because of that, but I appreciate your concern. How is the investigation going?"

"I seem to be running into various stumbling blocks." Like being pulled from the case.

"As in my uncle?"

"For one."

"Aunt Faye told me he was . . . a bit of a pain when you tried to question him. If it makes you feel any better, Gran doesn't like him one bit. Truthfully, he drives her nuts. She's very pro-police, and can't stand the fact he's taken this ultraliberal stance."

"I knew I liked her."

He smiled. "She appreciated your coming out to the house that night. Wanted me to thank you."

"I'm glad to hear she's doing better," I said, wondering where the hell Rocky was, so that he could question Lucas. I didn't see him anywhere and wasn't about to waste an opportunity. "Were you and Eve close?"

"Close?" he said, his gaze fixed on something in the distance—his uncle, leaning on his cane, deep in conversation with Paolini, I realized. Lucas looked back at me. "We used to be. Maybe it's part of the growing-up process. We were raised together, but the past few years she seemed . . . distant. Secretive, even."

"Any reason you can think of why Joshua Redding might be out with your cousin?"

"Joshua?" He shook his head. "No. My aunt told me Joshua was the man killed with Eve."

"Any reason why they might go see Marguerite O'Dell that night?"

"*That* I can answer. Joshua was infatuated with Marguerite. Always making excuses to be near her. Marguerite's the daughter of one of the women who helps Gran keep house. She and my cousin were in a club together, if you can believe that."

"Club?"

"A sorority club, according to Eve. When I asked her about it, she told me it was spoiled girls getting together and planning shopping trips to Paris. Frankly, I didn't believe her."

"Why not?"

He laughed. "Marguerite was the maid's daughter and came from the wrong side of the tracks. They couldn't have afforded a shopping trip to Paris unless there was some money coming in—never mind that they didn't even go to college at the same time. Marguerite's a few years younger than Eve."

"What do you think it was?"

He looked around, then leaned close. "I have no proof, but I think they were hooking. Marguerite to put herself through college, well—up until she got pregnant, then dropped out; and Eve for the thrills."

"You're sure about this?"

"You'd have to be dense not to notice there was a different man coming in each night. And Eve had a soundproof room built at the top of her stairs, one she kept locked. Mar-

guerite was at her place a lot. Gran, thankfully, didn't have
a clue, and Marguerite's mother thought Eve was a good in-
fluence, if you can believe that."

"Did your aunt or uncle know about this?"

"I seriously doubt it, but truthfully, I never asked them.
And somehow I can't imagine Eve telling them." He glanced
back toward his uncle and Paolini. "I should really go."

I thanked him for his time, then watched as he strolled
toward the house. I stared after him thoughtfully as Rocky
walked up just then with a full plate.

He set it on a nearby table, then popped a stuffed green
olive into his mouth, watching Lucas Harrington. "He give
you anything good?"

"More than you can imagine," I said, just as my pager
went off. The number was from the Hall, but I didn't recognize it. When I called, it was answered by Paul Britton, the
CSI who'd responded to Eve Tremayne's home the night of
her murder. "I got done processing all the prints from your
four-five-nine at the Tremayne place," he said, apparently
not knowing I'd been pulled from the case. "Figured you'd
want the results right away. The majority came back to Eve
Tremayne, not that there was any surprise there. It was her
place, after all. Now, what'd I do with that report . . ." I heard
a shuffle of papers, then, "Here it is. We got a hit on two la-
tents," he said. "The first one was on the doorframe in the
front room, where you saw the suspect touch it just before
he fled. The second was from the CD he dropped in the front
yard. You're never gonna guess who they come back to. Not
in a million years."

He didn't wait for me to ask. He just announced the name
and I nearly dropped the phone.

"You there, Gillespie?" Britton asked.

"Yeah. Can you repeat that?" I said, certain there must
have been a mistake.

He said the name again.

"Are you sure?"

"I'm looking at the print card right now. Pulled it from his arrest pouch myself."

"Son of a bitch," I said, thinking of the implications, the time lost, the wrong leads followed.

"What?" Rocky asked.

"Joshua Redding rose from the dead."

12

Rocky stared at me, a look of disbelief on his face. It was nothing compared to what I was feeling. We'd been duped by Daisy Redding—if in fact that was her name.

"Okay," I said to Britton, after several seconds. "If Joshua Redding is alive, then who the hell is that lying in the morgue?"

"Beats me. I only know what I got in front of me."

"Do me a favor. Get that print card down to the morgue, shove it under Flanders's nose and don't leave until he compares it to our John Doe."

"Will do."

I pressed End, then leaned back in my chair, watching Rocky stab at bright orange lox with his fork, then lay it on a bagel with cream cheese.

I tried to call the morgue. The line was busy. "We're in the goddamned twenty-first century," I said. "How the hell does someone make a mistake like that?"

"It helps to have people purposefully misidentify someone," Rocky said, taking a bite.

"If it were my case," I told him, "I'd pray Daisy Redding's still passed out on that couch."

Rocky sighed. "Good-bye food."

"Oh, please."

"Hey, it's not often you get to eat gourmet food in a garden with the movers and shakers in town."

"And if we don't get our asses to Redding's place, we'll be enjoying egg on our face to go with it," I said, starting for the house.

Rocky grabbed his bagel with lox and followed, while I chastised myself for being a half-step off in everything we'd done so far. And I had only myself to blame. "It's bad enough my life is that way," I muttered, then pasted a smile on my face as Paolini descended the steps toward us.

"Leaving so soon?" he asked.

"Duty calls," I said.

"I trust we'll have an opportunity to finish our conversation?"

I wasn't sure what Paolini could offer, but I wasn't about to write him off as a source of information. "You have a number where I can reach you?"

He gave me a card. "Try not to pass it on to your coworkers. I like my privacy."

"We'll be in touch," I said, and left it at that.

In the car, I tried calling again while Rocky drove.

"Morgue. Flanders speaking."

"Mac," I said. "Britton tells me the prints from my four-five-nine belong to Joshua Redding."

"Is that good or bad?"

"Good for Joshua Redding. Bad for the guy who's cooling off in one of your drawers. And really bad for us, considering that J. T. Tremayne named Joshua Redding as a suspect in his daughter's death."

"You telling me that sweet little thing that came in here and identified your John Doe lied to you?"

"I'm telling you she wouldn't have had the opportunity if something hadn't gotten screwed up somewhere along the way."

"I'll check up on it for you. Give me an hour."

I disconnected and tossed the phone on my seat.

"What'd he say?" Rocky asked.

"He's checking into it."

"Makes you wonder who else they got stuffed in those drawers. They sure it was really Eve Tremayne who got buried today?"

Christ, that would be all I needed. But Eve had prints on file, because she had done volunteer work in the department. And if that wasn't enough, I thought of her mother's reaction when she saw Eve's body. Daisy Redding might be able to fake tears, but the anguish I saw—and heard—was something only a mother could experience, I was sure.

Traffic on the 280 was at a thirty mph crawl, which was better than stop-and-go. "You ever hear of anything called the Garden of Eden Club?" I asked Rocky.

"No. Why?"

I told him what Standiford had mentioned.

He looked over at me. "What do you think he meant by it?"

"The entire conversation seemed like one giant double entendre to me. Eve's cousin, Lucas, mentioned that Eve and Marguerite O'Dell were hooking."

"You think Paolini's involved?"

"Don't know," I said, wishing the traffic would move faster. "This little matter with Joshua not being dead sort of interrupted everything."

"Shame on him for not getting killed. You know what we need," Rocky said, checking his rearview mirror. "We need a hovercraft. A patrol car that can just lift straight up, zoom past all the traffic, then land straight down. That, and a few heat-seeking missiles, and we'll have it made," he said, taking our exit.

The street where the Reddings lived was a straight shoot

of houses on both sides, all built in similar fashion, leading down a fairly steep hill. Some children playing catch on the front lawn of one of the houses stopped to stare at us. One of them waved and Rocky waved back. About a block down and to the right, I could see the Reddings' house, and what I thought was Daisy's blue car in the driveway. A black car, familiar looking, was parked in the street, blocking the driveway.

As we neared, I could see two men standing beside the car.

"Isn't that one of the Secret Service types we saw at the funeral?" I asked Rocky. "Our so-called John Smith?"

He lowered his sunglasses to take a better look. "Sure as hell is. But who's that with him?"

As he pulled up behind their car, I saw a third subject sitting inside it behind the wheel, obviously his partner from the funeral. One of the two standing beside the car turned and looked right at us.

"That's got to be Redding!" I said.

As soon as he saw me, he bolted straight for the house. Rocky braked and threw it in park. The other man started to follow Redding, but apparently thought better of it on seeing us. He got into the car, which sped off.

"What about them?" Rocky asked.

"Too late now," I said, getting out. Rocky did the same and we rushed to the house. The front door stood wide open. We drew our weapons. "Police!" I shouted, entering, Rocky on my heels.

Daisy was on the couch, right where we'd left her. She sat up, rubbing her eyes. "What the hell?" she said, then her eyes widened at our guns.

"Where's Joshua?" I asked.

"What?"

"Your so-called dead husband? He ran in here."

"I don't know what you're talking about."

Rocky moved past me to the kitchen. I followed, pausing at a note I hadn't seen there earlier on the table that read simply, "Black and White." At the same time, we heard the unmistakable sound of someone scrambling over a fence.

"He's jumping into the next yard," Rocky said, looking out the window.

Great. And here I was in high heels and a short dress.

We ran out the back. Scuff marks on the wood showed us where he went over. The fence was only six feet, an easy jump if one was dressed for the occasion. Since I wasn't, I grabbed a patio chair and carried it to the fence. Rocky climbed over first and I was about to follow when I heard a car start up in the front. "Daisy."

"You think she's going after him?" Rocky asked from the other side of the fence.

"Of course she's going after him. You don't misidentify dead people unless you're protecting live people."

"Pick me up on the other side," he said, tossing me the keys. "I'll see if I can spot him."

I hopped off the chair and ran back into the house and out the front door, not even stopping to shut it. The blue car was gone. Did it go up the hill or down? A crapshoot either way, but one with a logical outcome. I raced to our car, started it, and drove downhill. At the bottom I turned right, then right again. Back up the hill. I saw the blue car at the top, Joshua running toward it, Rocky after him. Joshua got in the car; it shot forward and sped straight toward me. As it passed, I saw Daisy's face, white, frightened. I slammed on the brake, tried to copy the plate, but the last two digits were covered with mud and unreadable. Rocky, huffing and puffing, ran up to me.

"Geez, that kid's fast," he said, leaning down, his hands on his knees as he tried to catch his breath.

"Should be. He rose from the dead," I said, writing down the partial number as he got in. "Buckle up," I said, flipping a U-turn.

"They went left at the bottom of the hill."

I did the same. I looked both ways. Didn't see them in either direction.

"Great."

"They had to have gone right."

"Assuming they went this way at all."

"What else can you do?"

"Go back. Freeze the house, then get a search warrant."

"Not as fun as a car chase."

"Gotta know where the car *is* to chase it," I said.

"Isn't that them?" Rocky said, pointing down the main street.

I looked. Sure enough, stopped at the red light was the small mud-splattered blue import. I signaled, then pulled out when it was clear. The light turned green and they moved on. I stayed a few cars back, hoping they wouldn't notice. After several blocks, they made a right into the parking lot of a mall. I followed, but just as I was about to turn in, a dark green Chevy Suburban cut in front of me, blocking my view of all but its bumper and the sticker on it that read, "When the going gets tough, the tough go shopping."

By the time I got in, we'd lost sight of the blue car. The place was packed—hundreds of vehicles parked everywhere. We drove around for a few fruitless minutes, finally ending up at a spot that gave me a view of the lot. I hoped I could see where they'd driven. Suddenly a horn blared behind me. The Suburban again, apparently waiting for the parking spot I was blocking. When I didn't move, she backed the behemoth away, apparently deciding not to wait.

I opened my door and stood on the running board, trying to get a better view, thinking had we been smart, we would have commandeered the Suburban and used it to look for Daisy's car. Rocky got out to look as well, but after a few minutes we gave up.

"What now?" he asked.

"If it were my case? Go back to the Reddings', secure it, get a telephonic search warrant, and hope something turns up."

Rocky picked up his cell phone. "I'll call Gypsy and get started on it."

I threaded my way out of the parking lot, back onto El Camino, and tried to retrace my path. After a few wrong turns, we finally made it. The Reddings' house was about midway up the hill. So was the goon car. Behind it was a second black sedan, occupied by two other men.

"Don't look now, but they're back," I said. "And they've got company."

Rocky unsnapped his holster just in case. "Who the hell are they?"

"Let's run their plates."

Easier said than done. As we pulled up, both cars sped off, tires screeching. I stabbed the gas pedal, trying to catch up. The goons' Cadillac turned right, the black sedan continued straight, and I followed it.

"Got 'em both," Rocky said when we reached the top of the hill. The black car raced toward the freeway, just as I got a look at the driver's profile, dark hair, bushy mustache. I let it go. More important that we secure the house and get the warrant.

I parked in the driveway. "The front door is closed," I said. "I never shut it when I chased after Daisy."

"Our two goons musta been in there. Hope they didn't find what we're looking for."

"Hope we can figure out *what* we're looking for," I said.

Rocky called in our warrant info to Gypsy, to type up

what we wanted it to say. That done, he got a call from Andrews. When he moved off a few feet, I had a feeling it wasn't good news for me. He came back a few minutes later. "Andrews says you're not to go in the house, or be involved in the chain of evidence," he said. "You can cover us outside, but that's it."

And here I'd been telling myself that there was no way I was leaving this house until we'd searched it. I'd gotten caught up in the case and forgotten the consequences of my actions. "He say anything else?"

Rocky hesitated.

"What?"

"If he sees your name come across one piece of paper in relation to this search, you might as well start polishing the leather on your gun belt, because he's gonna bust you back down to patrol."

"I get the hint," I said. "I'll just sit here on the fender of the car and watch." I might not be able to search, but I'd sure as hell be able to see what they were pulling out as it took place.

A little over an hour later, warrant in hand, uniformed officers to back him up, Rocky called a judge and got a telephonic approval to proceed with the warrant.

"Done," he told me, then went to brief the officers who would be making entry with him.

Having nothing to do, I ran the license plates from our thugs' cars. Before the report came back, Rocky had organized his entry team and they were moving toward the front door with two other uniformed officers.

"Gillespie," the first called out to me, holding up his radio. "Dispatch is on the air."

I was standing by the garage and had paused to hear what the dispatcher was saying. Rocky and the officers took a position at the front door, their guns drawn. The dispatcher repeated the plate of the goons' car and continued with, ". . . comes back stolen out of San Francisco. Second vehicle comes back registered to Bay Area Benevolent Society."

One of Nick Paolini's fronts. I wondered if Rocky had heard. He knocked on the door, then called out, "Police! We have a warrant." Standard procedure, even though we were pretty certain the place was unoccupied. He turned the knob, then jiggled it. "Locked," he said. "I'm going to kick it in."

I hugged the wall at the bottom of the steps.

Rocky moved back a few feet. He took aim, kicked at the door.

And the whole damn thing exploded in a flash of fire.

13

The explosion blew me to the ground about ten feet away. Shock set in and I didn't move. Pink tufts drifted in the air, settled on the ground around me. Cotton candy, I thought, until it occurred to me it was attic insulation. I was vaguely aware of an officer calling for Code 3 assistance. People ran toward us from all sides of the neighborhood. Someone helped me to my feet, and still I couldn't think. Couldn't move. My knees were weak, but as the seconds ticked by, I realized I didn't see Rocky anywhere. I looked around, calling out, "Rocky? *Rocky?*"

Heart pounding, I ran forward, not sure what I'd find, praying no one was hurt, knowing that was impossible. The two officers who had accompanied Rocky to the door were alive and conscious and completely singed. Their uniforms had melted in spots, looking much like someone had left the press on too long at the cleaners. One officer was sitting on the grass, the other standing, both clearly in shock. Bits of glass sparkled on their clothes and burnt hair, and blue paint and wood chips dusted them like confetti.

"Rocky?" I called out again. It was chaos—people running around, officers and citizens alike. No one heard me. A piece of the roof slid to the ground, shattering. I started to panic. "Rocky!"

And then I found him beneath the front door, flat on his

back in front of our car. The explosion had sent him flying like a ragdoll and tossed the door on top of him like a Frisbee. I lifted the door, pushing it aside. His face was singed, his eyebrows and hair melted in tiny beads. His pants had that same spotted effect from the heat.

"Oh, God," I said, feeling his carotid for a pulse. There was none. I put my ear to his mouth, hoping to feel a breath, something that told me he was okay. Nothing. His chest was still.

"Jesus, help me," I said, tilting Rocky's head back and opening his mouth. An officer, the one who had run my plate for me, kneeled beside me to help. I covered Rocky's mouth with my own, pinched closed his nose, and gave him two breaths as the officer started the chest compressions, counting aloud.

I felt for a pulse, saying, "Breathe, dammit." Again, nothing. We repeated our steps, and this time, when I placed my fingers on his carotid, I felt a flutter. My ear to his mouth, I felt the faintest of breaths, and I blinked back the tears. "Thank you," I whispered, to the officer, to Rocky, and to God.

I heard sirens in the distance, and knew they were coming for us; and then I looked up at the house. If there was ever anything worth finding in there, it had been blown through the roof or the windows, which were now gone. I stayed at Rocky's side, cradling him until help arrived. A few minutes later a fire engine pulled up; the firemen ran over. I watched as they strapped an oxygen mask on Rocky's face, and I felt detached, like I was a spectator in some live drama on TV. They worked quickly and efficiently, and I remembered saying, "He's going to be okay, isn't he?"

But no one answered. An ambulance pulled up, and they placed Rocky on a board, strapped him, then lifted him onto a gurney, wheeling him to the vehicle.

A fire truck was blocking my car in the driveway. My hands were shaking and my knees felt ready to collapse as the adrenaline fled my limbs.

I grabbed my cell phone out of the car, then climbed into the back of the ambulance, sitting next to the medic. The ambulance beeped as it backed up, then drove down the hill, the same way I had driven earlier. I hated this street. I hated Daisy and Joshua. I hated the Reddings and I hated the Tremaynes. Mostly I hated myself.

I felt like it should have been me on that gurney, and I knew it would have been, but I had pulled my father's photo from an album.

I'd set a chain of events into motion, gotten myself banned from the case. And in the end, all I could do was run a couple of plates, one stolen, the other belonging to a mobster—and I added the two thugs and Paolini to my hate list, while the siren wailed in my ears.

The ambulance ride took forever and my head started hurting, a sharp pain at the back of my skull that pulsed in time to the siren. I touched it, pulled my fingers back at the tenderness of the lump. But I knew nothing compared to what Rocky must be going through.

"Hang in there, guy," I said, wondering if he could hear me. I reached out, holding his hand, and he opened his eyes, looking at me.

"Do I want to know how I got here?"

"No." Even the hairs on his knuckles were singed. "You're going to be okay."

They wheeled him into the emergency room and I followed, giving what information I could. A nurse hustled me out to the waiting area and I was immediately conscious of people staring. I looked down at my clothes, noticing bits of glass, paint, and wood splinters embedded in the material. And everywhere was that pink insulation. I looked like I'd been rolling around in God only knew what. I paced for several minutes, trying to reach Lieutenant Andrews on my cell phone. Someone needed to tell Susan, bring her here.

I pressed End, then punched in Shipley's number. Voice mail. I sank into a chair between a woman cradling a feverish-looking toddler and a man with a bloody towel wrapped around his right hand. *Gypsy,* I thought—*she'll know what to do.* I called her phone. She answered on the second ring.

"Gypsy, Rocky's been hurt. There was an explosion."

"Dear God. Is he okay?"

"I hope so. We're at the ER now. I can't get ahold of anyone."

"The lieutenant's gone for the day. Something came up. Shipley and Zim are out."

"Someone needs to go get Susan. Bring her here."

"How are you?"

"I'm, um, okay," I said, surprised when my voice shook. "Our car's still out at the Reddings'."

"I'll get someone to Susan's right away. And we'll get your car. Don't worry about it."

"Thanks."

She hung up, and I set the phone on my lap, staring at it, trying to figure out what went wrong. He'd kicked the door. Had they rigged a bomb to it? Why? To set up Daisy and Joshua when they got back? Or to protect them from us, figuring we'd return?

Were they the men who had come and attacked Eve's grandmother in the garage? Joshua had been standing by them when we pulled up to his house, then ran when he saw us. Was Joshua a part of it? And who was in the black car? A couple of Paolini's men, no doubt. But what connection to this did he have, and what could explain Paolini's pretense of helping me?

A baby was crying, and I couldn't concentrate. The questions went round and round. I pressed against my eyebrows, willing the pain in my head to subside.

"Kate?"

I looked up to see Mike Torrance. The sight of him standing there in his business suit, tie loosened, was enough to make me want to run into his arms, just let him hold me. And had he made the slightest move, given the slightest indication that I'd be welcome there, I would have.

"Are you okay?" he asked.

"I'm fine. Rocky's . . ." I held up my hands. I didn't know what to say.

"Susan's with him right now. They want to keep him for observation. I'll give you a ride home." When he said that I realized I had lost all track of time. How long had I been sitting there?

"What about Susan?"

"Mathis is with her."

"I—okay," I said, allowing him to lead me outside.

A sickle moon glowed in the sky, royal blue with the coming dusk. Torrance and I walked through the parking lot to his car in silence. He unlocked my door and held it open. "What happened up there, Kate?"

I took a breath. "I don't know," I said, not meeting his gaze. "He kicked open the door, and—"

"And what?" he asked when I stopped.

"I should have been on that porch, not him."

"He's going to be fine."

"It doesn't matter. It's my fault he's there. If I hadn't—"

"Kate. What happened?"

"Rocky kicked the door and it exploded. That's the last thing I remember until I got up off the ground. And then I couldn't find him. And when I did, he wasn't breathing. He didn't have a pulse, he—"

"He's going to be fine."

"But I didn't know that," I said, trying to maintain my calm, and not succeeding very well. I stared across the lot at the street beyond. Anything to keep him from seeing the fear that still lingered with me. "I thought he was dead."

"But he's not," he said, taking my chin and turning my face toward his. "And you can't beat yourself up over something that you had no control over."

"I *did* have control over it," I said, wishing I were brave enough to just fling myself into his arms. It was that rejection thing I couldn't take, and the way this day was going, I figured I was better off putting on the brave front.

Torrance eyed me a second longer, and I had a feeling he saw right through me. But he said nothing, and finally stepped back, allowing me to get into the car.

As we pulled out of the lot, I said, "I'd like to go by Redding's house."

"We picked up Rocky's car on the way over, if that's what you're worried about. Mathis drove it to the hospital."

"I'd still like to go by."

He drove in that direction, but made no comment. There was still a fire engine and a patrol car there. Torrance parked across the street and we got out.

As I approached, I tried to put what happened from me, but the guilt weighed heavily. It was just one little photo. Not even the murder suspect. If I'd left it there . . . my action had caused me to be taken from the case and Rocky to be on that porch. But it was over, I told myself. Rocky was fine.

Funny how my brain was telling me otherwise.

One of the firemen saw me and waved. "How's your partner?"

"Better," I said. "Anything left in that house?"

"Feel free to go in and look around."

I turned to Torrance. "I can't go in, but you can. Would you mind? We—Rocky was trying to serve a search warrant."

"I have some time."

We walked up to the porch, stepping over splintered wood and shattered glass. Another fireman was inside, just exiting as we approached, and I asked him what happened.

"Someone left the gas on. I'm guessing your partner sparked it when he kicked the door."

I examined the shattered doorframe, what was left of it, but didn't cross the threshold. The fireman wandered over. "Find something?" he asked.

"I don't know much about arson, but is it possible that someone could have rigged the front door so that it set off the gas?"

"Could be. Gas is pretty combustible, and anything that might cause a spark can ignite it. Metal striking metal, lights switching on or off, water heaters if you turn on hot water—"

"Water heaters?" That was something I wouldn't have guessed.

"Pilot light," he said. "You're thinking this isn't accidental?"

"I'm pretty positive about that. I was in here not more than an hour before. The back door was open and the front door was open. When we got here, both were closed."

He took another look around. "It doesn't take long to build up enough gas. But we'll get more answers when the arson investigators get here."

"Do me a favor. When they come up with their results, can you have them give me a call?"

"Sure, you got a card?"

I didn't. Torrance pulled one of his from his pocket.

"Will do," the fireman said, putting it in the pocket of his turnout.

"Is it safe to look around?" Torrance asked.

"Should be."

Torrance eyed me. "Anything I should know before I go traipsing around? As in what I'm looking for?"

"I don't even know what we're looking for," I said, but gave him a quick rundown of the case so far, then remained by the front door, while he went through the place, room by room.

After several fruitless minutes, he returned and called it quits. "We'll need to send someone back when it's light," he said.

In a way I was glad. I was more than tired, and frankly, needed a very cold beer, never mind a shower. We headed down the steps to the driveway, stopping at the front door lying there. I tried not to think about the moment when Rocky had had no pulse. And that's when I saw the slip of something dark gray attached to the edge of the front door. I reached down and touched it, feeling the fine grit surface. "Look at this," I said to Torrance.

He got down on his haunches to examine it closer. "Flint paper," he said as a fireman came over to see what we had found.

"Ten to one there was another piece attached to the door frame and a match stuck between," I said.

"Assuming we could even find what's left of the door frame," Torrance said, standing.

I felt sick to my stomach and wondered who the target had been. And who the suspects were. I had naturally assumed it was the two men we'd seen, but that didn't mean that Daisy and Joshua hadn't somehow beaten us back here, turned on the gas, blown out the pilots and put flint paper on the door and frame so that whoever opened it would set it off. And we'd conveniently secured the scene, allowing the gas to build while we acquired a search warrant.

On the way back to the Hall, my thoughts were swirling in a dozen different directions, and to stay sane, I asked Torrance how he was doing on his investigation into the stolen stereos. Anything to keep from thinking about Rocky and what had nearly happened.

"Actually, we got a confession," he said. "That's where Mathis and I were when Gypsy got ahold of us."

"Case solved?"

"Sort of. He admitted to stealing the battery from your victim's car."

"The battery?" I said, staring out the window at the houses on the top of the hill near Daly City. Every house was the same and they always reminded me of the ridges on a dinosaur back. "And what, the stereo just walked off on its own?"

"He swears he didn't take it, because it was covered with blood and guts, as he put it. Strange thing is that he freely admitted taking other stereos from other vehicles towed in."

I drew my gaze from the rows of houses, looking at Torrance. "Is it possible he was telling the truth?"

"At that point, he had no motive to lie. Why?"

"Take me back to the Hall."

"You need to go home and get some rest, Gillespie. Or haven't you looked in a mirror?"

"I need to get to Evidence."

"You've been pulled from the case."

"Okay, then *you* need to get to Evidence."

"What's there that can't wait?"

"A CD," I said. I detailed the burglary of Eve's house and the CD with Joshua Redding's prints on it found outside the house. "He broke in there, I'm guessing specifically to get it. And Eve's father said that Joshua was blackmailing him over some past indiscretion. He thinks Joshua killed Eve."

"And this ties into the theft of the stereo from the car at the corp yard?"

"If there's no battery, there's no power to eject a CD from that type of player. If you're working quickly, you sure as hell aren't going to take the time to hunt down a battery. You think of any other reason someone would steal a stereo covered with blood and guts? I'm guessing that whoever stole it from the car may have thought the CD was there. Maybe after the hit, they were interrupted. Didn't have time to check the CD player and eject it. A couple kids reported the murder. Probably pulled around the corner right after it happened. Our hit men fled, figuring they'd go back for the CD player later."

"Only unbeknownst to them, our thief at the corp yard steals the battery, and they're forced to rip out the whole CD player just to see if there's a CD in it."

"Sounds good to me."

"And what's on the CD?"

"I'm guessing it isn't music."

"This ought to be interesting."

As soon as we got to the Hall, Torrance checked out the CD from Property and a few minutes later we were back in my office, popping it into my computer. I slid the compartment shut, figuring that if the CD player turned on, it was only music. I heard it rev, but then nothing happened. I clicked on the CD drive and a window opened, rows of little JPEG icons filling the screen, the titles on each listed as dates. The first date was a few weeks ago, the last date a year ago. I double-clicked on the most recent.

The picture opened.

"Eve was into S&M," Torrance said, matter-of-factly.

"Yes," I said, staring right through the screen that showed a photo of a man, naked, his hands in leather cuffs that were chained to the wall. Eve stood in front of him, dressed in a black leather bustier, fishnet stockings, and spiked heels. Completing her ensemble was a black collar with silver brads around her neck and a black leather whip in her right hand.

Torrance looked at me a moment, then said, "You're worried that your father might have been involved in this?"

I wanted to say something flippant, something like, "Who the hell can picture their parents having sex, much less kinky sex?" But I couldn't. I closed out the photo and opened the next, afraid that my father's likeness might pop up, even though the date showed a few months ago, not a few years ago. Dates on CDs could be changed, photos scanned in. We'd be here all night looking through them. "The thought crossed my mind," I said instead, closing out that photo and opening the next.

"She was an accomplished con artist, Kate."

"Meaning what?"

"You did say that Eve said she set you up, that what you suspected never happened."

And now she's dead and I have no way of knowing.

"Let it rest," he said, as though he could read my thoughts.

"Easier said than done," I said, clicking onto the next photo, then leaning in closer to the screen at the familiarity of the face I saw. A dark-haired man was tied spread-eagled against Eve's wall, wearing nothing but a black leather collar, much like a dog might wear, with a short chain hanging down the front. There was an assortment of whips and leather items set out neatly on the floor. As in the other photos, Eve stood in front of him and the man looked at her, his expression one of eager anticipation.

I narrowed my gaze when it hit me. "Standiford."

"Not quite how I pictured the ultraconservative supervisor," Torrance said.

"You think he lied about being faithful to his wife during his last election?"

"Or embellished the truth a bit."

"I don't remember seeing his photo in the album."

"You think his was the second missing photo?"

"Could be. If so, this sort of changes things."

"Everything except the fact that you need to get some rest."

I closed the photo and pulled out the CD. "We need to burn a copy of this before we book it. Gypsy's computer has a CD burner."

It took about ten minutes to boot up her computer, find a CD, and make a copy. By the time we finished and returned the original CD to Property, I was more than ready to go home, shower, and get to bed. Torrance drove me to my house, which meant I'd have to get a ride into work the next morning to get my car, which was still parked at the garage near Starbucks. I didn't bother saying anything, I was too tired.

My landlord Jack's car was in the driveway and Torrance pulled behind it and parked, turning off the engine. "I'll walk you up."

"That's okay," I said. I wanted to avoid the awkward moment I envisioned as I opened my apartment door and we both just stood there. But as I started to open my door, he reached over the center console, touching my shoulder.

"Kate."

I turned and met his gaze. Several seconds passed and finally, he said, "Get some rest."

"I will. Thanks for the ride." I got out, shut the door, waved, then walked in front of his car to the path that led to the back. He remained where he was until I started up the steps, then I heard him backing out, and I wondered what would have happened if I'd let him walk me up.

Dinky met me at my door, slipping in at my feet with a loud meow. I gave him a quick scratch, then made a beeline for the bathroom, stripping down, piling my clothes in one corner. My face was covered with dirt, my hair flecked with particles of glass and paint and pink fluff. I showered, got out, and heated up a frozen lasagna, thinking about the images on the CD and trying not to think of Rocky lying there in his hospital bed. But the two now seemed to be interlinked, and I wondered if someone on that CD knew of its existence and thought that Daisy or Joshua had it and had somehow arranged for the house to explode.

It wasn't until I finished eating that I recalled the note in Daisy's house when we'd chased after Joshua. I hadn't seen it after the explosion, but then, I'd had other things on my mind. Black and white. Black and white *what*? There were a lot of things that were black and white. Patrol cars for one. Probably not it, I thought, taking my dish into the kitchen. Black and white photo prints of the pictures on the CD I'd viewed?

I thought of my conversation with Eve's cousin, Lucas, this afternoon. How Eve and her grandmother had flown to Paris to get their gowns for the Black and White Ball. And since Eve was dead, and the words "black and white" were in a house moments before it exploded, well, hell. Someone obviously had to go to this Black and White Ball. And I was as good a candidate as anyone.

Whether Andrews would let me go was another question entirely.

14

Jack, my landlord, gave me a ride into work the next morning, and I drove straight from there to visit Rocky.

He was watching TV and I stood there a moment, wanting to apologize for him being there, but not sure how to say it. "Hi," I finally said.

"Hey, kid." He turned off the TV when I walked in.

"You feeling okay?"

"Not bad."

"Yeah, well, that just-toasted look is you."

He smiled. "Keep that up and I'm selling that Polaroid of you asleep at your desk to the highest bidder."

"How's the head?"

"I've had hangovers that were worse."

I pulled up a chair and sat by his bed, thinking he didn't look too bad—considering. His flat-top haircut was a bit on the uneven side where the hair had melted in spots, and his eyebrows looked like someone had tried to shave them off. The crow's feet wrinkles around his eyes were stark white, contrasting with the lobster red of his face, making it look like he'd fallen asleep for a couple of hours under a tanning lamp with his eyes squeezed shut.

"When you getting out?"

"Hour or two. Soon as the doc clears me. Apparently I had a slight concussion."

"Slight? You were out cold."

"Nothing a beer or two won't fix."

"Guess that precludes you from being a socialite?"

"Being a socialite where?"

"Black and White Ball tomorrow night."

I told him about the note I'd found in the Reddings' house when we'd chased after Joshua.

"Makes you wonder if they were planning some surprise visit, since Eve was going to this ball," he said.

"Or some follow-up," I suggested, "because Joshua is the suspect and there's some unfinished business to handle. Maybe something with this blackmail against J. T. Tremayne?"

"You think Andrews is going to let you go?"

"It could be considered a surveillance." I hoped. "That's not the most interesting thing going on, though. You remember me telling you about Standiford mentioning Eve's little club?"

"Garden of Eden, or something?"

"Turns out it's a club for politicians and businessmen with a penchant for S&M."

"How'd you find out?"

"The CD that Joshua Redding dropped when he fled Eve's apartment had photos of her sex partners instead of the music we thought was on it."

"In the act?"

"Big time."

"Ho boy. That'll create some motive for murder. Just saw on TV where Standiford announced he was considering not running against Tremayne after all. Seems Senator Harver's going to run for Governor and Standiford's thinking he'll run for Senator."

"No wonder no one knows who the hell to vote for. The politicians can't even make up their minds."

"Yeah, well, Standiford's name coming up certainly adds to the suspect pool."

"Between the whips and chains and other goodies," I said, "most of the other past sex scandals we've heard about on TV seem like pure Pollyanna in comparison. Something else is that I don't recall seeing Standiford's photo in Eve's book."

"Like his is one of those missing photos? Ought to give you some new perspective when you go snooping around that ball."

"Yeah," I said, then talked about the flint paper we'd found on the door, and then about life in general until I got up the nerve to say, "I'm sorry I got pulled from the case and you were hurt."

"What—Jesus, Kate. You don't think I'm blaming you for this, do you?"

"No, but you should."

"You put the flint paper on that door? You turn on the gas? No. So how the hell is this your fault?"

"You wouldn't have been kicking in the door if I hadn't been removed from the case."

"Wrong. If you hadn't gotten pulled from the case and you were on the porch kicking that door in, we'd still be standing there waiting for it to open. There'd be so much gas built up, it woulda blown an entire city block. So you see, ya saved probably a hundred lives."

I smiled. "I could kick a door. It might take a few more tries—"

"You're a wimpy door kicker, Kate, especially when you're wearing high heels. And if you did get it open, who's to say you wouldn't have been killed? Who's to say that fate has a funny way of working out and that whatever the hell you did to get pulled from the case wasn't what saved you from getting killed?"

"I removed my father's picture from Eve's photo album."

He looked at me for a second in confusion. "You mean, the night Eve was killed? That's one of the missing photos?"

"Yes. That's what happened."

"Holy shit," he said

"So I'm sorry for what happened. I just never thought that one little action would . . . snowball, I guess."

"What was it doing there?"

I told him.

He stared at the blank TV screen and several seconds went by, then, "You know what, Kate? I woulda done the same. Only I woulda been smarter. I wouldn't of snitched myself off to an IA lieutenant, of all people. To any lieutenant. You're too goddamned honest sometimes, Gillespie. You know that?"

"Thanks," I said.

"Nothing to thank me for. Now quit beating yourself up and start figuring out who the other missing photo might belong to," he said as his wife arrived. "I have confidence in you. After all, you brought me back from the dead." He smiled. "One of the officers snitched on you."

"Yeah, well, don't make me regret it."

He laughed again, a good sign, in my eyes. And when I started to say good-bye, Susan came up to me and gave me a hug. "Thanks," she said.

"You're welcome," I said, then left, feeling somewhat better. By the time I returned to the Hall, Homicide was deserted. Fridays were like that. I thought about Daisy's note again. Black and White.

Had to be the ball . . . but why? To contact someone who was on the CD? A little more blackmail action?

A few calls later, I had the number for ticket sales and discovered they were sold out. "Is there a Will Call?" I asked.

"I was pretty sure someone was supposed to be holding a couple of tickets for me."

"What did you say your name was?" the woman asked.

"Daisy Redding."

"Hold on . . ." I heard a click, then nothing for several seconds. Finally, "I have tickets reserved for a Mr. and Mrs. Joshua Redding. We have the deposit, but the balance hasn't been paid."

Interesting. I asked how much and nearly choked at the price, but it was for charity, after all, and I told her I'd be by to pay for them that afternoon, even though I had yet to get Andrews's permission to go. I telephoned my former partner's office, figuring I could go off-duty with Sam Scolari and no one could say a thing. He picked up on the second ring, but I knew better than to come right out and ask him. He'd be a hard sell on something froufrou like a ball, so I stalled by telling him about Rocky first.

"Wait a minute," Scolari said. "You're saying Markowski's toasted like a marshmallow and you didn't take pictures for me?"

"Didn't exactly cross my mind."

"Thanks for the heads-up. I'll bring my Polaroid when I see him."

"I'm sure he'll appreciate it. So, how's the PI business going?"

"Fine, I guess. Why?"

"A person can't inquire as to their friend's well-being?"

"I know you, Kate. You want something."

I fiddled with my pencil, wondering how much trouble I'd get into if I took Scolari to the ball. "You interested in being a socialite?"

"A what?"

"I'm going to wrangle a couple of tickets to the Black and White Ball. Should be a blast. All you need is a tux."

"What's up?"

I gave him a rundown on the murder and the reason I got pulled from the case.

"Shoulda kept your mouth shut on that one."

"Yeah, well I didn't. And I'd like to go to dig up some info on Eve Tremayne."

"What for? You got pulled. Be grateful and let someone else do the work."

How easy that would be. But I knew I couldn't. I'd promised Eve's mother. And if that wasn't enough, trying to find out who almost killed my current partner was. "If that was me in that hospital bed, Sam, you'd be doing the same."

"You know I don't do balls. I think you're gonna have to go the legitimate route on this one. Run it by Andrews."

"Not what I was hoping to hear."

"Sorry, Kate. But maybe he's cooled off by now."

The moment I hung up, Shipley walked in.

I gave him the details of the ball, figuring if I could get him to go, Andrews might be more inclined to approve.

"That one of those things where I'd dress in a tux, hold out my pinkie and sip champagne? Don't think so. Besides, I'm going out of town. There's always Zimwit."

"Zim makes Rocky look like the poster child for *GQ*."

"That's putting it mildly. Sorry I can't help you."

"Thanks anyway," I said, noticing Andrews had returned to his office. There was no way around this and so I got up and knocked on the doorframe. "You busy?" I asked.

"I have a minute," he said, sounding not quite so mad.

"Would going to the Black and White Ball be considered a surveillance in your book?"

"What for?"

I briefed him on what I had, including the note I'd found in the Redding house on through to the CD with Standiford's photo.

"You sure it was Standiford?"

"Pretty positive."

He shook his head. "And to think I voted for him."

"Doesn't mean he's a bad politician. Just that he's a kinky one."

"Yeah. I believe that in a heartbeat. Check with Torrance. Tell him I asked if he could spare someone."

"Torrance?" I wondered why he picked him of all people.

Andrews raised his brows. "It's either that or Zimmerman."

"I'll give him a call," I said.

I didn't know what Andrews knew of Torrance's and my relationship—or lack thereof—but figured now was not the time to bring it up. Besides, just because he asked me to call Torrance didn't mean Torrance had to go with me. There was always Mathis. He looked good in a tux. He looked good in anything. And the fact he was gay made it a very safe date, never mind that it was really an undercover assignment.

I turned to leave when Andrews said, "Low key, Gillespie. I do not want to spend the next day in the chief's office explaining why we brought bad press on the department at one of the city's premier events."

"Yes, sir."

At my desk I called Torrance's office, certain no one would answer this late on a Friday night.

"Management Control. Mathis speaking."

"Is Torrance there?"

"Left for the day. I'm using his office."

Maybe luck was on my side. "You doing anything this weekend?"

"Depends."

"Black and White Ball."

"One of those dress-up things?"

"Please?"

"Let me call Mike. I was supposed to baby-sit one of the corp yard employees for a sting. Got his name from our guy who confessed. I'll get back to you in about five. Where you at?"

"My office." I glanced out the window at the on ramp for the Bay Bridge. It was after six and traffic was still backed up. "Catching up on reports. Tell him that Lieutenant Andrews asked me to call. We're sort of shorthanded this weekend."

A few minutes later, he was back on the line. "Torrance would say yes to me going, except I can't be certain we'll be done in time. He says he'll get back to you, see if he can get someone else to go. He'd do it himself, but he has a prior engagement."

"No problem. Thanks anyway."

I hung up, feeling slightly depressed. Another Saturday night and I couldn't even get a fake date.

Such is life, I thought, heading home, wishing I'd grabbed a snack from a vending machine before I'd left. Traffic was so thick I was starved by the time I got to Berkeley. As soon as I pulled into my driveway, my landlord, Jack, poked his head out the kitchen door, his white hair gleaming beneath his porch light. "We're short a bunco player, Kate. You don't even have to be mentally alert, just a warm body."

Somehow, playing bunco with a bunch of senior citizens wasn't what I'd had in mind when I'd picked up my six-pack. "You sure you wouldn't rather call my aunt?"

"Already did. It's her bridge night. We're having tacos and margaritas . . ."

Food that somebody else cooked and didn't have the words "take-out" printed on a bag? "Okay."

Turned out that his wife made a mean taco, and her margaritas were so smooth, I was pleasantly plastered when I finally went home and heard the phone ringing. By the time I found it on the couch cushions, the answering machine had picked up.

"Sorry," I said, once the message stopped. "Couldn't find the phone."

"I hear you need a date."

Did the entire world know? "Who is this?"

"Torrance."

"Didn't recognize your voice. Maybe because the word 'date' was coming from it," I said, not sure if I'd said that part aloud or not, and truthfully, not caring. "And for your information, it's not a *real* date. I just need a backup."

"I'll pick you up around six."

"Six," I said, pressing the Off button, and if memory serves, promptly falling asleep right there on the couch.

I woke the next morning with a killer headache. Dragging myself into the bathroom, I splashed cold water on my face in an attempt to wake up enough to take a shower. That done, I turned on the TV just to have something to listen to while I dried my hair, then searched my closet in the futile hope that I might find something suitable to wear to tonight's ball.

Just my luck: the news came on, and with it, the Bay Area's favorite local liberal extremist, J. T. Tremayne, discussing none other than his daughter's death and his lack of faith in the Police Department. I was just in time to catch his quote of, "Because as everyone knows, if the killer isn't caught in the first forty-eight hours, the chances of solving the case diminish significantly."

"Oh, please," I said. "As if I could get anyone to cooperate in the first forty-eight hours."

I reached for the remote, shut off the TV, and turned on some music.

I was less successful in the closet endeavor. It meant one

thing—I had to go shopping. Not something I relished, even after popping about three ibuprofen pills. I hit the department store and finally settled on an ankle-length black velvet gown with rhinestones around the neckline and long sheer sleeves, not because the saleslady said it shouted understated elegance. Because it made me look thin, even with a hangover, and it nicely covered the angry red scar on my shoulder from a shooting a couple of years back. What more could a woman ask for in a dress?

That hurdle out of the way, I went home, finished cleaning my apartment, then promptly hit the couch, intending on napping only for a minute—and woke up about five-thirty, not sure if someone was pounding on the door or on my head or both.

I sat up, looking out toward the kitchen, and recognized Torrance's silhouette through the curtain.

Dragging myself up, I let him in, tux and all. I'd seen rented tuxes, Scolari wore them. This was no rental. He looked damn good, but I wasn't about to let him know, especially when I was pretty sure my hair was probably plastered to one side of my head. "You're early."

"As drunk as you sounded last night, I figured you'd need the extra time."

"It's been a long week. And I was hardly drunk."

" 'Hardly' being the operative word. You have pillow marks on your face, Gillespie."

"Hazard of being a couch potato. Make yourself at home," I said, turning on the TV, then walking toward my bedroom. "I'd offer you a beer, but we used it in the margaritas last night."

A glimpse in the mirror told me I was in worse shape than I'd thought. Nothing for it but a second shower, at least to tame the hair. At five after six I was putting on black nylons, then sliding the velvet gown over my head. A few touches from a curling iron to my hair, along with a little mascara and blush, and I was ready to go. I grabbed my coat, slipped into black heels, and found a black purse with a chain strap, one that would carry a small pistol safely next to a zippered compartment for my badge.

Torrance stood as I left the bedroom, did a double take when I dropped my coat on the couch in order to slip my gun into my purse. Since he'd seen my various guns on more than one occasion, I had to assume he was looking at the dress. I took that as a compliment. "I clean up well," I said on my way to the kitchen.

He smiled, grabbed my coat, then followed me. "I didn't think there was anything wrong with you before you changed."

"I bet you say that to all the undercover officers you have to escort."

"Saw right through me," he said, slipping my coat over my shoulders. "Ready?"

"Ready."

He played the gentleman all the way out to the car, opening my door for me, closing it once I was settled. A girl could get used to this stuff. Too bad it was purely professional, I thought as we drove to the city.

The Black and White Ball was actually a conglomerate of musical events, centered at City Hall and overflowing into the various buildings that surrounded it. Held every two years, it hosted groups playing classical music, rock, big band, and everything in between, all to support the San Francisco Symphony.

For the symphony, it brought in millions, was attended by thousands, and truth be told, made me wonder how in hell we were going to find anyone remotely related to the case, never mind a simple parking space.

Turns out parking was the easiest of the problems. The

streets surrounding the area were closed to traffic and parking, and Torrance simply showed his star to the officers working traffic control. We parked as close as we could get to Davies Symphony Hall, where the tickets were kept at Will Call. Torrance took my coat while I went to get the tickets.

A woman sat at a table, dressed to the nines, and asked me my name.

"Mrs. Joshua Redding."

She fumbled through some envelopes separated by letter dividers, couldn't find it on the first go-around, then asked in a voice worthy of British royalty, "And *exactly who* did you say was leaving them here?"

"Supervisor Standiford." What the hell, I thought.

The name sobered the haughtiness from her face and earned me an, "Oh. Then why didn't you say so?" She flipped the envelopes to the *R* section, pulled the invitation out. Imagine. "Enjoy yourself, Mr. and Mrs. Redding," she said, handing it to me.

"Thank you. And by the way, if someone shows up saying they're us, can you do me a favor? Stall them and call the police? We've had a little theft problem."

"Of course."

I gave the invitation to Torrance, who appeared amused. "You didn't tell me we were married."

"I only just found out myself."

"Does this mean I get all the husbandly benefits?" he asked, holding his arm out for me to take as we entered the ballroom.

"Only if I get alimony when this job is over."

I took his arm, tried to ignore the wicked look he gave, and definitely ignored his whispered, "Might be worth it."

It was showtime, and I had a murderer to catch.

15

We walked into a world very different from what I was used to. A world filled with glitter and riches, women in glamorous dresses and enough diamonds to put the chandeliers to shame.

I was totally out of my element.

I pasted on my best socialite smile, as if I even knew what one was, and allowed Torrance to lead me across the crowded room. "What are you thinking?" he asked after a considerable silence.

"That I'm the only woman in here with fake diamonds and real fingernails."

"I'd say that calls for a drink," he said, suppressing a grin.

"Definitely."

He left me alone while he went to one of several bars set up around the ballroom, bars that were very crowded, which meant it would be awhile. He wasn't gone more than two minutes when I heard, "Kate?"

At the sound of my name, I turned to see my ex-husband, Reid, standing with several people, one of whom was his current girlfriend, TV anchorwoman Beth Skyler.

I debated offering a polite wave, but his group of friends seemed to part in anticipation of my inclusion. "Reid," I said. "What a surprise."

"Beth is covering the ball on the late news tonight. What are you doing here?"

"The usual twenty-four/seven stuff," I said, hoping he'd take the hint.

He did, introducing me to the others simply as Kate, finishing with, "You remember my friend Beth."

"How could I forget?" I said, smiling at her. I should have given her a medal for getting Reid off my hands—even if we were still married at the time—but sometimes little details like that were lost in the translation. "Nice to see you again."

She offered me a pleasant smile, which turned radiant when Torrance walked up—radiant because she was going to set her sights on him or because it meant less competition for Reid, I didn't know.

Torrance handed me a flute of champagne, and I sipped at it, nearly grimacing at the sweetness, until I realized it was sparkling cider. Sometimes this job had its perks. Now was not one of them, I thought, as someone tapped me on the shoulder. "Kate, isn't it?"

I turned to see Supervisor Miles Standiford, and couldn't help but recall the image of him on the CD. He was definitely one of those people who looked better with clothes on, and that was stretching it. "Mr. Standiford. What a surprise," I said.

Before he could respond, Beth put her hand on his arm. "Is it true you intend to run for Senator instead of District Supervisor?"

He smiled politely at her. "I'm giving it some thought, but I'm torn. There's so much I feel still needs to be done for the city." And then he turned to me, his gaze direct, vampire smile intact. "I was hoping you might honor me with a dance."

I looked at Torrance. "You don't mind, do you?"

Torrance raised a brow, and I wondered whether he was

thinking about the CD photos of Standiford or giving me a subtle warning to remember Andrews's orders to stay low key. "Not at all," he said, taking my drink.

Reid moved forward and started to speak, and I promptly cut him off by glancing at Standiford and saying, "I haven't waltzed in ages. As long as you don't mind if I step on a toe or two . . . ?"

Standiford laughed, then led me onto the floor. "I'm a bit rusty myself, so we'll muddle through this together," he said. But before he had an opportunity to prove his point, Paolini came upon us.

"Inspector Gillespie. You look enchanting, as usual."

"Paolini," I said, stepping back, very conscious of the look of surprise on Standiford's face. "You know Mr. Standiford, of course?"

"By reputation," Paolini said, a comment I found curious.

Standiford eyed me warily. "Inspector? As in police?"

Before I could answer, Paolini said, "As in Homicide detail. And here I assumed the two of you were acquainted."

"Apparently not as well as I thought," Standiford replied. "But obviously you have work to do, if you're looking for suspects here, so if you'll excuse me." He nodded to the two of us, then left.

"Well, that was interesting," I said, watching him as he strolled off, doing the politician thing, stopping every few feet to shake hands with someone he knew.

"What was?" Paolini asked, looking clearly amused.

"Everything. Including your timely interruption. Did you intend to give up my cover, or was there a purpose to this visit?"

"Actually, there was. I came to suggest you keep your distance from the Tremaynes. They have friends who might not take kindly to your meddling."

"Friends such as you?"

"Put it this way, Inspector—in the world of friends and enemies, I am but a small fish in a big ocean. And those you know who seem the friendliest might not be."

"So stay away?"

He gave a nod. "Just remember that I gave you fair warning, Inspector. Do enjoy the rest of your evening," he said. With a slight bow, he turned on his heel. I watched him weave his way across the crowded room, thinking about what he'd said about how "those you know who seem the friendliest might not be." For some reason, Faye Tremayne came to mind, and I told myself that she bore watching.

"What did he want?" Reid asked me on my return.

"Paolini?" I said as Torrance handed me my flute of cider. "No, Standiford."

Curious, I thought, since Paolini was the last person I'd spoken with—a mob boss, no less. I wondered why Reid was asking. Guilty conscience about the Garden of Eden? Was that why his photo was in Eve's book? "He simply wanted to dance," I said lightly.

"I thought you didn't know how."

"There's a lot you thought about me, Reid," I quipped with a smile. "That's why we're divorced. By the way. You have any idea why my being a cop might turn Standiford off?"

"I'm not sure I understand," Reid said. And before I could question him further, Beth returned with her cameraman and crew at her heels.

"Reid," she said. "Do be a dear and get me a sparkling water. We're going live in just a few minutes. Senator Harver is here and I'm going to interview him."

"For you, anything," he said. "Kate? Mike?"

"I have one," I said, taking a sip from my glass.

"No, thank you," Torrance said.

Reid left, and Beth pulled out a lipstick and mirror from

a small evening bag. She eyed her reflection, then me. "Reid tells me that one of your victims might be Joshua Redding?"

"Did he?" Nothing like having a direct link.

"I knew his girlfriend, Marguerite, in college. She was a few years younger than him."

"His name came up," I said, wanting to know what she had to say, but keeping it vague on purpose, since she was the press. I had orders to keep this low key, and I trusted her about as much as I trusted Reid not to talk to her.

"Well, the whole thing's ironic if it is him. Great angle for a story, now that I look back on it all. I remember there was some sort of scuttlebutt over their relationship."

"And what was that?"

She pressed her lips together, then touched up a spot with her pinky. "Heard it on campus one day. I guess you could say my budding reporter's instincts took the whole thing as hogwash for the simple reason that if you're not there, the girls would talk about you. She had the same class, and one day just never showed, so the rumors flew."

"You mean she cut class?"

"No, I mean she just never showed up again," she said, tucking the lipstick back in the tiny bag.

"And what were the rumors?" I asked.

"One, that she was supposedly pregnant."

"And that's why she left school and never came back?" It seemed far too mild a rumor to worry about.

"It had more to do with who the father of her baby happened to be," she said. "Needless to say, the *alleged* father was going to run for office, but backed out at the last minute, and everyone assumed that he had the mob do away with Marguerite, since she was never heard from again."

"And who was the alleged father?"

"Someone I find totally ironic, in light of the upcoming candidacy announcements and everyone jumping on the holier-than-thou platform," she said, snapping her little purse shut.

She looked at me and smiled. "Someone you know, of course. Eve's father. J. T. Tremayne."

16

<hr>

"We're ready, Miss Skyler," the cameraman said, before I had a chance to comment on her statement. J. T. Tremayne, the father of Marguerite O'Dell's child?

Now that I thought about it, there was some resemblance between him and the little girl, Bonnie. I wondered at the implications, dismissing the rumor that the mob had taken out Marguerite, since her child was obviously there at Lillian O'Dell's home.

That certainly fit in with Joshua Redding's blackmail scheme. But why kill Eve if Tremayne didn't pay? If it was about money, it didn't make sense.

Then again, Tremayne was wealthy, and with Eve dead, that could make Bonnie his heir. A motive for murder on Marguerite's part?

While I was contemplating motive, another of Beth's crew brought over Senator Harver and his wife, Lara, an elegant couple in their fifties. He was tall, gray-haired, and slightly overweight. She was about a head shorter, her dark hair swept into a bun at her nape.

Interviewing him would be a feather in Beth's cap, since Harver was vacating his seat to run for the Governor's office—something he had every chance of winning, considering his political background, household name, and pristine reputation.

It made me think of Standiford, who had a similar reputation, though at a local level. And that made me wonder: was there such a thing as an honest politician? Before I'd seen the CD, I'd have cast my ballot for Standiford in a heartbeat—had he been in my district. He was very pro-cop. Should it matter that he was into kinky sex and had lied about his fidelity? Or did one cast one's vote for Tremayne, a man who had possibly fathered a child out of wedlock, who hated cops, and whose murdered daughter was into blackmail and kinky sex?

Tough choice, I thought, as Reid walked up with the sparkling water and handed it to Beth. She took a sip, gave it back to him, then stepped in front of the camera, just as Torrance pulled his pager from his waist. "I've got to take this call," he said.

I nodded and he walked toward the men's room.

The lights came on, and the cameraman gave Skyler a mike, did a countdown, and gave her the signal that they were going live.

"We're at San Francisco's most elegant fundraiser of the season, the Black and White Ball," she said. "As you can see, the guest list reads like a Who's Who of the city's elite, with a marked absence of Eve Tremayne, whose tireless dedication . . ."

I moved away, standing next to Reid, thinking about the rumor of who'd fathered Marguerite's baby. If it was J. T. Tremayne, it would certainly explain why Marguerite's pious mother, Lillian, was upset—her daughter fornicating with an employer's married son. Mrs. Tremayne had certainly made a vague reference at the morgue as to the status of *her* daughter being the one lying there. Why? Maternal grief? Or a jab at his fathering a child out of wedlock?

What bearing that might have on why Eve was killed, however, I didn't know—unless Joshua was the killer, as

Tremayne had insisted. Which made me wonder again about Standiford's reference to this "little club" of Eve's and how and why Reid was connected to it.

"Reid," I said. "District Supervisor Standiford was—"

Reid held up his hand, motioning me to silence. "She's good, isn't she?" he whispered in my ear. "She can really take a story and run with it."

How did you "run" with an entertainment piece? I smiled and pretended interest.

". . . But the event is far from somber, in light of what happened, due in part to the unexpected appearance of Eve's father, and her cousin, Lucas, who came to pay tribute . . ."

I perked up at the name. "Lucas Harrington?"

"Eve interviewed him earlier," Reid said. "Over by the bar."

I looked in that direction and saw Lucas standing beside two very beautiful young women. "Back in a few," I said, just as Beth started interviewing Senator Harver.

As I approached, Lucas said something to the two women, who both left without a word, then he smiled at me. "I suppose I shouldn't be surprised to see you here," he said. "More questions?"

"A couple. I found a CD that was dropped outside your cousin's house the night she was killed. I'm guessing that was what the burglar was after. It wasn't music."

This time his smile looked uneasy. "I hate to say it, but I have a fair idea of what it was."

"Do you?"

"As I explained before, my cousin had . . . a rather prolific and unusual sexual appetite. She had a bag with some things in it that I'm sure she meant to keep private, and would have, had the zipper not broken when she was loading it into her car." He stared down at his drink a few seconds, then back at me. "Let's just say that there was a lot of leather involved, along with some other items whose function I could only guess at."

"Is it possible she might have been blackmailing someone with these photos?"

"Truthfully, I never would have thought my cousin capable of blackmail, but then, until I saw the contents of that bag a few months ago, I never would have thought her capable of—" He stopped, his gaze catching on someone across the room, before he finished with, "Well, you know what I mean."

I glanced in that direction and saw his uncle, J. T. Tremayne, watching us. He was speaking with a dark-haired man, someone I didn't know. Before I could reply, Lucas said, "If there's nothing else, I have some friends I've neglected long enough."

He left and I started toward Reid and Torrance, only to be waylaid by J. T. Tremayne, who held out his cane, blocking my path. He was alone now and stood in front of me so that I was forced to step back or stare directly up at him.

"I would think you'd have some respect for the dead," he said.

"I'm not even going to pretend to understand what that means."

"My daughter is barely in her grave, and you have managed to crash her funeral, the reception, and the ball to which she would have come had she still been alive."

"I'd think you'd be interested in trying to discover who killed her, Mr. Tremayne."

"Oh, I am. Which is why I have asked Agent Morley to look into the matter."

"Agent Morley?"

"From the FBI," he said. "So stay away from my family, Inspector, or I shall be forced to have you removed from the case."

Wouldn't that just make his day if he knew the truth? I didn't respond, though. Instead, I took a step to the side, then moved past him, feeling his stare on my back as I worked my way through the other guests to where I had left Reid. Reid, however, was gone. Only Senator Harver stood there, patiently waiting while one of the camera crew removed the mike from his shirt.

The senator looked at me and smiled. "I saw you talking with Miss Skyler," he said. "Are you part of her crew?"

"No," I said. "Actually, I'm just an acquaintance. Her boyfriend is my ex."

"Ah, Reid Bettencourt," Harver said after the crewman left. "Nice young man. Ambitious. I told him he should go into politics."

"He'd probably be good at it," I said, thinking about his track record with women.

"And what about you? Are you in law enforcement, too? I vaguely remember Reid saying he was married to a police officer."

"Homicide."

He narrowed his gaze. "Not the inspector whom J. T. Tremayne has been *not*-so-subtly bashing on his rounds this evening?"

"That would be me," I said. "In all my glory."

"Well, I don't know if this helps, but what he's doing goes beyond the realm of acceptability. Even the FBI agent he was speaking to said the same thing."

"I appreciate you saying so."

"Well, I really must find my wife. I promised to walk her across to City Hall where the symphony is playing. Perhaps we'll run into you there?"

"Perhaps," I said as Torrance approached from one direction and the dark-haired stranger J. T. Tremayne had been speaking with approached from the other.

They arrived around the same time, Torrance taking a position by my side, his expression wary as the other man said, "Are you Inspector Gillespie?"

"I am. And this is my partner, Lieutenant Torrance."

"I'm Special Agent Morley, FBI," he said. "Mr. Tremayne was telling me a little about his daughter's case."

"He mentioned that he was going to ask the FBI to look into it."

Agent Morley brushed at his mustache, looking off in the direction of the bar where Tremayne was ordering a drink. "He did ask, which is why I wanted to talk to you," he said, his gaze returning to me. "Is there any reason why you think this is a Bureau matter?"

"At the moment, no. Unless Tremayne told you something that we don't know . . ."

"Nothing that tells me the case isn't where it belongs." He gave an exasperated smile, then held out his hand. "Sorry to bother you, but I told him I'd check into it."

"Not a problem," I said, shaking his hand.

He left and Torrance and I watched him head back to Tremayne.

"Is that what Tremayne spoke to you about?" Torrance asked.

"That, and to tell me to stay away from his family. Apparently he was upset by my presence here and at the funeral. You get your call taken care of?" I asked, changing the subject. No sense letting him think I was doing more than a simple surveillance.

"Mathis says they're tailing our second corp yard suspect. He's supposed to have most of the stolen property." We were both silent a moment, each lost in our respective thoughts. Finally he asked, "Any sign of why this place appeared on that note?"

"Not really," I said, almost ready to give up. I looked

around, saw Reid standing beneath the Exit sign near the lobby, looking with interest at something outside. I wanted to ask him about this Garden of Eden Club, to see his expression. "But maybe Reid might have an idea? If you wait here, I'll ask him."

It turned out that Reid was watching Beth Skyler and her crew setting up just outside the doors.

"You have a minute?" I asked.

"Sure," Reid said, barely sparing me a glance.

"Tell me about this Garden of Eden Club that Eve was involved in."

There was a long silence as he drew his gaze from the activities of the news crew outside and turned his full attention to me. "What did you say?"

"Garden of Eden."

"I had *nothing* to do with it."

I noticed he didn't ask me what it was. "Let me rephrase that. Supervisor Standiford seemed to think your name gave him carte blanche to discuss the club, all because I told him Eve and I had a mutual friend in common, that friend being you. Now, why is that?"

"He obviously misunderstood."

"Oh, bullshit, Reid. He was alluding to sex, and you were always prowling for it—never mind that your photo appeared in Eve's big book of conquests."

"Photo?"

"Yes. Now, what gives?"

I waited.

Reid looked away for a moment, then back, as though gathering some thoughts or lies or both. "I introduced Standiford to Eve. For whatever reason he seemed to think it was the greatest thing since absentee ballots."

"He didn't tell you why?"

"He didn't need to. I guessed why. Eve was easy."

"Easy?"

"More than easy. She was addicted to sex."

I raised my brows.

"I mean *really* addicted," he said. "She wanted introductions to people she didn't know. The District Attorney, local politicians, visiting dignitaries."

"For what purpose?" I asked, though I knew. She'd used my father the same way.

"What do you think? So she could sleep with them."

"That's heartening. Please tell me you weren't sleeping with her when we were together."

"I swear. I didn't even really hear about it until tonight, when Standiford told me he'd mentioned the club to you."

"He told you?"

"Yes. He said he assumed I knew about it, because I'd introduced them and he thought I was—um, supposed to be sleeping with her. But I wasn't, Kate—I swear," he said, crossing his heart. "I told her that she and I couldn't be together because of you, and to tell you the truth, she was pretty upset. Even jealous. I don't think she liked you."

Go figure. Aloud, I said, "When was this?"

"It was the night of the New Year's party at the Hilton. We weren't there for all of five minutes before you got called out on that homicide," he said. He shoved his hands in his pockets, looking at the ground before meeting my gaze, and I wondered if that wasn't a jab at why he believed our marriage had never worked. *Good try,* I wanted to say. But no cigar.

"And then what happened?"

"She kept hitting on me, so I finally introduced her to Standiford just to get some space."

There was a first, I thought. Even so, I tried to remember if there was anything significant about that party that night, but I couldn't. He was right. I was there all of five minutes before I had to leave. "And what did Standiford tell you this club was?"

"She and a few of her friends used it as a way of meeting men and sleeping with them. No big deal." He glanced out the door, then back. "Anything else? I don't want to miss Beth before she finishes filming outside, then leaves."

"If I think of something, I'll call you."

He took off through the doors as Torrance walked up. "Find out anything significant?"

About what he knows? Or who he slept with? That part I didn't know. "No," I said. "I don't know what else there is to do here, except mingle and try to blend in, or just leave. Maybe we're wasting our time."

"Then maybe we should dance."

"Right."

He held out his hand, which was my first indication that he was serious.

I tried to think of a subtle stall. "I'm not very good."

"I'll take my chances."

I put my hand in his and he clasped it tight, then led me past a number of the younger couples who streamed from the dance floor. Apparently they didn't favor the slower music, and suddenly I wanted to follow them.

What was I thinking, agreeing to dance?

To be mere inches from Torrance's face as he held me was something I hadn't counted on tonight. It was too personal, and my feelings for him were too complex. I didn't even fully understand them myself. We had too many differences that needed too much work. I didn't even think he liked me anymore. How the hell was I supposed to handle this?

Talk about the case, I thought as we stepped onto the floor, my evening bag gripped tightly in my right hand. A nice, safe topic. One that couldn't be construed as anything but work and professionalism.

"Mathis sure made progress on that corp yard sting, don't you think?" I said.

Torrance didn't reply. He merely placed his hand at the small of my back, and I felt the heat from his touch through the fabric. *Concentrate,* I told myself. "When you think about it," I said, "that was probably a pretty profitable business. Car brought in to be stored, steal the parts—"

"Kate?" His gaze was dark, serious, locked on mine, giving me the feeling that he knew everything I was thinking just now. And everything I was trying not to think about.

"Yes?"

"Shut up."

And then we danced. And there was nothing proper about the way he held me at all, because I could feel him against me as we moved across the floor. I closed my eyes, trusting him to lead, afraid to look at him. Afraid to see in his eyes that he'd asked me out of politeness—afraid to see that he'd asked me for reasons I didn't want to contemplate right now.

I told myself I was safe.

I knew Torrance.

We were in public.

But as the music came to a conclusion, we stopped right there in the middle of the floor, Torrance holding me still. I opened my eyes, telling myself I would smile, say thank you, and that would be it.

I knew otherwise the moment I saw his gaze fixed on my mouth. I could feel it in the tension of his body, and my heart sped up in anticipation.

"Mike? Kate?" I heard Reid call out as he neared us. Torrance stepped back, the moment was lost, and I remember thinking that this had better be good, or I was going to get fired for killing my ex-husband. "You'd better come quick," he said. "There's a plainclothes officer who told me that Joshua and Daisy Redding are out there now, trying to get their tickets from Will Call."

17

Torrance and I followed Reid from the dance floor, through the lobby, to the Will Call. At first I didn't see anyone who resembled Joshua or Daisy.

"Are you sure?" I asked Reid.

"There he is now," Reid said, pointing.

The woman in front of me moved aside and I recognized Daisy at once. She was looking over her shoulder in both directions as though worried she might be seen. Joshua had his back to us, speaking to the woman in Will Call.

"You have a weapon?" I asked Reid.

Being a DA investigator, he normally carried concealed, and he gave a short nod.

"Do me a favor. Cover the door to the ballroom. Don't let them past."

"Got you," Reid said, taking a position by the main entrance.

I looked at Torrance. "Ready?"

"Ready."

We strolled toward them, arm in arm to the casual observer. Reality was that his right hand was positioned to draw his weapon from his shoulder holster, left side, while my right fingertips rested on the butt of my small semi-auto concealed in my evening bag.

I took note of our surroundings. Twenty or more people

stood about in small groups, talking, laughing, blissfully unaware of our presence. Just outside, two security guards
lounged near the doors, watching the camera crew and Beth
Skyler out on the sidewalk, apparently giving an update on
the night's event.

Nobody paid us the least bit of attention, just how I
wanted it. Now, if our luck would hold . . .

A woman in a white sequined gown laughed at something
her partner had said, a shrill sound that pierced the quiet of
the room. We were maybe fifteen feet away when Daisy
startled at the noise. Both she and Joshua turned toward it,
searching; then, recognition hit them as they caught sight of
me. I pulled out my star, which was clipped inside my purse.

"Shit," Joshua said.

"Keep your hands where I can see them," I told him. Suddenly he grabbed Daisy's hand, dragging her toward the
exit. Torrance lunged, caught Joshua by the arm, but he
pulled free and they flew out the door.

"Son of a bitch," I said. Having no choice, I hiked up a
fistful of gown with one hand and ran after them, hoping the
security guards would help. They simply turned and stared
at the spectacle. The Reddings descended the stairs two at a
time, Torrance in pursuit. Their small blue Nissan, the same
car we had chased them in, was parked out front, near the
line of vehicles for the press, and I wondered how they'd
managed to finagle that. A security guard leaned against
their car, smoking a cigarette. Joshua pushed him away,
yanked open the door, and nearly shoved Daisy in. He ran
around to the driver's side, got in, and started it up. A second later it sped off, tires screeching.

Torrance raced for his car.

I hurried down the stairs. Torrance backed up his car and
I got in.

They had about a block on us and were driving without

headlights, making it difficult for us to see them at all until they hit their brakes and made a right. I pulled out the radio hidden in the glove box and called for a marked unit in the area to make a traffic stop. We were in luck—a radio car was two blocks away and quickly caught up with us, its flashing red and blue lights reflecting in our rearview mirror.

"Three-six-one-five," the officer said, radioing his call sign. "Coming up behind you."

"Three-six-one-five, copy," I responded. "We're following a blue Nissan, unknown plate, no lights, break." I waited a couple of seconds, keyed the mike, and continued. "Vehicle driven by a WMA late-twenties, Joshua Redding. Passenger female."

Torrance pulled to the side, allowing the radio car to pass. It sped by, then, "Three-six-one-five, I have the vehicle in sight. Ten–twenty-eight," he said, then read off the license plate. Silence, then, "Three-six-one-five, suspect vehicle failing to yield. What's the want on these two?"

Depending on the want, he would terminate the pursuit or proceed. "Questioning on a one-eighty-seven and arrestable on a four-five-nine," I radioed back. Not enough to arrest him on the homicide, so might as well take him in for burglary.

A minute later, the officer radioed in a yield on Market Street. Torrance blacked out his lights and pulled up beside them as the officer used his loudspeaker to order out first Joshua, then Daisy as we held them at gunpoint. He searched each, then handcuffed them. When they were secured in the back of the patrol car, the officer approached me. "What about the car?"

I figured Daisy might be more inclined to talk if she didn't have wheels available to her. "Tow it."

I walked up to the rear of the radio car and opened the back door on Daisy's side, hit by an overpowering smell of aftershave, whether from Joshua or the patrol officer, I couldn't tell. I purposely ignored Joshua for the moment, and asked Daisy, "You mind coming down to the Hall for questioning?"

"On what charge?" she asked, looking panicked.

"Oh, I don't know. How about the misidentification of a dead body, for starters?" I glanced at Joshua. "Especially considering the guy you're sitting next to is supposed to be the deceased."

Joshua gave a snort. "That's only a misdemeanor. You can't hold her for that."

"Okay," I said, slightly annoyed by his attitude. "How about helping a fleeing felon to escape? That would be you, Mr. Redding. In case you were wondering."

"Don't say anything," he told Daisy. I drew her out of the car, then shut the door as he screamed, "It'll be okay! Don't say a thing!"

She looked from him to me as I guided her toward my car, her eyes glistening with unshed tears.

"If you're taking your advice from him, I'd rethink it."

"Do I need a lawyer?"

"Just in case, let me read you your rights." I took out my Miranda card even though I knew it verbatim. Defense attorneys were sticklers on crossing all their damned *T*s and such, and heaven forbid you didn't pause at a comma or something. When I finished reading it, I asked her, "Do you understand each of these rights I have read to you?"

She bit at her bottom lip, glancing back at Joshua.

"Daisy, do you understand?"

"Yes. Can we hurry?"

I handed her off to another officer and said, "Take her to the Hall. I'll be there shortly."

The first officer was filling out the tow sheet and called dispatch for a tow truck and for the registered owner. A moment later, the dispatch returned with, "I have your ten-twenty-eight."

"Go ahead," the officer said.

"Ten-twenty-eight comes back to Bay Area Benevolent Society."

The name caught me off guard. I didn't expect Nick Paolini's front to be associated with a car driven by potential suspects in the murder of his attorney's daughter. "Ask her to confirm the plate," I said to the officer.

He did. The dispatcher repeated the license number. There was no mistake. "Mean something?" the officer asked.

"You know who Nick Paolini is?" I said.

"Who doesn't?"

"The car belongs to him."

Even with her numerous earrings, nose stud, and spiky blond hair, Daisy looked somewhat out of place in the booking cell when I got there to fill out her booking papers. Our typical suspects generally didn't wear white evening gowns. "How are you doing?" I asked, more to break the ice than anything. She'd obviously been crying.

"How do you think?"

"If I had to guess, I'd say upset."

She crossed her arms over her chest. "What did you want to talk about?"

"Me? Nothing," I said, as I wrote my name and badge number on the bottom of the booking sheet. "I imagine the inspector assigned to the case might want to talk to you about murder."

"I didn't kill anyone."

"No, but I'd lay odds that you know more about it than I do."

"And you're supposed to be the police."

Sometimes I wondered what it would be like to work back

in the days when it was okay to slap your prisoners. "You know, Daisy, I liked you better when you pretended you were the grieving widow."

She looked away.

"You heard that my partner was nearly killed when the Redding house blew up?"

This caught her attention. "I didn't have anything to do with that."

"Do you know who did?"

"Someone who wants me dead. Who do you think?"

"You?"

"Hello. You haven't noticed the other girl killed was blond?"

Now it was my turn to be surprised. "Are you saying that Eve was killed because someone thought she was you?"

"And Joshua with me. The car was his."

"It belonged to Eve's grandmother."

"But no one knew that. Joshua was the only one who ever drove it. For his job."

"Why was Eve driving it?"

"Her Porsche had a flat."

"Where was she coming from?"

"From my house. She came to visit. We were . . . old friends."

"She was visiting you at Joshua's house?"

"In Napa. I'm not really married to Joshua. I only said so to get my mother off my case and so I could make the report. He said people were following him. I thought he was missing. I didn't think they'd take the report if I wasn't related to him or was his wife or something."

"And your real name would be . . . ?"

"You mean you *don't* know?"

"Maybe you could just help me out here," I said, trying my best to ignore her sarcastic tone. But then it started to sink in what she was telling me about being old friends. That was right about the time the meaning of Daisy hit me.

It was a nickname, of course, which is why it didn't surprise me in the least when she replied, "Marguerite O'Dell."

"So we can add the charge of False Identification?"

"I don't use Marguerite anymore."

"Okay, Daisy, then. You mind telling me why you were in Paolini's car?" She didn't answer, so I followed with, "Do you know who killed Eve, or who the dead man you misidentified as Joshua Redding happens to be?"

Again no answer.

"Okay. Does this case have anything to do with Tremayne being the father of your daughter?"

It was a second before she replied. "He was a mistake that happened a long time ago. It has nothing to do with this and I doubt he even knows she exists."

"Then he *is* the father?"

"Bonnie's mine!" she said, her voice rising. "I raised her. I took care of her when she was sick. She's *my* baby. The best thing that ever happened to me . . ." Daisy looked away, blinking back tears.

"Is something wrong?"

She shook her head and brushed the tears from her eyes. "I left just like they asked when she was born. I didn't get in the way . . ." She looked at me, her gaze filled with anger this time. "It's not fair."

"Who asked you to leave? What's not fair?"

"Nothing," she said, crossing her arms over her chest once more. "Nothing."

"Then can you tell me about the Garden of Eden Club?"

Her gaze widened. She sat up. "I don't know what you're talking about."

"Sure you do. You, Eve," I said, throwing the names out there, having no clue where it would lead.

She stared at me a few seconds, her face paling. "I want an attorney and my phone calls. I don't think there's anything more I should discuss with you."

I waited a few seconds more, hoping she'd relent and just babble what she knew. She didn't. "I'll let you make those calls."

I walked out of there frustrated that I couldn't get more. Yet I'd gotten something, so I shouldn't count it as a total loss. I finally had Marguerite O'Dell, the elusive witness I knew by name only. I also had a clue as to Eve's whereabouts just before her murder. Napa. Which probably meant we should be looking for our second victim's identity up there.

I headed to the interview room where they had placed Joshua, wondering what he knew about this.

Joshua sat at the table, his right fingers tapping impatiently on the scarred tabletop. As soon as I walked in, he leaned back on the chair, crossing his arms over his chest, tilting his chin up. "Hope you got yourself some damn good evidence, cause I'm gonna sue your ass so fast, they're gonna name this police department after me."

So much for pleasantries. I decided to skip any small talk and head straight to Miranda. "I need to read you your rights—"

"Why don't you take those rights and shove them up your ass?"

"You know," I said, trying to keep my cool, and failing miserably, "I'm not the one facing hard time for burglarizing a dead woman's house. And I'm not the one being accused of blackmailing a candidate running for office."

"That's a lie."

"So if you want to talk about things getting shoved where the sun don't shine, you might want to take a long hard look at your reflection in that window there," I said, nodding toward the one-way glass. "And then guess which blue-eyed baby-faced young man in this particular room is gonna have a boyfriend named Bubba passing him soap in the shower."

"Yeah?" he said, his gaze flicking to the window, then back. "You think you're tough, bitch? I been in the joint and I can take care of myself."

"Joint? If you think being arrested as a juvenile and being housed with a bunch of pimply faced teens counts as the joint, then yeah, you got one on me. But reality is that as far as Bubba and the guys in the big house are concerned, you're virgin material and they're gonna have fun deflowering you over and over." I pulled out my Miranda card. "At least my fears are put to rest, now that I know you can take care of yourself. In the meantime, you have the right to remain silent . . ." I said, then continued to read him the rest of his rights. He dutifully listened, his glance straying to his reflection in the window every now and then, perhaps wondering about a future in the pen. "You understand each of these rights?" I asked.

He nodded, his expression somewhat more subdued than when I first walked in.

"I'm sorry. Was that yes or no?"

"Yeah."

I jotted down his answer and the time, then asked, "Now that we have that out of the way, you mind telling me what you were doing in Eve's apartment?"

"I wasn't breaking in, if that's what you think."

"You just happened to wander in?"

"As a matter of fact, yeah. I was just getting something that belonged to me."

"Some music?"

"Music. Yeah, that's it."

"What else did you take?"

"Nothing. Do I get my music back? I dropped it."

"You might think about springing for a new CD, since it'll be tied up in court for the next few years."

"What?"

"You knew what was on it?"

"I don't have a clue."

"How'd you get in?"

"I work there. I had a key. A couple of guys had been in there right before I got there. I figured they were going to set me up for the murder. And that's why Daisy went in and pretended that I was dead."

"I thought they were trying to kill Daisy."

"And me. That's why I sent my mom to Mexico and Daisy took Bonnie to her mom's house. I didn't know if they'd go after them, or just me and Daisy."

"You *and* Daisy?"

"Why else would they have gone to Mrs. Harrington's house unless they were looking for me?" he asked, leaning his chair back, his tough guy demeanor having returned.

"Good question. Maybe because you had something they wanted? Like info on this Garden of Eden Club? A particular CD full of photos?"

Joshua stared at me for a full second, his face showing disbelief. And just as quickly, he recovered, saying, "Two things. I want an attorney, and I hope you have a will."

"Why is that?"

"Because you're gonna be dead."

"Is that a threat?"

"Hell, no. It's just the plain and simple truth, so you might just wanna start looking over your shoulder, cause they're gonna do to you what they did to Eve."

18

Normally I wouldn't think twice about a threat from some two-bit crook like Joshua Redding. But having received a veiled warning from Nick Paolini, a warning that in my opinion carried a hell of a lot more weight, I wasn't about to walk around unarmed anytime soon. "You mind telling me who is going to carry through with this threat?"

Joshua sat there, tightlipped.

"All because of this club?"

Silence.

I stood. "It's like this, Joshua. If you don't tell me who or what this is about, I'm going to assume this threat comes from you. Which means I'm going to make sure your bail's increased so that you can sit in our jail and have plenty of time to think about it."

He gave a shrug, but seemed unfazed.

"You have a pleasant stay. And say hi to Bubba."

I left, and a jailer came in, taking Joshua back to a cell. It didn't take a brain surgeon to figure out that this case was going in a completely different direction than we'd first anticipated. Suddenly I began to rethink it. Had Daisy and Joshua been the original targets?

And what of the explosion at the Redding house? Who was the target there? Joshua and Daisy again? Someone waiting for their return after we'd chased them from the premises?

When I met up with Torrance, I ran it by him as he drove me home. We tossed the facts back and forth, both deciding that it all seemed to fit together . . . all except for Tremayne's suspicion that Joshua was responsible for Eve's death.

"The only thing that doesn't make any sense," Torrance said, as we neared my street, "is Joshua's interest in this Garden of Eden. Why take the CD?"

"Tremayne said he was blackmailing him over a past affair."

"With Marguerite?"

"Undoubtedly. Unless he's had others."

"So Joshua takes the CD as extra leverage, to make sure Tremayne pays?"

"Tremayne's running for office. I doubt he'd want any press on his daughter's extracurricular activities. Couple that with his having a kid out of wedlock, and I doubt he'd get a lot of voter support."

"Which means he could very well have hired a hit on Joshua and Daisy and accidentally had his daughter killed by mistake."

"Speaking of hits, Paolini warned me to stay away from the Tremaynes, because they have friends in high places."

"And low places too, if his hand is in it," Torrance said as he pulled into my driveway. He stopped the car and shut off the engine. "I'll walk you to your door."

Suddenly the entire case went out the window. This was my opportunity to say, "That's okay," or something equally intelligent, but my mind refused to cooperate. I had no excuses, no nephews, no ex-husbands nearby. There was only the frightening knowledge that if he walked me to my door, he might kiss me.

Even more frightening was the thought that he might not. He might just turn around and leave.

It was what I wanted, wasn't it? To be left alone? Not to

have to face him, or the reasons we were constantly at odds? Not to have to admit that some of the problems in our relationship might be my fault?

I couldn't speak, though. I merely opened the door, got out, and wondered what I was going to say at the top of the steps.

We walked up side by side, and I fumbled in my little purse for my keys, which were tucked safely in a small zippered pocket, but might as well have been padlocked somewhere, for all my finesse in getting them out. As I shoved the key in the lock, I told myself that I was going to be brave. I was going to look him in the eye, and what would be would be. I could do this. I could handle the outcome.

I turned the key, opened the door a few inches, then glanced up at him. The porch light flickered, and I couldn't tell what he was thinking, or what his intentions were. *Say something,* I told myself. *Something not stupid.* "Would you like a drink or some coffee or, um, anything?"

Could I sound any dumber?

"No," he said.

Torrance didn't make a move, and I felt like an idiot. I'd been wrong. About everything. Even about the look he gave me as we danced tonight. I took a breath, gave a smile to convey my cool detached professionalism, then said, "Well, good night, then."

The barest of hesitations, then, "Good night, Kate." And with that he turned and walked down the steps.

I felt crushed. And for what? What the hell did I expect? That he'd sweep everything I'd told him all those weeks ago under the rug? All the accusations I'd made that he put his job before me, used me, that he should let bygones be bygones? Should I just call out that I'd been wrong about him then, and I'd be wrong about him in the future, but that's the way I was, and I was sorry?

But I stood there, not moving. The story of my life, because I couldn't face it if I'd told him I was wrong and he just nodded, then continued on down the steps, because I was too stupid to say so a long time ago and he had moved on with his life.

Tell him, I thought. *Just tell him.*

Before I had a chance, he stopped. Turned. Closed the distance between us. He wrapped one arm around me, his other hand gliding up, threading his fingers through my hair, bringing my face up, leaving me no choice but to look at him, face him, my body pressed against his. He waited.

An infinitesimal moment, an eternal moment.

The time it would take to say no. But the only sound was that of my pulse rushing in my ears, and my only thought was this was what I had been waiting for. And his mouth descended on mine.

His kiss was forceful, pent up with emotions buried too long. His hand swept down my spine, his fingers splaying against my backside. And then just as quickly, he stopped, looked at me, and said, "Good night, Kate."

". . . Good night," I said. But by then he was halfway down the steps.

I sighed, went into my house, and waited for my pulse to slow. I was *never* going to understand that man.

The next morning, I awoke to the phone ringing. I reached for it, not quite awake. "Hello?"

"Kate, dear? You'll never guess who's on the news." It was my Aunt Molly.

"Who?"

"You are. Or you will be after the commercials. Channel two."

"What?" I asked, bolting up, suddenly wide-awake.

"They just announced it. Something about a police chase,

and they showed you running after someone. You want me
to tape it for you?"

"What? No," I said. "Let me call you back after I've
watched it."

I hung up, worried about what Skyler had sensationalized
last night's activities into, and even more about how J. T.
Tremayne would take it and spin it for his own benefit.

I had to see the damage on TV. Lieutenant Andrews was
going to literally kill me if I did anything to bring bad press
on the department. In his opinion, I was a walking PR nightmare. In my opinion it wasn't my fault that they always
seemed to catch me in a bad light, and J. T. Tremayne sure
as hell wasn't helping my reputation.

I ran for the living room, turning on the TV to Channel 2.
There was a hand soap commercial, and I stood there, waiting.

Beth Skyler's voice came on the air. "Last night's
fundraising festivities turned into a murder investigation
when Homicide Inspector Kate Gillespie questioned guests
about the death of Eve Tremayne, the very woman being
memorialized at that function." And just my luck, there was
an accompanying clip that showed me talking with Eve's
cousin, Lucas.

"The guests, including such notables as Senator Harver,
were shocked when two people showed up, both wanted for
questioning in Eve's murder and trying to gain entrance. Inspector Gillespie and her partner attempted to apprehend
Joshua Redding and a woman posing as his wife, Daisy
Redding," she continued, the next shot showing Torrance,
his back to the camera, running after the pair and me with
my dress hiked up to my knees, seconds later, hopping into
Torrance's car.

I sat on the arm of the couch, watching my career going

down the toilet as the picture cut back to the studio, where the anchorman asked, "Have they made an arrest?"

"Yes, Neil," Skyler said, her face filling the screen again. "But neither was charged with homicide, and our sources tell us that both have posted bail."

"Oh, God." I'd made sure the bail was enhanced. Something those two could never afford. Who the hell had posted it?

The phone rang again. It was my aunt. "Well, your dress looked lovely."

"Thanks," I said, trying to sound upbeat. Shielding my aunt from the stresses of my career made life easier on both of us.

"Have a good afternoon, dear. And don't worry about your legs. They looked fine, even on TV."

"Thanks," I said again, wishing that was all I had to worry about. "Bye."

I hung up, then hit the shower, forcing myself to concentrate on the case and not the spectacle on TV. How was it that Daisy and Joshua had somehow posted an exorbitantly high bail and gotten out? And why were they in a car registered to one of Paolini's fronts if they were potential suspects in the murder of his attorney's daughter? And who was our John Doe who was killed with Eve? I wanted to know about the Garden of Eden and who all the players were. I wanted to know plenty and the questions continued ad nauseam as I tried looking at them from different angles. Nothing seemed to click.

By the time I got out of the shower, I had put the case momentarily aside and convinced myself that what I had seen on the news wasn't all bad. Unfortunately, the telephone rang and my sense of ease fled when I heard Gypsy on the other end.

"Kate? Sorry to disturb you on your day off. Andrews wants you down here Code Two."

"The TV thing?"

"Let's just say there's been a lot of brass behind closed doors all morning and no one looks real thrilled."

Great. "I'm on my way. Sorry you got called in on this."

"You'll make it up to me. By the way. Very nice dress."

"Thanks. See you in a few."

I hung up, wondering where my career would be by the end of the day.

19

When I arrived at Homicide, the lieutenant's door was closed. Gypsy called him on the phone: "Inspector Gillespie is here, sir." Since she was taking the formal route, it meant that the lieutenant had an audience. Definitely not a good sign. She looked up at me and said, "He'll be with you in a couple."

"Thanks."

Shipley and Zimmerman were at their desks, and I could only hope they were here because of their weekend homicide and not because of me. Rocky's desk was noticeably empty.

Zim lifted his coffee cup. "Quite the classy act, Gillespie. Might even win you a daytime Emmy."

I ignored him. "You get to see Markowski?" I asked Shipley.

"Yeah. He's doing good. You really put your lips on his?"

"Obvious delusions due to the blow to his head. Dare I ask what you're doing here this morning?"

"Got called in," Shipley said. "But don't feel too bad. Even if we hadn't, we had to come anyway to finish up a report on the homicide we picked up this weekend."

"Dope dealer working pest control," Zim said, giving the non-PC term for a crook killing another crook and doing the public a favor. "Damn waste of a tree to make the paper to print it up on, if you ask me."

"Nobody's asking," Shipley said as I sat at my desk, staring at my blank computer screen. I was disappointed in myself for not having had the foresight to post Reid at the exit to keep Joshua and Daisy from running out and the entire debacle from being filmed. Right now I'm sure it mattered little to the powers that be that my foremost concern was in thinking it more important to keep the two of them from entering the ballroom and endangering the guests than appearing on TV.

There was one thing I could do while I was sitting there, however—find out who'd bailed them out of jail last night. I called the jail, told them what I was looking for, was put on hold. A few minutes later, the clerk came back, read the name of the bond agency just as Gypsy stepped in, and told me that Andrews would see me now.

"Well," Shipley asked. "Who posted the bond?"

"Nick Paolini," I said, as I headed for the lieutenant's office, wondering what interest a mob boss might have in these two players. Apparently quite a bit, considering there were *two* cars involved in this case that were registered to his front. The blue car that Joshua and Daisy were driving when they were arrested, and the black sedan we saw at the Redding house before the explosion.

That, however, wasn't going to explain why this wasn't kept low key, I thought as I knocked on the door.

I entered to a crowded room. Andrews was at his desk, J. T. Tremayne was seated beside his wife, and standing next to him was a man I'd never met. He was about my age and height, dark hair, dark suit, and stood with the air of someone who had spent several years in the military. "This is Inspector Gillespie?" he asked Andrews.

"Yes."

I looked at Andrews for clarification and he said, "This is Special Agent Marten Floyd. The case is being turned over to the FBI. He'll need you to brief him and turn over any notes."

I ignored Tremayne's smug expression, instead focusing on the look of apology from his wife, Faye. *"Those who seem the friendliest . . ."* Paolini's words of warning.

I put them from my mind and turned my attention to the agent. "Anytime you're ready," I told him, then started for the door. He followed and as we left, I heard J. T. Tremayne, his voice angry, saying, "That's it? I demand there be an investigation. This officer has been harassing me and my family."

"Management Control has already been notified," I heard Andrews say, just before he closed his office door.

"Right this way, Agent Floyd," I said, trying to keep my voice light. No sense letting Tremayne get to me.

At my desk I pulled the case files and said, "I'm surprised the Feds are taking this over. Last night when I spoke with Special Agent Morley, he didn't think it was a Bureau matter."

"Trust me. We don't normally like to come in and step on local agency toes. Someone's pulling some political strings and you and I are just the pawns." He opened the case file and started looking over the paperwork. "Anything missing?"

"My reports on the arrests last night of Joshua and Daisy."

"You interrogate them?"

"No. Just a few questions at booking. The case was reassigned, but the inspector is out on sick leave."

"They give you anything?"

"They denied having knowledge about the killings, then asked for their attorney."

He closed the files and stood. "They mention anything unusual? Off the beaten path?"

"You mean about the Garden of Eden Club?"

"Club?"

"I heard a rumor about this club earlier and found a CD with some rather incriminating photos on it, which I assume have something to do with it."

"And did either this Daisy or Joshua admit to any knowledge about it?"

"None."

"You have any thoughts on it?"

"I'll let you look at a copy of a CD we found and make up your own mind," I said, pulling the copy out of my desk drawer and popping it into the computer.

I clicked through a few of the photos, and he said, "You recognize any of these people?"

"Unfortunately I haven't looked at the entire thing. This photo is Miles Standiford. He's one of our District Supervisors who happens to be running against J. T. Tremayne for the same district."

"If this is a club, it's a little on the kinky side. You find any other CDs, or is this it?"

"This is all we found. It was dropped outside a burglary of Eve Tremayne's house the night she was killed. It's all in the report."

He thumbed through the paperwork. "I'll look it all over at the office. Mind if I take the CD?"

"Go ahead," I said. "The original is booked into evidence." I ejected the copy and gave it to him. "I don't suppose you have any ideas about this matter?"

"First I heard about any of this was when Morley, the SAC, called me this morning and told me to get down here and take the case." He glanced at his watch. "Either way, it's an FBI matter now. God only knows what we want with it."

Agent Floyd shook hands with me, gave me a card, told me to call him if anything came up, then left.

A minute or two later, Andrews opened his office door

and called me in. The Tremaynes had departed, and it was apparent that Andrews was not pleased by the entire affair. "What happened last night?" he said, his almost-too-quiet voice telling me that he was even angrier than I thought. "And how did it get all over Channel Two news?"

Although I'd given him the basics last night over the phone, I hadn't mentioned the news cameras, probably because it hadn't occurred to me that I was going to be the star attraction. "Joshua Redding and Daisy showed up. We—I needed to contact them regarding the homicide," I said, having a feeling that it wouldn't matter what I told him.

"And the Tremaynes' nephew?"

"I had no idea we were being filmed."

Andrews leaned back in his chair. "I said a *low* key surveillance, Gillespie. What part of that didn't you understand?"

"I'm sorry, but don't you find it odd that the FBI suddenly shows up on this? When I spoke with Special Agent Morley last night at the ball—"

"Apparently Morley changed his mind."

"But if Tremayne is going to such lengths to—"

"Gillespie? When I said off the case, I meant off. I do not appreciate having to spend my Sunday mornings in the Deputy Chief's office, trying to explain why my inspectors are highlighted on the news for cases they aren't even assigned to."

He stood, slipping on his jacket over his shoulder holster, his anger still evident in the way he carried himself. "I'm going home now," he said. "And I expect you'll do the same."

"Yes, sir."

Gypsy, Zim, and Shipley were gone, apparently hightailing it out of there to avoid being caught in this nightmare. When Andrews left, I was alone, wondering how I was ever going to dig my career out of this hole, or if I should even be worrying that I had a career left at all. I grabbed my keys from my desk and had taken about two steps toward the door when my phone rang. Ignore it, I told myself. I took two more steps, then said what the hell and went back to answer it.

"Gillespie, Homicide detail."

"They have my daughter!"

It was Daisy and she was crying. "Where are you?"

"In Napa. They took her! They promised me yesterday if I didn't say anything to the police they would give her back when I got here, but they didn't!"

"Slow down. Who took her?"

"Joshua told me no one would get hurt. It was just a way to make some money." I heard her take a deep breath. "He didn't say they'd take my baby!"

"Who took her?"

"I don't know who. The ones who killed Tom and Eve."

"Tom?"

"Brewer," she said. "Please. I need your help. You want the club, don't you? The negatives?" I heard an intake of breath, then a whispered, "Oh, God. I have to go." The line went dead.

I called Andrews's cell phone and told him. "You're off," he said. "That means off. Call the agent, tell him, and call Missing Persons, then Napa PD. Understood?"

"Yes, sir."

I dropped the phone in the cradle and picked up the agent's card, called his pager and left my number on it, then called his voice mail and left a brief message on it about what Daisy had told me. That done, I used Rocky's phone, keeping my line open, and called Daisy's mother, Lillian O'Dell, who sounded as cold as ever on the phone.

"Mrs. O'Dell? Inspector Gillespie, Homicide. Has your daughter been by there?"

"I haven't seen her since yesterday, when she came by to pick up Bonnie."

"You don't happen to know her address in Napa, do you? Or happen to know where she was going?"

"She didn't inform me."

"Have you spoken to her or Bonnie since?"

"No."

"She just called me to tell me someone had taken her daughter. She sounded scared. Do you have any idea what is going on?"

There was a hesitation, then a quiet "No."

"Mrs. O'Dell?"

"She told me she thought someone might be after her. I didn't believe her . . ." There was a trace of real emotion in her voice.

"Do you happen to have a picture of Bonnie?"

"I—maybe."

"I'm going to send someone by for it. Will you wait for them?"

"Of course."

I hung up and called Missing Persons. "Pierce? Gillespie. You remember Daisy Redding?"

"Yeah. What's up?"

"Her real name is Marguerite O'Dell, but she goes by Daisy. She just called to say someone took her daughter. I don't know when or where, but it sounds like a legit kidnapping."

"Jesus. How old is the kid?"

"Six, I think."

I heard him exhale. "Give me a couple minutes to get a team in here and I'll call you back for the particulars."

"Thanks."

Unfortunately, the address Daisy gave last night during booking was her mother's address here in the city. No help there, so I booted up my computer, ran the name Tom Brewer and then Thomas Brewer, and came up with a match in Napa. As soon as I had that, I telephoned Napa PD, asked for the watch commander, and a moment later, when he connected, I told him briefly what we had. He said he'd send a car by the house and do a welfare check, and if necessary, order some extra patrol on the place, then asked me to send a TRAK photo of Bonnie and they'd issue it to all the officers.

There was no doubt in my mind that Bonnie's abduction was directly related to our case. I could only hope that Napa PD would turn up a lead on victim Tom Brewer—something that might give us an idea on where Bonnie had been taken to.

I worried it wasn't enough, but what more could I do? All the bases were covered—all except the FBI agent who had yet to return my phone call.

Tapping my fingers on my desktop, I stared out the window at the weekend traffic heading toward the Bay Bridge. A child had been kidnapped and I had screwed up a case— or rather, my integrity in involving the case. And while I wasn't foolish enough to think that the kidnapping was my fault for taking a photo, I was still depressed enough over the entire incident to need a serious beer. And just crazy enough to think maybe I could do something more. Only problem was who could I take who wouldn't get into trouble, since I was technically off the case? And then it occurred to me: my former partner, Sam Scolari.

Couldn't fire a cop who was retired now, could you?

I called him at home. "Hi," I said when he answered. "You doing anything today?"

"Yeah, I was gonna watch the game on TV and eat pizza. Why?"

"Just wondering if you were interested in going to Napa with me. A favor."

"What d'ya got?" he asked.

I gave him the *Reader's Digest* version of the case, finishing with how the FBI took it over.

"The goddamned FBI? What the hell do *they* want with the case?"

"The CD, maybe? Or maybe it's simply that Tremayne pulled some weight."

"He's a freaking real estate attorney who's running for office. Since when is that a Bureau matter?"

"Apparently it is one now, and there's no one here I can take with me who won't suffer the consequences of an IA."

"I'm in."

"I probably can't pay you much."

"I'll put it on your tab. It'll be worth it, just to see what the hell the FBI finds so interesting about this case. Besides, there's a kid out there. I'll meet you at the Hall in a few," he said, then disconnected.

I hung up the phone.

"IA?"

I turned to see Torrance leaning against the doorframe of Gypsy's office, his arms crossed, his dark eyes filled with suspicion.

There was an awkward moment of silence before he asked, "Going somewhere?"

Two words came to mind: *Oh, shit.*

I gave him my most innocent smile, wondering how much Torrance had heard and how the hell I was going to get out of this one and still have a job. "As a matter of fact, I am," I said.

He waited, not moving, his look telling me he was prepared to disbelieve every word I told him.

Definitely not good.

Only one thing to do. Twist the partial truth. "Sam and I are going to Napa."

"Napa?"

"Wine tasting," I said.

"Really?"

I hated that word. I used it myself when I was trying to il-licit a statement, usually incriminatory, from someone. "Really," I said.

"You and Scolari?"

"Yeah. You know, get him out, doing stuff because his wife died."

"Never mind that he doesn't drink wine."

Obviously time to change the subject. I wanted Torrance out of here, preferably before Scolari arrived. "So, what are you doing here if not to do an IA?" I asked.

"Two things," he said. "The first I wish I could have done earlier, but I was tied up in meetings this morning. I came to apologize."

"Apologize?"

"For what happened last night."

My mind raced. For what? For the moment he *almost* kissed me on the dance floor? Or for the moment he *did* kiss me on my porch? As much as I might deny it to myself, I had wanted him to kiss me. Hell, I'd wanted more. And now here he was, apologizing for it? Either the feeling wasn't mutual, or he was suffering from his typical not-while-on-duty syndrome. Regardless, I didn't want him to think I was affected, so I figured my best defense was to brush it off.

I leaned back in my chair and gave a casual shrug. "That little matter on my porch? Don't worry about it. It was no big deal. You and I both know it didn't mean . . ."

His dark brows arched slightly.

A little warning bell went off in my head, as usual, too late. "You weren't talking about the kiss?"

"No, Kate."

". . . What were you apologizing for?"

"That I let Joshua Redding get by. That the news crew filmed you. That Tremayne tried to pin the blame on you."

"Oh." Boy, did I feel like an idiot.

"About this . . . little matter on your porch—you mind explaining just what it *didn't mean*?"

What the hell was I supposed to say? That I only pretended it was no big deal in case to him it really *was* no big deal? That I thought he might have been sorry for kissing me? Somehow, that didn't sound good, almost as though I didn't trust him or that he lacked integrity, which was basically what I had accused him of a few months ago—right after I'd told him to go pound sand.

He didn't like it then; he was bound to like it even less now.

"What I meant," I said, thinking fast, "is that we could have a helluva lot more fun if your morals weren't so . . . damned moral." And then it occurred to me: turn the tables and shift the blame. "You kissed me last night and then you left. I want to know why."

His gaze narrowed. "We were working."

"What do you have, an on-off switch?"

"Is that what you think?" he asked, his voice low, even. He closed the door behind him, then crossed the room toward me, stopping so close in front of my chair that I had to crane my neck to meet his gaze.

"Yes?" I said, frustrated.

"No, Kate."

His voice had an edge to it, and I realized that maybe turning the tables might not have been the best idea. Unfortunately, relationships weren't my specialty, and remembering my true purpose behind all this, getting him to leave before Sam got there, I tried to lighten things up a bit.

"Remember the old days when you could just hop in bed with someone and nobody thought twice about it?"

"You're not that type," he said.

"Maybe I've changed. I mean, we're not talking marriage here."

There was a heartbeat of silence, then he leaned down, grasping both arms of my chair, until his face was mere inches from mine. "Thanks for the clarification," he said, his dark gaze boring into mine, making me wonder if he saw right through my little show. "So, when do you want to sleep together?"

20

When do you want to sleep together? Talk about going out of the proverbial frying pan into the fire.

I swallowed past the lump in my throat. "That's a pretty specific question," I said, the expert in stalling tactics. "Assuming you're serious."

"I am, and it demands a pretty specific answer."

"What happens when morning comes?"

"I don't know," he said, his voice tinged with anger or frustration or both. "We've never gotten that far."

I think I stared at him for several seconds, not sure what to say. This was what I'd wanted all along, wasn't it? Why then was I so scared to say yes, I do want to sleep with you?

"It's okay, Kate," he said after a while. "You don't have to answer that question. I—"

"Tonight," I said, surprising myself.

He didn't say a thing, and I could have counted my heartbeats in the ensuing silence—until the phone rang, breaking the tension.

I answered it. Pierce from Missing Persons, wanting to know the particulars on the case. I spent the next several minutes going over it with him, very much aware of Torrance watching me the whole time.

Had I really just said I'd sleep with him?

Oh, God.

And just as I hung up the phone, Scolari walked in.

"Everything okay?" he asked, looking from me to Torrance, and I knew why. To him, Torrance was IA.

"Fine," I said. *Just act normal.* "Torrance was wondering where we were off to."

"Wine tasting," Scolari replied, without missing a beat.

When I stood, Torrance glanced at my computer to see Brewer's Napa address right there in plain view.

"It was for Missing Persons," I said, but his gaze told me that he undoubtedly knew where I was headed.

His words confirmed it. "Don't do this, Kate."

"There's a kid out there."

"And Pierce and his team are handling it. As is Napa PD."

"But—"

"And I'm here because Andrews ordered you home."

"He asked you to do this?"

"That's the other reason I came. He seems to think you have this misguided sense of wanting to save the world. I tend to believe him. Now, go home. You've done all you can."

"He's right, Kate," Scolari said.

"Fine," I said. "I'll go to Scolari's and watch the game. Okay?"

That seemed to satisfy him, and as he turned to leave, it occurred to me that we hadn't finalized this other matter. The one that had nothing to do with police work. He strode out of the office, and suddenly it was important to me that he knew I hadn't been lying about that, at least.

I ran to the door, stepping out into the hallway, but there were two inspectors from the Robbery detail standing just a few feet away, so I said simply, "I'll call you after the game." He looked at me and I waved, then ducked back into the office before he could say anything. If nothing else, that told him that I wasn't going to Napa, and that I was serious about tonight. I guessed I'd find out soon enough if he was.

Scolari eyed me as I grabbed my keys and purse. "Something finally going on between you two?"

"Don't know what you're talking about."

"Right. You want to drive or you want me to?"

"I'll follow you."

When I got to Sam's, he popped the tops off two beers and handed me one, then turned on the TV. We had no sooner settled on the couch then my cell phone rang.

It was Faye Tremayne.

"I know who killed Eve!" she said in a rush. "It was Joshua Redding!" Judging from the background noise, she was on her car phone.

"How do you know?"

"Because I saw him digging around in the tool shed. I heard him swearing when he couldn't find them. Then he took off in his car."

"Find what?"

"The negatives."

I stilled. Thought of my father and the photos, Eve telling me she had the negatives. But that was years ago. "What negatives?" I asked, motioning for Sam to turn down the TV.

"The negatives that Eve had of—of the men. Lucas told me that a few days before she was killed, she had borrowed his scanner to put some negatives on a CD."

"Did he see what was on the negatives?"

"I don't think so. But he said they were in a box, and now he thinks that's what was stolen the night she was killed, the night they attacked Mother. Then Mother told me she had seen Joshua with the box in the tool shed this morning. So I went to look and I found it."

"*You* have the negatives?"

"Yes," she said, and I heard a horn honking in the background. "You are going to arrest him, aren't you?"

"Where are you?"

"I'm following him right now."

Christ. "Following him where?"

"North on one-oh-one. We're about to cross the Golden Gate Bridge."

"No," I said, figuring that Joshua was probably en route to Napa. "You get off on the turnout. *Do not* cross that bridge."

"He killed my daughter!"

"And if that's true, then you're in danger."

"I'm not letting him get away. Now get out here and arrest him."

Demanding shades of the Mrs. Tremayne I used to know. "What are you driving?" I asked, getting up to grab a pen and paper from the kitchen counter.

"A gray Mercedes. He's in a black BMW."

"I'll need both your license plates and your cell phone number."

She gave them to me. "You are coming?"

"I'm on my way now," I said, handing the slip of paper to Sam, then grabbing my keys. "But I want you to back off. I have his license. I'll call CHP."

"I'm sorry, Kate. I can't. You do understand, don't you?"

She disconnected before I could say anything else, and I told Sam, "Eve's mother is following Joshua northbound on one-oh-one. She seems to think he's the killer."

He picked up both beers, took a swig of his, then put them into the refrigerator. "On the off chance we get back before the beers go flat," he said.

"We can only hope. I'll drive, you call CHP and Sonoma County with the info."

"Check. What about Andrews?"

"I'll call him . . . eventually," I said, knowing he'd order

me off if I did. Waiting to call couldn't hurt. I figured they
had about a ten-minute lead on us, depending on how fast
they were driving, and kept my fingers crossed that CHP or
a sheriff's patrol would pick them up before too long. CHP
had dispatched a patrol car to the southernmost Marin exit,
but traffic was heavy and when we reached that milestone,
we saw the patrol car and no sign of Mrs. Tremayne or
Joshua's vehicle. I pulled over and the highway patrolman
told me he hadn't seen them.

"Any luck getting through to her?" I asked Sam.

He'd attempted to call Faye Tremayne several times. "Her
phone's turned off."

"Great."

I thanked the officer and we continued northbound.

About forty minutes later, we were heading up Highway
29 into the Napa Valley. In comparison to the city, Napa
held a peaceful allure. A promise of greenery and beauty,
rolling hills dotted with oaks and rustic-looking wineries
set amid acres and acres of vineyards, a mixture of old-
growth vines and modern vines, the sort grown on wire trel-
lises in pristine rows. It was one of those places you could
drive through and just soak in the scenery, not having a
thought in the world except which winery to visit or where
to eat lunch.

We hit a fork in the highway, Highway 29 in one direction
and 221 in the other, both leading to Napa. I chose 221,
wondering which direction she might have taken, and about
five minutes later, she called me from a pay phone at a shopping center off 29 and Imola, telling me her cell phone had
died, but she had just seen him turn down a road not too far
from where she had stopped.

"I think he got lost," she said when we arrived. "He kept
driving up and down the highway before he finally turned
down a road."

"Did you get the name of it?"

"No, but I can tell you how to get there."

"The negatives," I said. "Where are they?"

"They're at Mother's."

"You told me you had them."

"And I do. At my mother's," she said, giving me an odd look as she got into her car, and I wondered if she purposefully intended to mislead me, or was I just too eager to get them to pay attention. And as we followed her, I wondered if my father's image appeared within that box. Or the negative for the missing photo from Eve's album. The one I didn't take. I wanted to know who it belonged to. Another victim of misled desire? Or a murder suspect?

Before I could contemplate that, Faye Tremayne stopped at the corner of a street about a half mile away. I looked at the sign and saw it was the same street that our male victim, Tom Brewer, had lived on.

Mrs. Tremayne pointed to the east. "He drove all the way to the end," she said.

Scolari and I glanced down the street, but didn't see anything. Just to be safe, we called Napa PD and asked if they could have a marked unit meet with us. We were in luck. A patrolman was just a few blocks away. Apparently he'd been the officer assigned to check out Brewer's address. "Been by there a couple times already," he said and looked at his watch. "Thirty minutes ago the place was locked up tight. No one home."

"You mind going with us to check again? We think someone might be there now."

"Not a problem," he said. And after instructing Mrs. Tremayne to remain behind, Scolari and I followed the officer down the stretch of dusty road that dead-ended into a dirt cul-de-sac after about a quarter mile. Brewer's place was a small ranchette painted olive green and situated on the edge of a vineyard that backed up to the Napa hills. A gravel driveway led to the house and a black BMW was parked in front of it.

We parked our car behind the officer's, to the west of the driveway, then to avoid making any noise in the gravel, we traversed a bed of pansies to the front lawn, which had needed a mowing several days ago.

Several newspapers were scattered by the door as we stepped up onto the wide porch and I wondered if anyone had noticed that Tom Brewer was missing.

The front door was locked. "Let's go have a look around back," I said.

The three of us made our way to the rear to the west of the house, feeling the hot sun reflecting off the side of the building. We found the back door also locked, and other than the BMW parked out front, there was no sign that anyone was home or that the place had been disturbed.

There was, however, what appeared to be a barn situated about a hundred feet to the rear of the main house. I noticed the double doors standing slightly ajar, then heard a slight shuffling noise from behind it. I pointed in that direction and both Scolari and the officer nodded and we started that way, drawing our weapons.

We were just about to check the circumference of the building before taking up a position on either side of the barn doors when we heard the crunch of feet on the drive behind us and I spun around to see Faye Tremayne. "Son of a bitch," I whispered. Her gaze widened and she froze at the sight of our weapons.

"I'll get her the hell out of here," Scolari said, "then come back and cover that side door."

He hurried toward her and I moved to the edge of the property, where the sun beat down on the grape leaves. The air was still, heavy, almost stifling in its heat, and I shielded my eyes from the glare, looking out over the vineyard of dark gnarled wood, thick twisted vines, a vineyard probably older than me.

I heard the noise again coming from the back of the barn and put my finger to my lips, alerting the officer. Scolari was pointing to a bench at the side of the house, telling Mrs. Tremayne to sit there and wait. A breeze picked up, swirled down from the hills, and brought with it at first the scent of grape leaves. And then something more subtle. Spicy. Like aftershave.

We stilled ourselves, listened.

Heard a whooshing noise. Something came at us, dark. Low to the ground, from beneath the vines.

Wild turkeys. They darted past into the yard and Scolari spun around, drawing down on them.

I exhaled and hoped it was just us startling the birds. Until the barn's side door swung open. Joshua raced from it toward the house. I called out. Scolari flew down the gravel drive toward the front, and the officer and I followed on the opposite side, but he was too fast for us. He hopped in the black BMW, started it, and backed up, dirt and pansies flying from his wheels.

The officer radioed for help, hopped in his cruiser, and chased after the BMW. And then we heard a scream from the back of the house.

We ran to the barn to see Faye Tremayne standing at the partially open doors, pointing. "In here," she cried, then started backing away, shaking her head, her hand covering her mouth.

Not sure what we'd find, Scolari and I stood on either side of the doors. I eyed the partially open barn door to my left, the weathered, flaking paint. "Shall we?"

"Now or never."

I grabbed the door, pulled, and aimed my weapon.

The door swung open and the sunlight streamed in. My gaze went past a small tractor. And just beyond it, on the floor, a woman, face down, her short, spiky blond hair matted with blood.

21

"It's Daisy," I said. I made sure the building was clear, holstered my weapon, then rushed in, Scolari behind me.

Kneeling, I reached over, placed my fingers on her carotid, felt a pulse, then noticed the slight rise and fall of her back as she breathed. "She's still alive," I said, pulling out my cell phone to call 911.

Faye Tremayne stood at the door. "Shouldn't you help her up?" she asked once I'd finished the call.

"I don't know how she's injured," I said. "She's breathing fine on her own, so we'll watch her until the ambulance gets here." Head wounds bleed a lot, sometimes making them look much worse than they actually are. But I wasn't about to chance moving her in case there was something else wrong.

About five minutes later, we heard the approaching sirens of the ambulance and police. "Hang in there," I said to Daisy, hearing the EMTs run up the drive. They came into the garage, and we moved back, out of their way.

"Do you know what happened?" one of them asked.

"No. We found her here just as she is."

He checked her pulse and then evaluated her for further injuries. When they rolled her over and onto the gurney, I noticed an envelope on the ground, perfectly square and about the size that a CD might fit into. As soon as they lifted her onto the gurney, I used my fingernail to flick the envelope over. The clear round window on the other side told me it was empty.

"Look at this," I told Scolari.

"Apparently there's more than one CD floating around?"

Before I could comment, the Napa police arrived, different officers than the one who'd accompanied us earlier, and as soon as we identified ourselves and explained the nature of our investigation, they called detectives. Within an hour the pastoral setting of country property was lost beneath a plethora of high-tech crime scene equipment.

Sometime later two men wearing suits approached. "You the San Francisco cops?" the older of the two asked.

"Yes," I said.

He introduced himself as Bobby Venegas and his partner as James Grove. Scolari and I shook hands with them as I made the introductions on our end.

"I understand you think this is related to a homicide and kidnapping in the city. I'd like to hear more about it."

Scolari took Faye Tremayne back to the bench to wait and I went over the basic details of the case with the detective, while he took notes.

"Let me get this straight," he said, angling his head toward his partner, who was questioning Faye not too far away on the bench near the house. "This lady's daughter, Eve Tremayne, was murdered with Tom Brewer in the city, who happens to live here with my victim . . ." He checked his notes. ". . . Marguerite O'Dell, AKA Daisy Redding, girlfriend slash pseudo-wife to Joshua Redding, who happened to be driving a car registered to the Bay Area Benevolent Society, which is a front for the mob. Daisy calls you, tells you she's up here, that her daughter's been kidnapped, and you discover her unconscious moments after Joshua Redding flees the scene."

"In a nutshell, yes."

"Can of worms if I ever heard one," he said.

"Oh, it gets better," I said. "The FBI took over the case. Technically we're not even supposed to be here."

He cocked an eyebrow. "You know why they're so interested?"

"Either Faye Tremayne's husband has a lot of pull, or they're interested in something called the Garden of Eden Club."

"Somehow I'm guessing you're not talking horticulture or Bible study."

"No. I have a CD with photos of politicians and businessmen involved in S&M–type stuff that was taken at one of our victim's residences. I'm not sure why Daisy came back here, unless it was to look for her daughter, but she asked for my help, then asked me if I wanted to know the members of the Club. Before she could tell me anything else, she said she had to hang up, because someone was coming. She didn't say who."

"How long ago was that?"

"Hour and a half before we got here? I called the agent who took the case over, but he never got back to me. I also called your WC, and the officer who came out with us originally said he'd checked the place about a half hour before and no one was here."

"Ten to one he didn't check the barn," he said, writing as he spoke. "You said that Faye Tremayne called you about some negatives and led you up here?"

"That's right."

"It'll be interesting to hear what she tells my partner about this. We'll have to put you down in the report. That gonna cause any problems since you weren't supposed to be here?"

Truthfully, I was more worried about what was on those

damned negatives. I didn't want anyone to recognize my father if he did appear on any.

"I've been in worse straits," I said. "To make it legit, I'll call my lieutenant so he doesn't find out from someone else, let him know I'm here." *In case he wants to call out IA on me,* I told myself, trying not to picture Torrance's expression should he be the one Andrews discussed the case with.

The detective nodded and I pulled out my cell phone, then moved a few feet away for some privacy and called Andrews at home. "How's the game?" I asked.

"I hear police radios, Gillespie. Please don't tell me you're doing something you're not supposed to be doing."

"Would you believe I came up to Napa for a little wine tasting with Scolari?"

"And what? Took a wrong turn? Drove over the speed limit? Just tell me you weren't working the Tremayne case."

"I didn't intend to. I called Missing Persons, had them take the report, like you asked. Then I called the agent and tried to pass on the info I got, but he never called back."

"So you had to drive up there?"

"Faye Tremayne called me when I was at Sam's." I told him how everything had transpired. "We have a tentative ID on our second homicide victim, Tom Brewer. He happens to work for one of Paolini's fronts. Bay Area Benevolent Society."

There was a long silence on the other end. "Now what?"

"I expect Napa PD will do a search warrant on the place. Daisy's in the hospital, out cold, and we have yet to discover what it was she was going to give us or why she was assaulted or where her missing daughter is. From what I heard on Napa PD's radios, Joshua managed to evade the officer."

"You have that agent's number?"

"Yes, sir."

"Call him again. Let him know so he doesn't think we

were holding anything back from him. You think this is related to that CD you found?"

"I do."

Again another stretch of silence. "All right. I'm going to
get Zim and Shipley back out, start working things on this
end. Something's up, and I'll be damned if we sit on our
thumbs while the FBI diddles around with their own agenda.
Any suggestions for where our guys should start?"

"Daisy's mother, Lillian O'Dell. And Eve's grandmother,
Mrs. Harrington. Might be a good idea to put a couple officers on both places in case Joshua heads to either. If I had to
guess, though, he's en route to the Harrington place. Eve's
grandmother has a box of negatives there that belonged to
Eve, and according to Mrs. Tremayne, Josh tried to steal
them."

"Where are the duplicate case file notes?"

"On Rocky's desk."

"Keep your pager and cell phone on. I want you to stay
there and interview this Daisy or Marguerite, or whatever
the hell she's calling herself today."

"How long do you want me to wait?"

"As long as it takes her to come to. Get a motel, sleep in
the hospital, I don't care. Just talk to her and find out what
the hell this Eden thing is all about and if it has anything to
do with who took her kid. Once that's done, I want you back
here and turning over anything to Shipley. I'm assigning the
case to him," he said, which was a relief to me. It meant Zim
would have minimal involvement.

"You realize I'm up here with Scolari?"

"Lucky he's retired, or I'd suspend him for this. Tell Scolari he's deputized till you get back. Now do me a favor. Call
that agent and do *not* get me into any more trouble."

"I wouldn't think of it."

"Yeah, and I need a bigger bottle of antacid," I heard him say before he hung up.

I called Agent Lloyd's pager, left my cell phone number on it. After that I called his voice mail, leaving a short message about what had happened, before returning to Scolari and Detective Venegas. "I've got my lieutenant's blessing. Looks like we'll be staying, at least until we get to interview Daisy."

Venegas nodded. "I'll check with the hospital in a bit, see when we can interview our victim. I'd like to talk with the neighbor across the street, see if she knows anything. Saw her sitting out there when I drove up. You're welcome to come along."

The neighbor's house was situated on the opposite end of the dirt cul-de-sac, and as we approached, we saw a woman, forty-something, sitting on her porch, watching the activity.

Detective Venegas introduced us, and we learned her name was Irene Jones.

"Is Daisy going to be okay?" she asked, looking a bit frightened.

"We think so," Venegas said. "You mind telling us when's the last time you saw her?"

She glanced at the Brewer house as though trying to re-member. "This has something to do with Eve Tremayne's murder, doesn't it? I had a feeling . . ."

"Why is that?" I asked.

"I read about Eve getting killed in the paper. She was here that same night."

"You're certain?" Venegas asked.

"She was standing right there," Irene said, pointing to the overgrown lawn in front of us. "My son was playing catch with Tom and Daisy's daughter, Bonnie, and I was right here on their porch when this white Mercedes pulls up. That's when this woman got out. I saw her picture on the news. It

was definitely Eve Tremayne who got out of that car, and
that's when it turned really strange."

"How so?" Scolari asked.

"Well, that guy who drove up in the black BMW a little
while ago? He was in the car with her. He gets out of the
passenger side and they walk up to Tom and the kids, and
this guy says, 'See?' And the woman, Eve Tremayne, is
looking at them and says, 'Oh, my God!' Tom even turns
white and says he needs a drink, which is pretty much what
Eve Tremayne said, and the three disappear into the
house."

Detective Venegas flipped a page in his notebook. "Any
idea what they were talking about?"

"Definitely," she said, crossing her arms. "You didn't
have to be a rocket scientist to figure it out. Same eyes. Bonnie and Eve Tremayne are definitely related. Which I guess
means that Tom isn't really the father."

Which confirmed in my mind that J. T. Tremayne was the
father. "When's the last time you saw Eve?" I asked.

"I was doing my dinner dishes. Saw her from the window,
so it must have been around seven the night she was killed.
She left in the Mercedes."

"Anyone with her?" I asked, thinking about the murder
scene in the city, wondering if it really *was* Tom Brewer in
that car with her.

"I'm not sure. Tom and the guy who came with her were
standing on the porch arguing. But I had something boiling
over on the stove, and when I took care of that and looked
back, they were gone."

"You see anyone since?"

"No. But my husband said he saw that other guy the next
day by their barn. The one who drove up with Eve."

Joshua Redding.

"When's your husband going to be home?"

"Tomorrow morning about seven. He's on the road. He drives a truck."

Detective Venegas stood. "Tell your husband we'll be here first thing in the morning," he said. "In the meantime, is there anyone we can call for you?"

"No. I'll be fine. I'm going to wait for my son to come home and then I think I'll go stay at my sister's until, well, until all this gets settled."

After we crossed back to the Brewer's property and met up with Scolari, Detective Venegas asked, "You get the idea that someone's been killing all these people because this child of Daisy's looks like Eve Tremayne?"

"I suppose that's a distinct possibility. Daisy's little girl told my partner that Daisy got upset after the 'pretty lady visited,' " I said. "It certainly makes me wonder if that's why Eve's parents wanted an attorney before they'd give me a statement when they came down to the morgue to identify their daughter's remains."

"They wanted an attorney?" Scolari asked in disbelief. "Why is it that politicians and rich people circumvent the judicial process when it comes to investigations of this sort?"

"Because they have something to hide?"

"Makes you wonder what it is," Venegas said. "Didn't you say that the hit on your two victims could have been mistaken identity?"

"A possibility."

Scolari said, "Maybe Tremayne's thinking of upping his political career and was worried that Daisy and Joshua might ruin things if they let it get out he had a daughter out of wedlock."

"Maybe that's why he dropped out the first time, six years ago."

No one commented as a uniformed evidence tech walked

up and addressed Detective Venegas. "We couldn't get any fingerprints in the barn. Too much dust from the doors being open."

"Thanks," he replied, then said to me, "You think you can get me a photo of this Joshua Redding?"

"Shouldn't be a problem," I said. "He was booked in our jail last night. Mind if I ask what's next on your agenda?"

"I'm thinking we do a search warrant, but not tonight. We'll post a team on the place. Ain't nothing in there that can't wait till morning. In the meantime, you two interested in going to dinner later? Assuming you're hanging out in our fair city for the night."

I looked at Scolari. He gave a shrug that told me he was okay with whatever I decided. "I guess we're staying until Daisy can be interviewed," I said. "Any recommendations on where?"

"The River Rest Lodge," he said, as his partner and Mrs. Tremayne reached our side. "Clean, reasonable, close to stores and restaurants, and they like cops."

"Sounds good. Point us in the right direction and we're there."

He gave us the address, then looked at his watch. "Let's say I call you around six? That oughta give you time to rest up and my partner time to start the paperwork."

"Very funny," his partner said. "This report is yours unless you're buying dinner tonight. At Mustard's?"

"Mustard's it is," Venegas said.

"We'll wait for your call," I said. Then I asked Mrs. Tremayne, "Are you going to be okay to drive home?"

"Yes. Is Marguerite going to be okay?"

I hesitated. A couple of days ago, when she was thanking me for removing Daisy from the funeral, she'd referred to her as "that horrid girl." Then again, it was her daughter's funeral. She was entitled to be upset over a disturbance.

"More than likely," I said, then walked her to her car. "Where are you going from here?"

"To Mother's. I'm going to pick her up and take her to our home until this is all over."

"Probably not a bad idea," I said.

She opened her door, then stopped, looking at me. "I just wanted to thank you. I know I haven't always been—"

"Don't worry about it, Mrs. Tremayne."

And then she got in her car and left.

Scolari and I headed to our car and then the motel. "You sure you don't mind staying?" I asked.

"Don't worry about it. Besides," he said. "What's one night in the grand scheme of things?"

"Yeah," I said, as I pulled into the lot. It took us not quite ten minutes to get there. That was when I remembered that on this particular night I had sort of made plans.

Scolari's room was a few doors down in the smoking section. I told him that I was going to rest for a bit, and he said he was taking a walk to the store to get a few things. Like every homicide cop I knew, I kept an emergency overnight bag in my trunk for just such occasions and brought that in with me, tossing it onto the bed. I pulled my phone, pager, gun, and badge from my belt, depositing each on the nightstand, then arranged the pillows against the headboard and sat to make my calls. I had several of them to make—Andrews, Torrance . . .

It was that last call I wasn't looking forward to. *Hi, it's Kate. Just wanted to let you know that I was serious about tonight but have to back out, because I didn't plan on getting tied up out of town when I was lying to you in the first place, even though I changed my mind and didn't go, but now I'm here . . .*

Right.

I closed my eyes, figuring I could pretty much write off

my relationship with Torrance, such as it was. I knew him. He'd say it was okay and then that would be it. Over. It didn't matter how I ended up in Napa. I went and he'd told me not to. But it was a call I had to make.

So here goes nothing, I thought, and picked up the phone.

22

Then again, what the hell was I thinking? I was here spending the night in a motel in Napa all by myself. So what if Scolari was a few doors down? Maybe if I *did* explain to Torrance how I'd gone to Sam's like I'd said, and that due to circumstances beyond my control, I was here. Why not come and spend the night?

In theory it sounded good, so I called Torrance's cell phone, since that was the number I knew by heart. I got his voice mail. I waited five minutes and tried again with the same result. When his message came up, I was tempted to disconnect. Suddenly my theory wasn't sounding so good.

"Hi, this is Kate," I said, before I lost my nerve, even as I stared at the stark motel room, thinking this was not how I pictured this happening. I gave a quick explanation on how I'd ended up here, hoping it didn't sound too lame, then added, "I'm staying at the Napa River Rest Lodge . . . and was wondering, um, if you wanted to stop here—by here, you know what I mean. I'm in room . . ." I glanced at the phone by the bed. "One-sixty-three. We're going to dinner at six."

I hit End, wondering if he'd come by or call back. I supposed it would depend on how upset he was that I had attempted to hide the reason for my coming here in the first place. Then again, maybe I was worrying for nothing.

Maybe I had totally misread everything Torrance had said and he figured I was bluffing and he really had no intention of sleeping with me.

And if I were smart, I thought as I sat on the bed, I'd make that assumption, so that I didn't have to worry about getting my feelings hurt. Tired, I leaned against the pillows and flipped the phone shut. I hadn't closed my eyes for more than a few minutes when it rang, and I wondered if it was Torrance.

It was Agent Lloyd.

"I got your messages," he said. "You're still in Napa?"

"Yes."

"Find anything significant up there?"

"Not really. Daisy did have an empty CD case on her. Whether there was a significant CD in it at one time is unknown."

"What are your plans?"

I hesitated. Stepping on Bureau toes was not something I was comfortable with doing, even if my orders came from higher up. "Since you didn't return my pages, my lieutenant wanted me to stay here, interview Daisy as soon as she's medically cleared."

"My fault. I'm working on something in the South Bay and couldn't get back to you right away. Unfortunately I only now checked my voice mail. What are you doing about her daughter?"

"We have Missing Persons on it, and Napa PD is working on it up here."

"I'd like to be there when you interview her. Let me know when you set it up?"

"Shouldn't be a problem. I don't know if it'll be tonight or tomorrow, though."

"You staying there or you heading back for the night?"

"I'm holed up in the Napa River Rest Lodge. NPD may

do a search warrant in the morning, looking for whatever it was Daisy was going to give us on the club."

"Jesus. This thing's spinning faster than I can figure it out. I'll make some calls from my end, see if we have anyone who might've heard of this mystery club. If I'm lucky, I'll get done with what I'm working on in time to make the morning search warrant."

"See you then," I said.

I flipped the phone shut and set it on the nightstand, then closed my eyes, tired after the events of the past few days. I awoke to the motel phone ringing. Detective Venegas calling about dinner.

"Meet you at Mustard's," he said. "Can't miss it. Up the road about ten miles on the left, just past Yountville."

"We'll be there."

I called Scolari's room, told him to meet me at the car, and about ten minutes later we were pulling in. It was a small restaurant in the heart of the valley, crowded with people spilling out into the parking lot, waiting for a table. I'd heard of it but had never eaten there, and looking at the crowd, wondered if we'd get the chance.

The two Napa detectives were standing by the door waiting for us.

"This place is packed," Scolari said as we worked our way into the small lobby by the bar.

"Not a problem," Venegas said. "Chef's a good friend of mine. Called him up and voilà, table for four."

True to his word, we were seated immediately. I let the others order first, thinking I'd get an idea or two, but they all chose the same thing, pork tenderloin, obviously a guy thing.

I scanned the menu, then ordered the halibut, which came grilled to a delicate crunch on the outside and hot and moist on the inside. Fish cooked to perfection was a very good thing. "Maybe we can get a change of venue from San Francisco to Napa once this case goes to trial," I told the others after we had finished. "I'd be willing to make a sacrifice in having a long drive to eat here for lunch."

"Very big of you," Scolari said. "Especially considering anyone has yet to make an arrest."

"Any theories bouncing around?" Detective Venegas asked, after ordering coffee and dessert for everyone. "I mean, theories other than our victim being attacked by this Redding guy? Seems to me it's all related. We solve this, you probably have a good link to your homicide and your kidnapping."

"After talking with the neighbor," I said, "it seems clear that Eve made a specific trip out here to see this child, and that trip set into motion a chain of events."

"Yeah," Scolari said, "like she only just learned of Bonnie's existence and maybe wasn't too happy. Maybe something to do with her father's political run? Isn't that sort of a repeat on what happened six, seven years ago? He was the front runner, only back then, there wasn't any kid."

Venegas nodded. "Makes you wonder if maybe the rumor's true, that this kid's the reason why he dropped out the first time around? Our Vic would've been pregnant right about then, wouldn't she?"

"Yes," I said, recalling the comment made by Tremayne's wife in the morgue about that being *her* daughter lying there. A jab at the knowledge of this illegitimate child, even though he assumed she didn't know? "And here's Joshua sending him a photo of his kid and a blackmail note the moment he decides to run again."

"That fits," Scolari said, looking at me. "Maybe this Joshua character tries to blackmail Tremayne because of this election. Tremayne places a hit on them, accidentally kills his own daughter, then kidnaps the kid because a quick paternity test proves that he's the father and had plenty of motive to want them out of the picture."

"When I first interviewed Tremayne," I said, "he mentioned that Joshua was going to make Eve pay if he didn't."

"Pay how?" Venegas asked.

"That's a good question. Because why would he drag Eve all the way up here to see this kid she never even knew existed, unless it was important to Eve that her father win the election? Would she have paid money to Joshua to remain silent about her newly discovered half-sister?"

Scolari said, "The neighbor saw Joshua and Tom arguing right before they took off. Maybe Joshua killed Tom because Tom found out that Joshua was planning to blackmail Eve and her father."

"That's assuming Joshua is the killer. The only killer. I think they were the victim of a hit." I explained the autopsy findings, the bruises on their arms indicating that someone held them with enough force to leave marks.

"Maybe they got the bruises earlier."

"It's possible, but a big coincidence. And Daisy told me that she made the initial Missing Person report on Joshua, because he had told her that he was being followed. She also alluded to his having done something not above board. Something where he promised her no one would get hurt."

"Why would Joshua attack Daisy?" Venegas asked, once our dessert had been served.

"Maybe," his partner said, "she was going to rat on him about the blackmail. Or turn something over to the police that he wanted to use for blackmail. This Garden of Eden stuff. She did have that empty CD envelope. Maybe he took the CD, whacked her, and ran."

"Now that stuff," Venegas said, "seems to me would be a motive for murder."

Scolari nodded. "Maybe it's got nothing to do with

Joshua. Look at Standiford. His picture's on that CD you found, but missing from the book. Maybe Eve was blackmailing him and he figures if he's gonna make a run for Senator on his conservative platform, it might not look so good and he has Eve taken out. But then when these negatives turn up missing, and one of them is with him and Eve, he figures he'll lie low and just run for local office. All's he's gotta do is then deny, deny, deny until the photo pops up. Politicians do it all the time."

"That sounds logical," Venegas said. He put his credit card on the table, refusing our offer to let us pay for at least our share of the meal. "Tell you what," he said. "You get the change of venue, you can buy the next dinner."

We finished our dessert and coffee, then returned to the parking lot, where we stood for several minutes while Detective Venegas and his partner gave us a verbal tour of some of their favorite wineries. Agent Lloyd called while we were standing there. "Inspector Gillespie? Just wanted to fill you in on what I've learned about the Garden of Eden Club. You got a minute?"

"Several," I said, leaning against my car.

"Shouldn't take long. I called one of my friends who used to work out of the San Francisco office. He said that he heard rumors of this thing going on as long ago as seven, maybe eight years. Said the sex thing was part of it, but it also had something to do with drugs, and they suspected a woman was running it as a prostitution ring to finance it. A Lillian O'Dell. Anyone you know?"

"Yeah. She's the grandmother of our kidnap victim. You sure that was the name, not Eve Tremayne?"

"Definitely Lillian O'Dell, according to my source. For whatever reason, the bottom fell out of the investigation about six years ago and they couldn't prove anything. You going out there?"

"She'll have to wait for tomorrow," I said. "I don't plan on rushing back to the city tonight, unless we locate the little girl, Bonnie."

"Just as well," Agent Lloyd said. "I'm driving up there when I finish here. It'll probably be pretty late, so I won't disturb you. You need anything?"

"No, thanks."

"See you tomorrow, then," he said, then hung up.

"Everything okay?" Sam asked.

"So far." I told him and the two detectives what the agent told me about the Garden of Eden Club.

Scolari leaned against the car next to me, tapping a cigarette out of his pack. "You're saying the nun you interviewed was running a drug op?" he asked, lighting up a smoke.

"Allegedly," I said, when my phone went off again.

I had pretty much given up on Torrance by this time, and I hid my disappointment at the sound of Lieutenant Andrews's voice.

"Scolari still there with you?" he asked.

"Standing right in front of me. How's things on your end?"

"Interesting, to say the least. J. T. Tremayne denied knowing anyone up in Napa, according to Zim. We just finished talking to his wife when she got back a little while ago and she said the same. Both were pretty adamant that Eve would have had no reason to be up there either. But we did get the box of negatives. You want to tell me what we're looking for?"

"You know the photo album I told you about?"

"That would be the photo that I'm still not happy with you about?"

"Yes," I said, wishing I'd had the sense just to leave the damn photo there. My father was dead. It shouldn't matter. But it did, and I had taken the photo, and there was nothing

I could do about it now. "There was a second missing photo from the back of the book. We don't know if it was taken by Joshua Redding when he broke in, or if someone else took it."

"Which means we want to know whose photo it was."

"The photos in the album and on the CD seemed to me as though they were in chronological order. If the negatives you have are dated, I'd start with the most recent. See if the photos match up to the album, and figure out which one is gone."

"I'll have the CSIs get started, see what we can find. One other thing—Pierce wants to know what's up with the grandmother, Lillian O'Dell."

"Meaning what?" I asked, thinking of what Agent Lloyd had said about Lillian running a drug op.

"He went over there to see if she had a picture of Daisy O'Dell's kid, and she was gone."

23

Great.

Andrews hung up and I told Scolari and the two detectives about O'Dell turning up missing.

"That's all you need," Scolari said, taking a last drag off his cigarette. "Another witness disappearing in the middle of this investigation."

"Or suspect," Venegas said.

"Maybe she went to go hang with Joshua Redding's mother down in Mexico." Scolari flicked his cigarette into the parking lot, watched the embers bounce. "Well, at least we had a good dinner," he said, shaking the detectives' hands. "Appreciate you two hosting us for the night."

"Yes," I said, shaking their hands as well. "Thanks for dinner. Great restaurant."

"See you in the morning," Venegas said.

We drove back to the motel and Scolari walked me to my room. "You coming in?" I asked.

"For a few," he said, taking a seat at the table. "What d'ya think about this O'Dell woman running a drug op?"

"She didn't look like a druglord or -lady, as the case may be," I said, pulling off all my gear and putting it on the nightstand. "She looked like a frigid, religious woman."

"Don't you think the fact her name came up at all is

enough to put you on alert?" he asked, taking out his lighter, then patting his pocket for his cigarettes.

"This is a no-smoking room, Sam."

"They always are." He tapped his lighter against the table-top. "So where does Joshua figure into all this?"

"I don't know. Jealous lover, spurned while he's rotting as a handyman?"

"You think he took the kid?"

"I'm not sure. There's too much about him I don't know."

"You check with Narcotics to see if his name's come up recently?"

"No, but I will. I wonder if Lillian O'Dell's name has ever come up."

"Worth checking out."

After that we discussed the search warrant to be served in the morning. Several minutes later Scolari looked at his watch. "Time for me to hit the hay."

"Yeah, me too. See you in the morning."

He left and I shut the door, locked it, then saw that he had forgotten his lighter. Too tired to go after him, I left it where it was, turned off the light, and turned on the TV, more for company than anything else.

When I heard a knock on the door a couple minutes later, I knew it was Sam, probably wanting a cigarette. I grabbed the forgotten lighter and looked out the peephole.

It was Torrance.

Here.

Because I had told him I wanted to sleep with him.

I opened the door and he entered, walking into the center of the room, not saying a thing.

I closed the door, turning toward him.

He looked at the lighter in my hand. "You taking up smoking?"

"Sam left it," I said, shoving it into my pocket. His gaze

bore into me and I realized what I saw there was not the look of a man about to make love. It was the look of a man very much not happy. "Why are you here?"

"Not for the reasons you think, and I won't be long."

"I probably don't want to know, do I?"

"What you don't want to know," he said, "is what it's like being lied to, because someone wants a way around rules and regulations. Of all people, I expected something different from you."

"I know it looks bad, but I did go to Sam's and it wasn't my intention to come up here. And when we were in my office I wasn't trying to lie to you. I was trying to change the subject. It was all I could think of."

"You're definitely the first who has offered your bed."

I stared at the carpet. It was better than seeing the disappointment in his eyes.

He stood there a moment longer, then said, "Good-bye, Kate."

I moved away from the door, up against the wall to allow him room to leave. And that was when it struck me. Not good night—good-bye. With a finality. As though if there had ever been a ghost of a chance, there was none now.

He started for the door and when he moved past me, I put my hand out, stopping him. He looked at me but said nothing, and I knew that this was it. That I had about a millisecond to right an insurmountable wrong. That if I let him go this time, let him walk out that door . . .

"I'm sorry," I said again. "But I wasn't lying. Lack of judgment, yes. Lack of timing, definitely. But when has that ever been my strong suit? And I didn't tell you something that wasn't true. It's something I've wanted to say for a long time. Something I've wanted to happen for a long time. And . . . I'm sorry."

His gaze locked on mine. I reached up and touched his

face, and he closed his eyes as though fighting some inner demon.

"I'm sorry," I said again. "I—"

"Damn you." He caught my hand, kissed my palm, then pulled me to him and his mouth found mine, his kiss fierce, possessive. I knew in that moment that everything I had imagined, even what I had experienced with him, was about to pale in comparison as he unbuttoned my shirt, and then reached around and unhooked my bra. Tension, sweet, sharp, coiled within me as his hand brushed against my breast, then trailed down my belly as he held me there against the wall, a prisoner to his touch. My knees nearly buckled and he leaned against me, his mouth next to my ear. "You don't want to know how many times I've imagined—"

The rap on the door startled us both. I listened, hearing nothing but the rapid beating of my heart and our breathing. "It's . . . probably Sam. Forgot his lighter."

"To hell with his lighter," he whispered.

A second knock.

And then a loud bang.

Torrance spun, dragging me to the floor, knocking the lamp down with us. The room went dark and the door burst open. I felt for my gun on the nightstand. Heard another shot. Saw the muzzle blast of Torrance's gun. A thud as someone fell to the floor. A darkness filling the doorway. Another suspect. The glint of a weapon.

I fired. Again and again.

A second thud. Light spilling in from the breezeway.

Showing two bodies on the floor in front of me.

And one beside me.

24

I scrambled to my feet, my weapon aimed first at one, then the other suspect. Neither moved, but I wasn't taking a chance, trying to cover both. I could see only one gun, that belonging to the suspect nearer the door, just a few inches from his hand. I wanted so badly to look at Torrance, see if he was okay, but he was slightly behind me, and I had no idea if there were only two suspects or if anyone else was outside, waiting.

Then I heard the sound of someone running across the parking lot, yelling something I couldn't distinguish over the pounding pulse in my ears.

"Torrance?" I said, my voice sounding shrill.

The suspect to my right moved. I trained my gun on him just as a figure ran up to the door.

I looked, aiming there.

"It's me, Kate." Scolari. Thank God.

"Torrance is shot."

In that moment of distraction, the suspect rolled slightly, raised his gun.

Before we could move, a deafening blast rang in my right ear as Torrance fired. The suspect's body jerked, his gun fell to the ground.

"Scolari," I said. "Cover the guy by the door."

"Check."

From the corner of my eye, I saw Torrance over the edge of the bed as he scooted himself up, leaning against the wall.

"You got him covered?" I asked Torrance.

"Yeah," he said, his voice sounding raspy. "Cover the first guy."

"Cuffs?" I asked Scolari.

"Got 'em."

I aimed my weapon at his suspect, while Scolari holstered his own, then pulled his cuffs from the shoulder holster beneath his jacket. The doorway was awkward to work in, Scolari having to step over the suspect's legs and lean forward to grab his right hand, twisting slightly as he slapped the cuff against the wrist. Half the metal ring opened, flew around the wrist, and clicked shut on the other side. He stepped over the body, grabbed the other wrist and did the same, then checked him for weapons. "Clear."

I took my cuffs from the nightstand, tossed them to Scolari, and he cuffed the second suspect as well. Then I grabbed my phone and scrambled over the bed to check on Torrance. "You okay?"

"I'm fine," he said, looking pale. His left hand was tucked beneath his right arm, and I could see blood seeping between his fingers. I couldn't tell if he'd been shot in the hand, the arm, or his side.

My fingers shook as I punched in 9-1-1, then put the phone to my ear, listening to it ring and ring. Scolari came over, took the phone. "I got it." Outside in the distance, I heard sirens, then Scolari saying, "I need the Napa police. There's been a shooting at the Napa River Rest Lodge and we have an officer down. San Francisco PD . . . two suspects, both shot . . ."

I moved off the bed and knelt beside Torrance, setting my gun next to his on the ground.

"I'm fine," he said again, closing his eyes.

I felt sick to my stomach, even slightly dizzy as the adrenaline started to wear off. If I felt this bad, he surely felt worse. "You don't look fine."

He opened his eyes, then gave me a crooked half smile as he reached up with his right arm, his hand shaky as he grasped my shirt. "You sure as hell do."

I looked down, saw what he saw, and what Scolari had to have seen.

"Great," I said at the blast of sirens outside and then the sound of officers shouting orders. At least my bra was sort of covering me, I thought, as I reached back and attempted to close it. No luck. I figured I'd better do some buttons before a dozen cops came bursting in and were treated to the same sight.

I managed four buttons, hurriedly tucked in my shirt, and redid the top button of my jeans. A good thing, too—the room lit up like a sports arena from a flood of spotlights aimed through the door. Scolari put his gun on the nightstand, then held up both hands as he stood in the doorway. "You better get up here, Kate."

"You going to be okay?" I asked Torrance.

"Go," he said.

I took Torrance's and my weapons, put them on the center of the bed, and grabbed my star from the nightstand. I tucked it on my belt, then joined Scolari, raising my hands as I stood in front of him.

"You, in the doorway," came a faceless voice from the light. "Slowly step out, keep your hands up where we can see them."

Blinded by the spotlights to everything in front of me, I stepped over the body in the doorway, and realizing how it must look, prayed we weren't being covered by some overexcited rookie on his first big call. All it would take was one shot, and in the adrenaline rush, everyone else would follow suit and we'd go down in a hail of gunfire.

I continued moving out to the parking lot until the voice said, "Stop." I stopped. "Turn around, slowly." I did so, seeing Scolari in the doorway for a brief moment, comforted by his familiar presence. When I faced the direction of the officers, the lights blinding me again, I remained still, waiting for the next order. "Drop to your knees."

As I knelt, feeling the hard asphalt through my jeans, someone yelled, "Hold your fire. She's a cop."

I heard rather than saw the officer approach and then someone reached down to help me to my feet. "Inspector Gillespie?"

I couldn't see his face at the moment, couldn't remember his name.

"It's me, Venegas. What's going on?"

"My partner, Mike Torrance. Inside, shot. He needs an ambulance."

"It's pulling up now. What happened?"

"Two suspects busted in the door, shooting. I have no idea who they are. I can only guess it's related to the case."

"Call Scolari out. Let them clear the room." Two other officers joined us, both uniformed, one a sergeant, the other a lieutenant, their radios giving off a periodic beep, which signaled emergency traffic only.

"Sam," I said. "Come on out." Then, to Detective Venegas, I said, "There are at least five firearms in there. Torrance is against the back wall at the foot of the bed."

By then Sam was at our side, and not taking chances, he kept his arms raised until he was told otherwise by Venegas. "We appreciate your cooperation, Scolari. You okay?"

"Yeah. Torrance isn't."

The detective nodded, keyed his radio and said, "Three subjects within. One, an officer down, at the back of the room, foot of the bed. Two suspects, cuffed. Several firearms throughout."

"Ten-four."

The lieutenant keyed his mike, gave his call sign, and said, "Go ahead with entry."

We were moved back, behind the line of police cars and out of the spotlights. Only then did I see the several officers posted on either side of the room. Three made entry, one stopping at the door as the other two continued on. It seemed like an eternity before I heard, "Code Four. Officer down, two in custody. Code Three ambulance."

I think that was when it hit me—when the paramedics rushed in. My knees buckled and Sam caught me as I leaned against the car for support.

"He's going to be fine, Kate."

"This is all my fault."

"Whoa. What the hell are you talking about?"

"I *told* him to come to my room. If I hadn't . . ."

Sam drew me away where we wouldn't be overheard. "And if he *hadn't,* you might be dead. He's alive. That's what counts. Now let's get to the ambulance, see if you can ride over with him."

Torrance was on the gurney, about to be raised into the ambulance, when we got there. He was covered with a blanket, an IV tube taped to the back of his right hand. I wanted to go to him, see how he was, but his eyes were closed. I prayed he was sleeping.

"You mind if his partner rides with him?" Scolari said to one of the paramedics.

The paramedic looked at me and said, "You his partner?"

"Yes."

"Are you hurt?"

"No."

"Hey, Joe. Grab me a blanket."

Joe was in the back of the ambulance, ready to lift the gurney. He reached beneath something, pulled out a hospital blanket, and handed it to his partner, who unfolded it and said, "Put this on."

"Thanks." I draped it over my shoulders, only then realizing that I was cold.

"Just give us a couple and we'll make room for you."

They lifted the gurney, pushed it in, the wheels collapsing. When it was locked in place, Joe hooked Torrance's IV bag to a rack, then removed his rubber glove and reached down to me. "Ready?"

I looked at Sam. "The car keys are on the nightstand."

"Don't worry. I'll get there."

I hugged him, then took Joe's hand and stepped up into the back of the ambulance. And as I sat there and watched while he continued to prep Torrance for the ride to the hospital, I was reminded of a different night about two years ago, when I was shot during a search warrant, and it was Scolari who rode to the hospital with me. I was scared. I'd only been shot in the arm. I didn't know how seriously Torrance was hurt. I looked at Sam, who stood there watching me, not moving until the doors were closed and the ambulance drove off.

I knew from experience that the ride would seem an eternity to Torrance if he were conscious, and every bump and dip the vehicle made would be felt in excruciating pain. His eyes were still closed, and I didn't dare touch him for fear I'd wake him.

We arrived and I walked in with the medics, figuring the nurses would hustle me out to the waiting room. But Joe said, "She's his partner," and that was all it took.

I was in there with him, standing out of the way, in the corner, not even sure he knew I was there. The doctor walked in, lifted the dressing, and Torrance caught his breath and opened his eyes.

"How you doing?" the doctor asked.

"Fine," he said, his voice low, barely audible.

"Any pain?"

"Some."

"Scale of one to ten, ten being the worst."

"Eleven."

"I'll bet. Probably took a slice of your rib. Maybe cracked it." He looked up at the nurse. "We'll need to get an X ray." Then to me, he said, "Doesn't look too bad. For the most part a flesh wound. You can feel the slug right here, lodged against his rib."

I wasn't sure I wanted to look, but he moved aside and so I approached. When Torrance saw me, he said, "Hey."

"Hey."

His dark gaze was filled with pain. "Can I ask . . . something?"

I nodded, brushing the back of my hand on his cheek, and he reached up with his left arm and crooked his finger, indicating I should come closer.

I put my face next to his, figuring it must hurt him to talk. "What?"

I could feel his breath on my ear as he said, "Rain check."

I closed my eyes and bit my lip. Kept silent that had I not persisted, this wouldn't have happened. And when it appeared he was waiting for an answer, I said, "I promise."

"And Kate?" His whisper was barely audible.

"Yes?"

"For this, it had better be damn good sex."

That was when I knew he'd be fine, and I felt the prick of tears beneath my eyelids. I kissed him lightly on the mouth, and he closed his eyes once more, a soft smile on his lips.

Scolari arrived with the detective right about the time they wheeled Torrance off to X ray.

"How's he doing?"

"With a few pain pills, he should be back to his normal self in no time at all."

"Venegas says the FBI wants to get a statement from you. I'll go have a smoke, while you talk."

"They got here quick," I said.

Detective Venegas met me around the corner of the ER lobby, away from those who were waiting to be seen. "The administration is letting us use one of their offices. You don't mind coming in and giving us a statement now, do you?"

"No," I said, though I was tired and could have slept where I stood.

I followed him to a carpeted office, a meeting room, to judge by the large table and number of chairs around it. Two men were seated at one end, and both stood when we entered. I recognized the dark-haired man immediately. Agent Morley. He introduced me to his partner, Agent Thompson, and I shook hands with him.

"You okay?" Morley asked.

"In one piece," I said.

He indicated I should sit, and they did the same, then opened their notebooks. "I know you've been through a lot tonight," Morley said, "but if you can hang in there for a few minutes more and tell us what happened, maybe draw us a diagram so we can get a better understanding? It'll be a while before we can get out to the scene."

He passed me a legal pad and I drew a quick diagram as I narrated the events of the evening. The room wasn't that big, and when I drew the two Xs next to the nightstand—one representing me at the wall, the other Torrance in front of me—Detective Venegas raised his brows but said nothing. He had seen the state of my clothes when I walked out of that room, and I suspected he knew that Torrance and I weren't standing there idly conversing. The FBI agents made no reaction or comment to Torrance's presence.

"You two were damn lucky you didn't answer the door right off," Agent Morley said, rubbing at his top lip as he studied the drawing. "There's a bullet hole right in the center. Looks like they were anticipating someone coming up to the peephole to look out."

I stared at my sketch, the location of the *X*s, recalling how we hadn't wanted to answer the door.

Scolari was right. If Torrance hadn't been there, I would've gone right up. Looked out the peephole. Been too dead to feel guilty.

That knowledge did little to help.

"Any idea who these guys were, or what they wanted?" Agent Thompson asked.

"The only thing I can come up with is the two guys Markowski and I saw that day at the Redding house."

"Markowski?"

"He's my real partner. Off on injury leave from when the house blew up."

"Your partners take out extra insurance when they work with you?" Detective Venegas asked.

"The smart ones do."

Venegas smiled.

Agent Morley jotted down a few notes. "And what about these two you saw at this Redding house?" he asked.

"I didn't see the driver." I told them about their appearance at the funeral, how one of them grabbed Daisy and was later seen at the house. I also repeated my theory that the original murders of Eve Tremayne and Tom Brewer looked like a hit, and if not a hit, a homicide where there were two suspects present, each holding the arm of a victim as the victims sat in their car.

Agent Morley nodded, rubbing at his upper lip again as though studiously considering the possibility. "Looks that way," he said. "But how'd they know you were up here?"

"Good question." And one I couldn't answer right off. I couldn't think. My brain was on overload at the moment.

Agent Thompson asked me, "You know Agent Lloyd?"

"Yes. He came to the Hall and picked up the case."

The two agents looked at each other, then back at me. "Can you tell us what your interaction with him has been? From the beginning?"

Curious, I told them about Lloyd's visit with the Tremaynes, and then told of my call from Daisy about her missing daughter, which had brought me to Napa. I gave them the card that had Lloyd's name on it. They took it.

"Do you have any idea who you shot?" Agent Morley asked.

"No. It was dark, and afterward I was busy tending to my injured partner."

Agent Morley laid out two photos on the table. "These are the men who were shot."

The first I recognized as the man from the funeral and later the Redding house before it exploded. The second, however, was a different matter entirely, and I paled at the significance of what I saw, who I'd killed.

"Someone you know?" Agent Thompson asked, while the three of them watched me closely.

"Yes." I closed my eyes, wondering how I was going to get through this night, wondering if there was a mistake.

I had killed Agent Lloyd from the FBI.

25

"It's Agent Lloyd."

"Agent Lloyd has been on administrative leave these past few months," Morley said.

"You didn't send him?"

"No, we didn't send him, Inspector."

I stared at the three of them, the two FBI agents and the Napa detective, trying to recall what it was that Paolini had told me. *Sometimes in the world of friends and enemies . . .* Paolini had known, tried to warn me. And I wondered why. "He came with the Tremaynes. My lieutenant asked me to turn over the case . . ."

"Do you know what he was after?" Morley asked.

"He seemed interested in the CD taken from a burglary of Eve Tremayne's house right after she was murdered. I gave him a copy," I said. "It had some sexually graphic images of Eve Tremayne and other men on it. Lloyd called me tonight and told me he'd found out that a woman we'd contacted, Lillian O'Dell, was operating a dope-prostitution ring that was connected to what we saw on the CD, but the source dried up about six years ago. Other than that, I don't have a clue, and have to guess that his info is suspect."

The two agents nodded, looked at their notes. "We'll get back to you if we have any more questions," Agent Thompson said. "Detective Venegas, thank you for your assistance."

"Anytime," he said, then stood. "I'll take you back to your partner." I got up and followed him from the room.

We walked down the hallway, side by side.

"You get the idea they're scrambling to cover their asses on this one?" he said.

"I'm so tired, they could be telling me that I wasn't really here right now and I'd believe them."

"Can't blame you," he said, stopping in front of the ER lobby. He held out his hand, and I shook it. "I'm sorry it turned out this way," he said. "I'll get Scolari for you."

"He's probably outside smoking."

"See you in the morning?"

"Thanks."

Sam found me a few minutes later, and he held up his cell phone. "Andrews wants to talk to you." He pushed the Send button, then handed it to me.

It rang and Andrews answered. "Scolari told me what happened. You okay?" he asked.

"I'm okay. Torrance isn't."

"Do I want to know why he was in your room?"

"No."

I heard him exhale in the silence that followed, then, "Anything else I should know?"

I told him about the FBI and Lloyd. Scolari listened in.

"Jesus Christ," Andrews said. "If you're trying to make me old before my time, it's working. Did Scolari tell you about Lillian O'Dell?"

"No. I just got back from talking with the FBI."

"I checked with Narcotics. Lillian O'Dell has a prior arrest for drug dealing."

"How long ago was that?"

"About twenty years ago, which means she's either

changed her ways, or just gotten better at not getting caught. We'll talk more in the morning. As soon as Torrance is stabilized, I want you back here. That understood?"

"What about interviewing Daisy?" I asked.

"You know the rules. Three days AL for an officer-involved shooting. Go have your blood drawn if Napa hasn't done it as part of their protocol."

"But—" It wasn't the blood I was worried about. That was SOP. It was the getting back to the city part I didn't like. I wasn't ready to leave Torrance.

"Don't try to buck the system, Gillespie. You're on administrative leave as of now. Shipley and Zim will take it from here."

"Yes, sir."

"That means my office, tomorrow morning. Do I make myself clear?"

"I'll be there."

I disconnected and handed Scolari his phone. "Thanks," I said.

"I'm going to take a wild guess that you don't want to spend the night back at the motel?"

"Brilliant deduction, Watson."

"You wanna stick around here, or you want me to take you home?"

I glanced toward the ER. "I'm not going anywhere until I know Torrance is okay."

I found a nurse and had her draw my blood for the protocol shooting investigation. Afterward, Scolari and I waited together in the lobby, side by side, his arm around me the whole time. He kept telling me I should get some sleep. Right. After what seemed like an eternity, a nurse finally came out and told us that Torrance was in recovery, doing fine. And then, an eternity after that, the same nurse, Micki by her name badge, came back and told us that he was now in his room and sleeping. She started to walk away, then stopped, turned around, and said, "My husband's a cop. You want me to take you up to see your friend?"

"Please," I said.

Sam and I went up there together. We looked in. Torrance was on the far bed, his chest moving up and down in an even pattern, the IV bag a vivid reminder that all was not as it seemed. As we stood there, Micki went to the nurses' station, spoke softly with the floor nurse, then came back. "There's an empty bed," she said, nodding into the room.

I looked at Sam. "Go ahead," he said. "I've gotta make a few calls anyway."

Once they left, I sat in the chair instead. It was closer and I could hear his breathing. The sound was comforting, even though I already knew he was going to be okay. I sat like that in the darkened room for hours, just watching him sleep—something I couldn't have done myself if I'd wanted to.

Every time I closed my eyes, I saw him looking at me, then spinning away . . . down to the floor, out of my reach.

Who could have done this? Why? Who knew we were there?

Just about everyone, it seemed. Daisy had asked me to meet her. She certainly could have told Joshua, assuming he wasn't there telling her what to say in the first place. Faye Tremayne knew. She was there when Detective Venegas recommended the motel, which meant Venegas and his partner knew. And FBI Agent Lloyd knew, which sort of made everyone else's knowledge pale in comparison.

I looked at Torrance's face, hoping his thoughts were more peaceful than mine. I didn't know what time he stirred, turning his head my direction, but it was no longer the black of deep night, more the gray of predawn.

"Kate," he said.

"Hi."

He lifted his hand, reached over. I clasped my fingers in his until he fell asleep again.

It was well after eight when Sam woke me. Apparently I had finally drifted off and a nurse had come in and covered me with a blanket.

"I brought your jacket from the motel," Sam said, draping it over the back of my chair. He lifted his pant leg, showing me his backup weapon in its ankle holster. "You wanna borrow my thirty-eight for the time being?" A valid question, since Napa PD or the FBI would undoubtedly be keeping our weapons during their part of the investigation.

"You have something for yourself?"

"I'll dig up something. Mathis is on his way. Saw him downstairs."

"Mathis is here?"

"I called him last night. I told him we'd see him in the cafeteria in a few. Detective Venegas is there waiting."

"Andrews put me on AL. We need to go back to the city."

He gave me an odd look. "Go splash some water on your face. Wake up a bit."

I looked at him a moment, trying to figure out why he was being so stern. I felt like a fog was surrounding me and I couldn't think. But I slid off the chair, glanced at Torrance, who was still asleep, then hustled into the bathroom, washed my face, rinsed my mouth, brushed my fingers through my hair, and straightened out my clothes.

AL? I needed some serious caffeine running through my veins to think I was going to let a little AL stop me from going to that search warrant this morning to find out what happened, and wondered if the stuff here in the hospital was strong enough. When I finally came out, Scolari was standing in the doorway.

I looked at Torrance, reassured myself he was still there, still breathing, then turned back to Scolari. "Ready?" I asked.

He smiled. "Glad to see you've woken up a bit. Let's go. We're already late."

A few minutes later we walked into the cafeteria, where Venegas was seated at a table. "They put you on AL yet?"

"Last night," I said.

"Then what I'm going to tell you won't make that much difference anyway. It's one of those good news, bad news things," he said. "And who knows? Maybe the good out-weighs the bad." He dumped some photos out of a large manila envelope, then slid them toward me. "We found some evidence in our suspect's car that ties in with your homicide."

I looked at the photos. The first was of a black Cadillac parked in the motel lot. The second was a close-up of the ve-hicle's open trunk and inside it a tan leather purse. The third shot was of the purse and its contents spread out on a utility table, I assumed at Napa PD, and my gaze caught on a key chain with several keys and a small pewter cat dangling from it. I recognized the pewter cat. It was the same as the cat on the key chain in Eve's grandmother's house. The one her cousin Lucas had given to me the night she was killed.

Beside it was a tube of lipstick, and I knew without see-ing it open what color it would be. I pointed to it with my finger. "Bright pink?"

"Yeah," Venegas said.

"Any ID?"

"This." He pulled out a photocopy of Eve's driver's li-cense. "Hard to imagine someone who looked this angelic could do the things you saw on that CD."

"She definitely had innocence down to an art," I said, star-ing at the photocopy. The good Lord only knew she'd had me fooled. And everyone else she'd ever met. It was that very innocent quality that I remembered seeing in Daisy as well, and I could see a resemblance between the two, making me wonder if it was mistaken identity, as Daisy had claimed. I handed the photos to Sam and he took a look.

"Guess that answers the question of who killed Eve."

"And fits with your hit theory. We got two dead guys who undoubtedly were both at the scene of your double homicide, which makes it pretty clear that Lloyd's involved, or he wouldn't have this stuff in his car. Can't get too much tidier than that."

"What's the bad news?" I asked.

Venegas gave an apologetic smile. "We got more time for breakfast, because you can't do your interview. Daisy took off from the hospital sometime last night when our attention was focused elsewhere. Apparently once she came to, she decided that she didn't need medical attention after all. Who knows? Maybe there were one too many Feds walking around the place last night. Made her nervous."

"We know for sure she took off and someone didn't help her out?"

"Could be. Just about everyone's looking for her. The place is crawling with Feds. You want something to eat?"

I ordered toast and coffee. Scolari had a bowl of oatmeal.

"Did she have any visitors last night?" I asked.

"One," Venegas said. "Tall blond guy, according to the nurse. They wouldn't let him in, but who knows?"

"Joshua?" I said.

"Don't know. If it was him, makes you wonder if he came to help her or hurt her. But that's not the kicker. Apparently the hospital got a call yesterday from your pseudo-agent Lloyd, telling them not to let anyone interview her until he gave the okay. Which is why we were waiting around with our thumbs up—well, you get the picture."

"Great. And here I was down the hall, when I could have checked in on her . . ."

"With your mind on other things," the detective said.

"Besides," Scolari replied. "It wasn't like she was suspected of being a flight risk. Daisy was a victim, last we heard, and her daughter was missing. And Agent Lloyd was an agent as far as we knew, too."

"We put out a BOL on her," Venegas said. "But other than that, we don't have much to go on."

"What else can go wrong?" I asked.

"The judge could refuse to sign the search warrant for the Brewer place."

I looked at Venegas and he held up his hands. "Just kidding. Anytime you two are ready, we'll head over."

I stood, pushing my chair back. "Forgot my jacket in Torrance's room."

"We'll wait for you in the parking lot," Venegas said.

I took off down the hall, trying to think about everything, piece it all together. According to the two FBI agents, Lloyd was on administrative leave, and had been for quite some time, which meant he was suspected of doing something wrong in the past.

So if they didn't send him to get the case, how did he know I had it?

The Tremaynes. He had to have contacted them. Either they were working with him, or he had convinced them he was legitimately on the case.

And there was that little matter that he came specifically to kill me, which meant he was worried about something that I was on to. But what? Obviously he thought I was a threat to him, because I was certain it was me and not Torrance they were after. And what of Lillian O'Dell's drug trafficking history? Could she possibly be behind this? She seemed so nonthreatening, just like her daughter, Daisy. *In the world of friends and enemies . . .* I thought as I neared Torrance's room, then heard Mathis's voice coming from within.

"What the hell were you thinking, Mike? You're this close to leaving for the FBI."

My first thought as I stepped into the room was that Torrance was awake. A good sign.

"It was a mistake," Torrance said. "I never should have been there—"

I froze in the doorway as he and Mathis stared at me.

It was a mistake. His words echoed in my head and all I could do was stand there. *Move,* I told myself. *Move.*

"I . . . forgot my jacket," I said. I went in, grabbed it.

"Kate . . ." Torrance's face was pale, his expression stricken.

I tried to smile, act like it was no big deal. I'd heard something I shouldn't have, and I wished myself a million miles away.

It was a mistake.

"I have to go. I'm late," I said, then turned on my heel.

"Kate, stop."

But I didn't, and I knew it wasn't fair. It wasn't like he could get out of bed, drag his IV after me.

"Gillespie," Mathis called out. I ignored him too, hurrying down the hallway.

What did I expect? I was the one who had initiated all this. I was the one who had practically forced him to my room with all my talk of let's sleep together. I didn't want to be anyone's mistake, I told myself, shoving open the doors and stepping outside into the cool morning air. I saw the others in the parking lot and strode that way, determined not to let it get to me. Apparently I failed.

Scolari handed me his thirty-eight, which I tucked into my waistband. "What's the matter?"

"Nothing," I said. "Just tired."

He narrowed his gaze, then glanced up at the hospital. "Torrance doing okay?"

"Fine. Mathis is up there with him. Where'd you park?"

He pointed. "You sure you don't want me to drive?"

"Positive. Let's go."

We arrived at the Brewers' house but had to park a good ways down the road due to the line of dark-colored sedans already there. "Guess Napa PD pulls out all the stops," Scolari said.

Detective Venegas's partner met us as we walked up. "So much for serving our search warrant," he said.

"What's going on?" Venegas said.

"FBI came by and pulled rank. They got a federal judge to sign a warrant, because of their rogue agent. Won't let us near the place. I tried to call you. Couldn't get through, so I figured you must still be at the hospital."

"Having breakfast," Venegas said. He looked mildly annoyed but didn't seem too worried.

I, however, was. "This is the second time the Feds have taken over this case."

"First," his partner said. "Lloyd was an impostor."

"Then how the hell did they hear about it?" I asked, pointing to the Brewer house. "How the hell did they know you were going to do a search warrant on this place?" I looked at Venegas to watch his reaction. "How the hell did they know that Lloyd had been killed?"

"They showed up at the scene."

"You call them? Because when I left there, I didn't even know who we'd shot. It was dark. The lamp broke."

The two Napa PD detectives looked at each other, then at the house in question. "Son of a . . ." Venegas said, drawing his gaze back to me. "What the hell have you gotten mixed up in?"

26

I watched the FBI agents as they stood in the front of Brewer's property. "I don't know what I've gotten mixed up in," I said. "But I'm not going to find the answers standing here."

I saw Morley and Thompson conversing with two other agents I hadn't met before, both men gray-haired and balding, the shorter of the pair holding a clipboard. I walked up to them.

"Inspector Gillespie," Morley said. "What can we do for you?"

"I have some questions, if you don't mind."

He glanced at the shorter agent, who gave a slight nod as he wrote something down, then said, "We have a few minutes."

"I'd like to know how you knew about the shooting last night. And what you're doing here searching the Brewer house."

"I wish we could tell you," the shorter agent said, still looking at the papers on his clipboard. "But that information is classified."

"Well, classify *this*," I said. "My partner was shot last night by one of *your* agents. Now I'd like to know how the FBI *knew* he'd been shot if he wasn't working on behalf of the Bureau. Because if your men were hovering that close, then they must have been watching him. And if they were watching him, then why the hell did he and the bastard with him manage to break down my door and start shooting?"

The shorter agent handed the clipboard to Thompson, then said, "This looks fine. Get a subpoena to the phone company. I want a record of every call that came in or out of this place during the last few months."

"Yes, sir." Thompson took the clipboard and headed to one of the vehicles parked in the cul-de-sac.

When he left, the agent looked up at me, and there was no doubt from his expression that he was the agent-in-charge—that, and his ID card, hanging on a chain around his neck, which had "SAC" emblazoned across it. "You have to understand our position," he said. "This is a sensitive investigation involving high-level people, one we've been working on for quite some time."

"And you have to understand my position. If I don't get some answers, I'm going to make sure there's a very *public* investigation as to why my partner is lying in that hospital with a bullet hole in his side."

The SAC pressed his lips together, clearly displeased. I didn't care at that point. I had an agenda, and I wasn't leaving until it was met.

He narrowed his gaze at me. "What I'm about to tell you is confidential, the culmination of months of investigation by Morley, Thompson, and a number of other agents. If it gets out, there are those, even in your DA's office, who may tip off our suspects," he said, making me wonder if he was referring to Reid somehow, and hoping he wasn't.

"We'd turn up a lead," he continued, "only to be one step behind, no matter what we did."

"Sounds familiar," I said.

"Yes—well it was Morley who finally suggested that maybe someone within the Bureau was involved, someone familiar with the investigation. He suspected Lloyd, and he and Thompson were following him last night."

"We don't know," Morley said, "whether Lloyd realized he was being tailed. Thompson was on point, but lost him when a car passed him, cutting him off. We split up, hoping to locate him. We didn't discover he had turned into the motel lot until we heard the sirens. And by then it was too late."

"Unfortunately," the SAC said, pulling out his pager and checking the message, "that's all the information we can release right now. I spoke with your lieutenant this morning to make him aware of what is going on. If you'll excuse me, I need to make a call."

He replaced his pager on his belt, then took out his cell phone and stepped away.

I stood there a moment, looking after him when Morley said, "We're about to be run over." A white van pulled into the gravel drive, and Morley guided me to the grass as it stopped and two agents got out.

The van separated us from his boss, so I decided to take the moment to query Morley out of the SAC's hearing. "What were you doing at the Black and White Ball?" I asked, as we watched the agents unload equipment from the van.

"The same as you, Inspector. Looking into Eve's death. Which is why I had to pretend it wasn't a Bureau matter when her father approached me."

"So Lloyd killed Eve?" I asked, even though I'd seen the evidence in the trunk of his car.

"No doubt about it."

"Why?"

He looked at me, shoving his hands in his pants pockets, and at first I thought he wouldn't answer, until he glanced toward the SAC, then back. His voice low, so as not to be overheard, he said, "Eve was going to turn state's evidence. Apparently there was more to her operation than just sex."

"Blackmail?"

"We now believe Lloyd was using the images to ensure that the men depicted would introduce a certain bill, make a generous donation, overlook something in an investigation. It all depended on their professions . . . and their pocketbooks. Why do you think Lloyd was so intent on asking you where the other CDs were? There was money to be made, but if she testified . . ."

"You're saying she was killed to keep her from testifying?"

"Precisely."

That would certainly put a hole in the mistaken-identity theory that Daisy had posed. "What about Daisy and the kidnapping of her daughter? And why are you so intent on searching this house?"

"Let's just say the SAC is not totally convinced that her attack and the kidnapping are real. Personally, I think Joshua Redding is behind it."

"Why is that?"

"His position working for Eve's grandmother gave him access to both houses. Tremayne alleges that Joshua tried to blackmail him. Another theory is that Nick Paolini is involved. That perhaps he has been the force behind Lloyd's blackmail operation and that maybe Redding was a simple pawn, trying to horn in on the action, or make a name for himself."

"And what do you hope to find in the house?" I asked.

"Records that will tie all this to Paolini," he said, his gaze straying to the SAC, who was directing the newly arrived agents into the house. "I better get going before I'm missed." He started off, then stopped after a few feet. "You know, there is one thing you might check on your end."

"What's that?"

"Find out which of the Tremayne clan brought Lloyd into the investigation." He gave a shrug. "Who knows? Maybe it's got nothing to do with Paolini at all."

He returned to the house and I made my way through the myriad government sedans to where Scolari and the Napa detectives were waiting. "Any luck showing the lineup to the neighbor's husband?" I asked.

"Yeah," Venegas's partner said. "He met us as we pulled up. Positive ID on Joshua Redding being at the house the morning after the murder."

"Seems to me," Venegas said, "if Daisy reported him missing and he was at her house that same day, she'd be a bit suspect. That maybe Daisy was lying about him being missing to begin with? Maybe her kid's not even missing and she's in on this plot the FBI's investigating?"

"It would seem that way after all this," I said, thinking about what Morley had told me. "She was in my office that morning doing a damn fine job of not knowing Joshua Redding's whereabouts and playing his grieving wife. But for all that she's an accomplished actress, there was a definite moment of shock when she came to the morgue."

"That it wasn't Joshua?" Scolari asked.

"Exactly," I said, recalling her expression.

"You think her daughter really is missing?"

"She definitely sounded upset about that," I said, as we walked back to our cars. I looked over at the Brewers' house, watching the agents move in and out, ignoring us as we stood there. "You let me know if they find anything of significance?" I asked Venegas.

"Soon as they let *me* know."

We all knew that wouldn't materialize and so said our good-byes. By the time we left, I was running on empty. I put my keys in Scolari's hands. "Do me a favor—get me back to the Hall in one piece?"

I slid into the passenger seat, staring out the window, trying not to think about anything but the trees and the grass. Scolari, unfortunately, had other ideas.

"You want to tell me what's going on between you and Torrance back there?"

"Not really."

He gave an exasperated sigh. "You and Torrance ever sleep together before last night?"

I said nothing.

"Didn't think so."

"And how would you know?" I asked, perturbed.

"I sat across the desk from you for a year. I know you."

"My luck. Everyone seems to know me but me."

"Yeah, and I know Torrance well enough to figure out his being there was out of character for him."

I looked over at Scolari. "What do you mean by that?"

"You telling me he didn't know you were lying to him about going to Napa?"

I slid farther into my seat, feeling guiltier than ever. And then I closed my eyes against the sinking feeling in the pit of my stomach as I thought of the way he touched me, kissed me. "I don't want to talk about this."

"You want me to pretend I didn't see what I saw last night? Because then I'll have to pretend I didn't see you being upset when you came down from his room this morning."

I closed my eyes. "He told Mathis his being there was a mistake. I walked in on them and heard Mathis ask him what the hell he was doing there."

There was a long stretch of silence, then, "You ever know Torrance to do anything on a whim?"

"No."

"Because in my book, that's how people make mistakes. They do things on a whim. You walked in on the middle of a goddamned conversation, Kate. And knowing you, you didn't stick around to find out what it was, did you?"

"I saw the look on his face. It pretty much said it all."

"Maybe you better ask him what he meant, is all I'm saying."

He looked over at me, reminding me right then of my father, chastising me for something, and I closed my eyes, thinking I'd catch a nap. But as I drifted off, I kept hearing the words, "It's a mistake . . . a mistake . . . a mistake . . ." And then it was Eve's face I saw, looking at me over her makeup mirror. "You're making a mistake, Kate."

"No," I said, holding up the photos she'd dropped. Photos I was never meant to see. "*You* made the mistake. If you're trying to blackmail my father, he'll never pay."

"This isn't about money."

"What is it, then?"

"Nothing to worry about. I'm going to add him to my collection."

"Your what?"

"My photo album. Practice makes perfect. I needed to know if the camera worked. I needed to know if I was convincing. Basically I wanted to see if it could be done," she said, looking into her mirror, using her finger to touch up a spot on her bright pink lips. "And it can . . ."

She looked at me again and smiled. "It's all about power . . ."

I woke with a start, confused about where I was as the car jerked to a stop.

"You okay?" Sam asked.

"Yeah. What happened?"

"Idiot in front of us decided he missed his turnoff to Sausalito."

I stared out the window, thinking about Eve, her words echoing in my head: "It's all about power . . ."

Paolini had power, I thought, as the Golden Gate Bridge emerged from the fog. Was he behind any of this? I started thinking about all the people we had contacted since Eve was killed. All the people who now seemed to be missing. Joshua's mother. Joshua. Daisy's mother. Daisy.

And most important, Daisy's daughter, Bonnie.

Traffic came to a halt and as we sat there, inching our way toward the bridge, I became worried. The FBI seemed to be more involved in the political scandal and fallout, trying to pin things on Paolini—at the expense of a child who might be missing and in danger. Maybe Paolini was behind it, maybe Joshua was behind it. What mattered was that the child was still missing and I had a direct link to one of the suspects.

I took out my cell phone, then pulled out the card Paolini had given to me at Eve's funeral, calling the number on it.

"What are you doing?" Sam asked.

"Calling Paolini. Daisy and Joshua were in a car registered to him. If there's something that the FBI overlooked, I can almost guarantee that Paolini hasn't. And whatever he knows about all this, I intend to find out," I said as I waited for the call to connect.

"Inspector," Paolini said after I identified myself. "To what do I owe this pleasure?"

"To the fact that you've withheld some important information from me in this case."

That netted me only silence.

"Look," I said. "I have a partner who's lying in a hospital room with a side full of lead that was meant for me. I've got a six-year-old child who has allegedly been kidnapped and her mother out there who may be in danger. Surely even you have scruples when it comes to women and children?"

"I am thinking a crab cocktail would be nice. Alioto's?"

I glanced at my watch. Nine-forty-five. "When?"

"Ten, fifteen minutes."

"I'll be waiting."

27

We drove straight to Fisherman's Wharf and as we got out of the car, my phone rang.

It was Andrews, and he did not sound happy. "Tell me you're on your way back to the city."

"Um, yeah. Why?"

"One, because you should have been here by now. Two, because I wanted to let you know what the CSIs came up with. They matched most of the recent negatives. You were right—they were chronological, which made it easy to figure out which photo was missing. Looks like what Eve did was take a suggestive but clean shot for her book, followed by more explicit photos which resemble what you had on that CD. You'll never guess whose photos they found."

"Whose?"

"None other than the man who is running for Governor. Senator Harver."

So much for Harver's clean, conservative platform. "Any word on Bonnie's kidnapping?"

"Missing Persons is still on it. The SAC from the FBI called me this morning. He thinks it was a setup to take the attention away from Joshua Redding's blackmail scheme. That he has the kid stashed somewhere," he said, just as a few sea lions started barking. "Where the hell are you?" he asked.

"Fisherman's Wharf . . . I was getting hungry. Starved, in fact."

"Gillespie, you're on AL. Now get back to the Hall before you get into trouble."

"What trouble could I possibly get into here?"

"Gillespie . . ."

I scraped my finger across the speaker of the phone. "Bad connection. Let me grab a quick shrimp cocktail and I'll get right over there."

I turned off the phone before he could order me off as Scolari and I walked through the parking lot toward Alioto's. The restaurant was situated in the middle of Fisherman's Wharf, one of the quintessential tourist attractions of the city, and undoubtedly why Paolini had chosen it. We wouldn't be staging some arrest or setup in the midst of tourists.

We waited just outside the restaurant. About five minutes later, Paolini arrived, accompanied by a broad-shouldered younger man who wore a gray suit with a charcoal gray shirt and matching silk tie—a bodyguard who obviously favored gangster chic. Paolini, looking more the businessman than the gangster, wore a subtler navy suit, extremely well cut and from its shimmer, undoubtedly costing a small fortune. He strolled down the breezeway, his walk confident, something I suppose came from knowing we had nothing on him.

He smiled, held up his hands. "What do you want to know?"

"You bailed out Joshua and Daisy."

"I happen to be rather fond of Daisy and her child. As for Joshua Redding, let us just say that we shared the same interests. I figured it was a worthwhile investment."

"Then tell my why every single person involved in the death of Eve Tremayne is connected to you in one form or another."

"If you think I had something to do with her death, you are mistaken."

"Yet she was found in a car driven by one of your murdered employees, Tom Brewer, who lived in a house owned by one of your fronts."

He looked away and I thought I saw a flicker of emotion. "Tom was the caretaker of one of my properties up in Napa."

"What was his involvement?"

There was a second of hesitation, then, "If you want to continue this conversation, I suggest we take it where we won't be overheard."

He immediately walked back the way he had come. Scolari gave me a look that said, *What the hell?* But when Paolini's goon indicated we should precede him, I said, "Maybe you don't watch TV. Cops don't like guys with guns walking behind them."

The man didn't reply. What could he say? He simply followed Paolini, and we followed him. Farther down, Paolini stopped at one of the big crab cookers on the walkway and ordered a crab cocktail from the man tending it. I couldn't help thinking that Paolini seemed out of place in his several-thousand-dollar suit, eating from a paper container with a plastic fork. Not that I was about to tell him to hurry up and eat the damned thing. I had a case to solve. All we could do was wait as he finished. Finally he tossed the container into the trash, but kept the small bag of oyster crackers.

"Let us walk," he told me. "They can follow."

Great. I glanced at Scolari, who nodded.

"Where to?" I asked.

"Around the corner. I like to feed the gulls."

We ambled through the tourists, some watching the crabs boil and others sorting through bins of seashells. We turned right at the end of the covered walkway, then followed it along until we came to the docks. There was a small alcove with a bench where a family sat eating crab cocktail. A toddler chased pigeons so used to people that they fluttered only a few feet at his antics.

Paolini and I moved past them to the railing overlooking the boats moored in the water. A sea lion basking on the dock opened an eye but otherwise ignored us, and I watched as Paolini opened up his small bag of crackers. He took one out and tossed it into the air. Immediately several seagulls swooped down, all vying for the tidbit. They landed in the green water and waited for more.

"What is it you want to know?" he asked.

"You were telling me about your man, Tom Brewer."

He looked out over the water for several seconds before answering. "Six, maybe seven years ago, when Tremayne was running for Supervisor, he learned that he was to be a father—again. Knowing this might upset his wife, who held the purse strings, he came to me and asked if I could help. I merely set up the young lady with a job and a home, assisting my caretaker in my Napa vineyard."

"In exchange for what?"

He smiled. "I might need a favor one day . . ."

"Unfortunately for you, he dropped out of the race."

"A patient man learns to cultivate his contacts."

"Does that have anything to do with his daughter's interest in a business that brought in high-ranking clients with unusual sexual practices?"

"I see you found the CDs that everyone seems to be searching for."

"You mean there's more than one?"

"That is my understanding."

"How many people are searching for them?"

"Whoever knows of their existence would have an inordinate interest, I expect."

"And you wanted them because . . . ?"

"I'd think the answer to that would be obvious."

"Having a little dirt on some of the married politicians depicted within?"

He gave a slight smile, but didn't answer. He didn't need to.

"Why did you warn me off?"

He took a cracker and crumbled it, letting the crumbs drift to the water below, then watched the gulls peck at the bits. "I did that because you and I have a history, Kate Gillespie," he said, looking over at me. "I do not always like what you do—something I suppose is to be expected in my business."

He turned his gaze to the water once more. "However, I respect you, and there aren't many people I will say that to. You play fair in a game where the rules are not always known—a quality that I believe could be your downfall . . . as was evidenced by this shooting last night."

"Meaning what?"

"Meaning that you are up against a force that makes its own rules."

"Is that any different than you or anyone else I've ever dealt with in this job?"

He gave a grim laugh as he tossed more crumbs, then looked out at the boats, forgetting the birds for a moment. "Perhaps not at first glance. But don't forget there is a difference. Though I might not play by the rules, I am not the entity that *makes* the rules. Have you ever heard of Skull and Bones or Bohemian Grove?"

"Bohemian Grove," I said. "That's the Republican summer camp up by the Russian River?"

He gave a slight cock of his head, then tossed a few more crackers down to the gulls, a look of satisfaction on his face as they seemed to squabble over the crumbs. "Both clubs involve men of power, and rumors and the utmost secrecy. Eve's club is similar in many respects."

"This is about politics?"

"Not in the least . . . and absolutely. It is definitely about power, and Eve liked it and hated anything that got in her way or stopped her from getting what she wanted. She took photos of her exploits, and to her downfall, it got out."

"Why would the FBI be involved?"

"Put it this way, Inspector. Anyone who has an interest in Eve's legacy is either protecting himself or someone else, or buying some insurance."

"I heard a rumor that Senator Harver may be pictured on one CD."

"Funny. I heard the same thing."

Just to make sure I had covered all my bases, I asked, "Do you know who kidnapped Daisy's daughter?"

"Not yet," he said, crushing the remainder of the crackers in his palm with a force that turned his knuckles white. He looked at me, his gaze dark, filled with intense hate. "But whoever it is, they better pray that you find them first."

28

"**W**hat'd he say?" Scolari asked, once we were headed back to the Hall.

"That Eve was involved in something similar to the Bohemian Grove stuff." I gave him the rundown.

"He give you any indication exactly what these similarities were?"

"None. You know anything about that stuff?"

"Considering they never invited me, not really. I've heard it's where the Who's Who of politicians go to play, that they conduct business and pleasure on the same grounds. Come to think of it, wasn't there some scandal a while back involving the Sheriff and hookers and busing them in for a night with the boys?"

"It sounds familiar, but frankly I didn't pay much attention."

"Might want to look it up. See what you can find."

Scolari accompanied me to Homicide for old times' sake. When we got there, Andrews took one look at me and said, "You're on AL, Gillespie. Where were you?"

"I told you, the Wharf."

"Eating crab cocktail."

"Actually, watching Paolini eat crab cocktail."

"In my office. Now."

"I'll wait out here," Scolari said, sitting in one of the

chairs against the wall near Gypsy's desk. "How's it going, beautiful?" he asked her.

"Just fine, Sam," she said, never looking up from her computer. "You planning on taking me to lunch like you promised . . . ?"

I followed Andrews into his office, closing the door behind us.

"What happened last night?" he asked me after he'd taken a seat at his desk.

I told him everything—almost. The part about Torrance I circumvented by saying that he decided to come up to talk, and knew I wasn't fooling anyone.

When I finished, Andrews said, "And the FBI questioned you last night?"

"Yes." I told him what Morley had told me about Lloyd, the ongoing investigation into Eve's activities, and that she was going to turn state's evidence in the political blackmailing scam and that they suspected that Daisy's attack and Bonnie's kidnapping might have been a setup.

"What did Paolini have to say?"

I related that as well.

He was quiet a moment as he looked down, rubbing at his temples. His eyes were red, his face unshaven, and I figured he'd been up all night. "You're to meet with Dr. Clement for your post-shooting interview, then straight home."

Dr. Clement was the department shrink, and had about as much personality as a doorknob. I looked at my watch, wondering how I might get out of this. Ten-thirty.

Andrews must have guessed my thoughts. "You will *not* skip this interview. Do I make myself clear?"

So much for that idea. "Yes."

"And you *will* go home at its conclusion."

"I will not leave here without heading home." Andrews held my gaze for several seconds as though trying to decipher the truth of my words. Finally he gave a nod of dismissal. I left and found Scolari still talking to Gypsy. "I have to see the shrink, then go home," I told him.

"Now?"

"Now."

"You want me to wait?"

I glanced in at Andrews's office, saw him staring out the window. "Yeah. Maybe you can play around on the Internet while I'm tied up."

By the time I finished all the requisite interviews, it was after three. Scolari was drinking coffee with Gypsy. Andrews was gone, as was everyone else.

"How'd it go?" Scolari asked.

"Apparently Dr. Clement still doesn't think I'm crazy enough to retire on a psych."

"Only because on the insanity scale, Homicide cops are off the chart and he doesn't know how to read numbers that high."

"You find out anything?"

"Yeah, my password doesn't work anymore. Lucky for me, Gypsy's got a fondness for strange websites."

"Lucky for him," Gypsy said, "no one else is here."

She handed me a list of all the websites they'd found and I took it to my desk. Scolari followed.

"Anything stand out?" I asked as I booted up my computer.

"Not really. Paolini didn't give you any better hint as to what we were looking for?"

"Just that Eve's club, the Skull and Bones, and Boho Grove are similar for men of power, rumors, and secrecy. When I asked him if it meant politics was involved, he said, 'Not in the least . . . and absolutely.' "

"What do you think he meant by that?"

"Typical political ambiguity, I guess." We clicked through

several sites, reading, scanning, and skipping. A couple of them alluded to secret meetings with political agendas. One of the more interesting websites alluded to the men dressing up as ancient druids and I stared at the photograph, one taken by the infiltrator from quite a distance. Nothing I saw told me much, but then, wasn't that what Paolini had hinted? That what I was looking for might be there, but I wouldn't find what I was looking for?

Ten seconds later, I read one of the names on a website that listed some of the better-known guests from the President on down to local politicians and businessmen. And lo and behold, if Supervisor Standiford's name didn't pop out as one of those who had been there. "Check this out," I said, tapping the screen.

Scolari read the name. "He's the one who told you about Eve's club?"

" 'Eve's *little* club,' is how he phrased it . . ." My voice faded as I read a paragraph on a young woman's description of her summer working at Bohemian Grove. There was a photograph of the place and I recognized the backdrop. The photograph I'd seen of Eve, one I'd thought had been taken at some sort of summer camp. She had been at Bohemian Grove and returned a different woman—craving power. I told Scolari of the photo.

"So Eve had a summer job there."

"Reid said she was a sex addict."

"So she had a summer job there with a bunch of men who probably took advantage of her."

"Or she took advantage of them?" I glanced at Scolari, who seemed intrigued by my line of thinking.

"Where you going with this?"

"A bunch of dirty old politicians who can't say no to sex, coupled with a sex-starved girl who has a penchant for power."

"Isn't that what her cousin had suspected? Eve was a prostitute?"

I leaned back in my chair and stared at the computer. "Whatever she was, it was to the rich and politically famous."

"If she's out screwing hope-to-be-Governor Harver, and he was guaranteed no one would find out it was him . . ."

"And here comes Joshua with his little pictures, and starts a blackmail scam . . ."

"It's not like Harver can get his money back. Maybe he put the hit out on Eve? Or pressured Lloyd to take care of things?"

"Maybe. Andrews said his photo was in the box of negatives that they recovered from Eve's grandmother's house."

He sat in Rocky's chair and put his feet up on the desk. "They sure there's another CD out there? Or could you have missed a photo on the CD you've got?"

"Maybe I did. Who knows?" I picked up the phone and called down to Property. "Johnsen? Gillespie. I need to check out a CD from the Tremayne burglary." I gave him the case number.

"Hold on." A minute later, he was back. "Got it here, waiting for you."

"Can you do me a favor? Burn me a copy, and keep the original?"

"Not a problem. I'll have it waiting for you when you get here."

I checked out the CD copy from Property and a few minutes later, we were back in my office, popping it into my computer. I slid the door shut. Scolari stared at the photos.

"Holy shit," he said. "Tell me the naked guy who's tied up against the wall with the full-on woody and the clamps on his nipples isn't Standiford."

"That would be him in all his glory."

"Nice. Lotta people in the voting public that would like this little tidbit to find its way to the press."

"Don't lose sight of the real purpose."

"Maybe that *was* the real purpose?"

We clicked on each of the photos, Scolari making faces at a few of them, definitely reacting to the pain aspect.

When we'd finished, he said, "See anything on there that screams out you missed something?"

"No pun intended? Not a thing. *You* see anything on there that would send the FBI scrambling to cover some tracks?"

He shook his head.

"That's what I don't get," I said, yawning.

"Okay," Scolari said. "Let's look at this logically. Piece it out." He took a pen and piece of paper from Rocky's desk, then drew a circle in the middle, writing Eve's and Tom's name. He drew another circle below it, then connected the two with a line. "You got your first peripheral victim, Eve's grandmother. You got your burglary of Eve's house by Joshua." Another circle for Joshua's house. "You got your explosion." That circle was connected to one he drew for Napa and said, "Two victims there. First Daisy, then Torrance."

I tapped the first circle he drew. "We assume that Eve was killed because of her involvement with her Garden of Eden Club. If she was going to testify against someone, then we have to do away with the mistaken ID theory. Tom Brewer may have been a victim of being in the wrong place at the wrong time. The hit men followed me. They could very well have followed her. Forced her off the road, turning down that deserted street."

"We're assuming Paolini didn't order the hit? He bailed your two suspects. And I think we have to assume that anyone who wants a copy of the CD might kill to get it?"

"It seems logical, *assuming* it was the same suspects who hit Eve's grandmother's house, attacking her."

"They did say they had the wrong place."

"As in they were merely *looking* for something there?" I said. "Thought she had something they wanted? Something maybe Eve or Tom told them right before they were killed?"

"Hoping the suspects might go away, leave them alone? I don't have it. It's at such-and-such a location?"

"That could work," I said, studying the chart. I pointed to the Napa circle. "Daisy said she had something. She becomes a victim, and then Torrance."

"Which I'm guessing was meant for you."

"But why?"

"The CD you found?"

"I don't buy that. Our so-called Agent Lloyd knew we had the original here, when I gave him the copy . . ." I hesitated, studying the chart.

"What?" he asked.

"Hold on, I'm thinking." I was trying to recall what the agent had said. Finally it came to me. "Lloyd had to have been at every one of these places at one time or another. And when Lloyd came here to the Hall, he wanted to know if I'd found any other CDs."

"Pretty much confirming this isn't the only one?"

"Paolini said the same thing. I'm thinking that if Lloyd went to the trouble of trying to kill me, then he, or whoever he works for, thought I had something incriminating, or that I might discover it . . . or maybe I already had?"

"Okay, all we gotta figure out is what it was you didn't figure out."

I picked up the chart that Scolari had drawn, looking at each of the locations, but the longer I stared at it, the harder it was to concentrate. The day, the night before, had finally taken its toll on me and I doubted there was enough coffee to keep me awake. "I can't think," I said, stifling a yawn. "I know I'm missing something, but what, I haven't a clue."

"I'll drive you home," Scolari said. "Wouldn't want you falling asleep at any red lights."

We'd both done that on occasion after working an all-nighter. "Okay," I said, grabbing my jacket. I slipped it on. "Ready anytime you are."

I started for the door and my phone rang. I looked at it, frankly too tired to care who might be calling.

"You gonna get that?" Scolari asked.

I sighed. What I really wanted to do was go to bed. "Yeah," I said, returning to my desk and picking up the phone. "Gillespie, Homicide."

"Are you the police officer who came to my grand-mother's house?"

I hesitated at how young the voice sounded. "Is this Bonnie?"

There was silence on the other end. I remembered my nephew at that age, nodding into the phone, not realizing that the person on the other end couldn't hear his nod. "Bonnie?" I said.

"What?"

"Where are you?"

"Over the sun triangle next to the bell."

There was a loud clunking noise, as though the phone had been dropped. Then I heard crying. I waved to Scolari, motioned him over to the phone. He put his ear next to mine and listened in.

"Bonnie?" I asked. "Bonnie?"

"Hello?" A woman's voice. Frightened. Bonnie crying in the background.

"Who is this?" I asked.

"Um, it's Daisy."

"What's going on?"

"Um, I'm supposed to tell you to bring the other CD."

"What other CD?"

There was a hesitation, then, "J-just the other one. You're, um, supposed to know what it is."

"Bring it where?" I asked. "I don't have it."

"They'll . . . k-kill us if you don't bring it. No one else . . . just you," she said, then started crying. *"Please . . ."*

"Daisy?"

The line went dead.

29

I listened to the dial tone. "Son of a bitch," I said, hanging up.

"Take it easy," Scolari replied. "You can't control everything."

I pulled off my jacket and hung it up on the rack, then took a couple of paces. "Who the hell is behind this?"

"Seems to me you got a couple choices. Who's still outstanding?"

"Harver, Standiford, maybe Paolini, and then there's Joshua and, I hate to say it, Daisy."

"Good a suspect as any."

"It's her own daughter."

"And this is the first time a mother's ever been suspect?"

"No. But she was crying when she called me yesterday to say Bonnie was gone. And now that I think about it, when Torrance and I had them stopped after the ball, she seemed worried then. Like Bonnie was missing then, but she was afraid to say . . ."

I thought about my interview with her. Her behavior. Then her call the next day. "She said that they told her if she didn't say anything, they'd bring her daughter back. She never said a word. That shows *some* maternal concern to me."

"Or maternal stupidity. She shoulda reported it to begin with."

I threw him a dark look.

"Okay, so maybe she's not suspect *numero uno*. But Joshua could be."

I sent an alphanumeric page to Andrews from my computer, telling him to call me on Rocky's line as soon as possible. I wanted to keep my phone line open in case Daisy or Bonnie called back.

About two minutes later, Rocky's phone rang. Lieutenant Andrews. "What's going on, Gillespie?"

I told him about the call.

"Get Shipley and Zim there, Code Two. Notify Missing Persons. I want them in as well. I'll be there in about ten. And see if you can raise Markowski. If he feels up to it, we could use him."

About ten minutes later, I was briefing a full office. Lieutenant Andrews, Shipley, Zim, as well as Pierce and Girard from Missing Persons. Markowski showed about five minutes into it, looking as though he'd spent two weeks in the Bahamas without sunscreen.

Once I finished, Andrews asked Pierce, "You have any suggestions?"

"Normally I'd say do a door-to-door in the neighborhood where Bonnie was last seen, but do we even know *where* she was last seen?"

Andrews looked at me.

"The last we know of," I said, "is at Daisy's mother's house. Lillian O'Dell saw Bonnie the day before yesterday."

"Only one problem," Pierce said, "Lillian O'Dell disappeared right after Daisy reported the kidnapping, so we have no way of verifying anything from her."

"Could she be a suspect?" Andrews asked.

"Why not?" Rocky replied. "She coulda kidnapped the kid to raise her the right way, out of Daisy's wild lifestyle."

"What she did report," I said, "is that Daisy allegedly

picked up the child from her house. And Daisy called me from Napa to report the abduction."

Pierce said, "I suggest we get some of our volunteers and do a door-to-door around the grandmother's, then contact Napa PD and see if they can do the same. If we're lucky, someone might have seen something. A car, suspect loitering around, who knows."

"Joshua Redding was driving a black BMW up in Napa," I said.

Pierce wrote that down. "Okay, that could be something. How about in the phone call? You hear anything that might clue us in on where they were calling from?"

I shook my head. "No. Only what Bonnie told me before the phone was taken from her." I remembered the noise of the phone hitting something and her crying, and my heart wrenched at the thought that someone might have hurt her, never mind that she was probably scared to death. "She said she was 'Over the sun triangle next to the bell.' "

"How old is she?" Shipley asked.

"Six," I said.

Shipley smiled. "Sounds like something my kid would say. You know, makes no sense whatsoever, until you see what they're talking about, then it makes perfect sense."

Andrews was jotting notes on the dry-erase board, the pen squeaking as he wrote. "How about this other CD?" he asked me when he'd finished writing.

"I'm assuming there is at least a second CD. One that is more incriminating than the CD we found."

"Any ideas where?"

"Not yet."

"Okay, let's assume you do know what it is and you found it. What then?"

"She said I'm to bring it. No one else, just me."

Andrews said, "Not likely we're going to let that happen.

But we can let them believe it for the time being. Any indication where?"

"None. I'm assuming she'll call back."

"Shipley, you call the phone company for a trap?"

"Already done."

Andrews looked at me. "You are on AL. You shouldn't be working this after the shooting last night."

"I realize that," I said.

"How do you feel?"

"I couldn't imagine not working it."

He gave a sharp nod. "Markowski? Doctor release you for duty?"

"As of this morning."

"You think you're up to this?"

"I'm like Gillespie. That kid was as cute as a button. No way I'm not working it."

My phone rang. The entire room stilled. I waited until Andrews gave the signal to answer and then I picked up. "Gillespie, Homicide."

". . . You have an hour."

"Daisy?"

"An hour to find it. I-I'll call you back."

She hung up.

I related the call, then said, "We need a negotiator doing this."

Andrews stood. "You're right. Gypsy? Contact the Op Center, tell them to get HNT down here. I want a hostage negotiator to answer her phone the next time it rings. Make it Code Two. And someone get a damn recorder on her line. Shipley, check with the phone company, see if they got anything on that last call."

"Ten-four," he said.

To me Andrews said, "You got any ideas on where to look for this thing?"

"Eve's house is the only place I can think of. Maybe we missed something when we searched it the first time? Or overlooked it in the evidence we booked?"

Andrews rubbed at his temples. "We'll need to go through the evidence you booked. As for searching the place again . . . an hour isn't very long."

"We have a search warrant," I said. "Gypsy probably still has a copy of it on her computer. We can use it as a boiler-plate."

Andrews looked at Gypsy for confirmation.

"It's there," she said. "Change a few things . . . the date, what we're looking for . . ."

"Call HNT for the negotiator first. Then call down to the court and get a magistrate to stand by for a signature. As soon as the warrant is finished, Gillespie can take it down and walk it through."

"Yes, sir."

Ten minutes later, search warrant in hand, I was back in Homicide. The two from the Hostage Negotiation Team were at my desk. Steve Carillo, older guy about Rocky's height, and next to him Lee Patterson, tall, blond. Both had been negotiators for years. Andrews was briefing them, but stopped when I walked in.

"Everything set?" he asked.

"Set," I said.

"You, Markowski, Shipley, and Zim on the search." He glanced at Scolari's thirty-eight tucked in my waistband. "You have another duty weapon?" he asked, since Napa PD had mine.

"In my locker."

"Get it before you leave. Okay, if there's nothing else, then everyone knows what to do. No one plays Lone Ranger," he said. "I've called out SWAT in case we find the kid and need to stage a rescue op. Let's go."

Eight minutes later, the four of us were standing in front of Eve's house and I looked up at the second story window that faced her grandmother's courtyard in the front. I hadn't noticed it before, but it was tinted with a film that reflected the church tower from the street behind us. I figured Eve had the film placed so that if anyone looked up, they would simply assume it was there to reflect the sun, never guessing that the window was blocked off from the inside, the room soundproofed.

We walked up the steps and Rocky tried the door. "Locked," he said. "And no offense, but I ain't gonna kick it in."

Couldn't blame him there. "Zim. Go next door, see if we can borrow the spare key from Mrs. Harrington."

"Check." Zim headed across the grass, then around the boxwood hedge to Eve's grandmother's house. He returned a minute later, the key dangling from the pewter cat charm. "Mrs. Harrington wasn't home, but Lucas was. And the Tremaynes were there, too. They didn't look real happy when he handed over the key. I have a feeling they're headed this way." He unlocked the door and opened it. "Guess someone's packing her stuff up," he said.

The entryway was filled with cardboard boxes, most empty. Zim had a camera and started snapping the before photos. I walked in to look around. Framed paintings had been removed from the walls. Knickknacks had been removed from the shelves. Most everything had been packed. I laid a copy of the search warrant on the dining room table.

"What's going on here?"

We all turned to see J. T. Tremayne and his wife, Faye, standing in the entryway.

Tremayne took one step toward us, his gaze narrowed. "I said, what is going on here?"

"We have a search warrant," I said, nodding to the copy I'd set on the table.

J. T. walked over to the table, limping slightly more than when I'd last seen him at the ball. He leaned heavily on his cane as he read the order.

"I don't understand," Faye said. "Why would you be searching Eve's house again?"

"Evidence to a murder and a kidnapping," I said, glancing at my watch. Fifteen more minutes to find what we were looking for, and if the upstairs was as empty as the downstairs . . . "I'll take the upstairs. Rocky, you come with me. Shipley, take the downstairs. Zim, escort the Tremaynes from the property."

"Stop!" Tremayne said. "You will *not* go through my daughter's house."

"If you so much as get in our way, Mr. Tremayne," I said, "I will arrest you."

"You can't arrest me."

Sometimes it surprised me how dense some attorneys could be. "I can and I will. At the moment, I don't have time for your bullshit, and unless either of you can tell us where *your* daughter is, Mr. Tremayne, we have no choice but to continue the search."

"My daughter?" Tremayne asked, glancing at his wife, who didn't look pleased at all.

"She's missing," I said. "Kidnapped. Her and Daisy, it seems."

"If you think—" he started, then pulled out his cell phone. "This is ridiculous. I'm calling my attorney."

"Feel free," I said, "so long as you park your butt in a chair or remove yourselves from these premises. I don't care which."

His wife, normally so calm, started to redden. "These are *my* daughter's things. I don't want someone else going through them."

"I'm sorry, but it has to be done."

"Then I want to be there. I insist—"

"Actually," Tremayne said, "I need to speak with the inspector . . . privately."

She looked as surprised as I felt. Tremayne *wanting* to speak with me? Why the about face? I led him to the living room.

"These things that you're looking for," he said, once he was away from his wife's hearing. "I assume you are talking about the . . . things from Eve's private life?"

"Such as . . . ?"

"Her addiction to sex and all the things that went with it?"

I waited.

He looked down at the floor, taking a deep breath. "This is not an easy topic of discussion," he said. "I know you were in here right after she was killed. My nephew told us. So I know you saw everything in that room. I felt it was necessary to get it out before my wife saw it. She doesn't know anything about it," he said. And I thought either they were both lying, or there was a little communication problem in their marriage, since his wife had clearly told me at Eve's funeral that she knew about Eve's sexual conduct, but that her husband did not.

"Are you sure your wife knows nothing about this?" I asked.

"Well, yes . . . I think, I don't know. That's not important. What is is that she was already upset with me over my past indiscretions. She lost her daughter. I didn't want her to lose her memories of how she remembered Eve, too, if that makes sense to you."

"I can certainly understand your concerns. What exactly did you remove?"

"Everything that was either metal or leather or—do you need to know exactly?"

"I'm looking for something in particular, so knowing what you took will help."

"If you walk into any adult store in the Mission District, you'll get a fair idea."

"Any movies or pictures?"

He shook his head. "There was a camera. In the wall . . ." He glanced over his shoulder at his wife, undoubtedly to make sure she was still out of hearing. "The way it was set up, I figured she was taking photos of . . . what she did. There were no CDs when I got here. I figured you had taken them in your first search."

"How did you know I was looking for CDs?"

"That FBI agent told me. The agent who came with us to your office that day."

"Have you spoken to him since?"

"No."

"Who sent him?"

"Morley, I guess."

"Morley didn't tell you it wasn't a Bureau case?"

"Well, yes, but I assumed he had changed his mind. He called me this morning and asked me the same—is this re-lated to the kidnapping?"

"The kidnapper is demanding the CD for ransom."

"Dear God," he said.

"Who helped you pack up Eve's personal things, and where are they?"

"Lucas helped. As far as I know, they're in the dumpster behind my office. I didn't know what else to do with them. You aren't going to say anything to Faye, are you? About Eve's . . . activities?"

"We will certainly try to protect your wife the best we can."

"Thank you."

We returned to the dining room, and I asked Faye about Agent Lloyd, if she knew how he came to be on the case.

"I think my nephew Lucas sent him," she said. "He told me that Agent Lloyd was working on the case and would be by to ask questions. Why?"

"Nothing I can go into right now," I said. I pulled Zim aside, since he had something of a rapport with J. T. Tremayne, and asked him to convince them to return to the Harringtons' while we conducted our search. To my amazement, they both readily agreed, leaving us alone. As Zim walked them out, I could hear Mrs. Tremayne asking questions. How long would it take? . . . What were we searching for? . . . Zim fielded each query with a vague answer that seemed to satisfy her.

On our end things weren't so easy. We had yet to find a single CD and the computer itself had nothing of interest on it. We started upstairs and discovered that the room there had been completely emptied of everything but the furniture. Not a piece of leather or a costume in sight.

Shipley walked in and looked around. "Judging from the outside, I figured this room would be bigger."

"Probably because it's soundproofed," Rocky said, "to keep the neighbors from hearing the screams of blissful pain from Eve's customers. What do you figure she's got? Three feet of insulation to keep the noise in?"

"Who knows?" I said, standing on my toes to see on the closet shelf.

"I'll get you a chair," Rocky said. He set down his radio on the table, then brought over the chair.

"Thanks." I stepped up, but the shelf was clean.

"Maybe a hidden compartment or safe?" Rocky asked.

"If it's here," Shipley said, "I can't find it. I checked behind every nook and cranny. No CDs. Not even a whip or chain. Tremayne definitely cleaned the place out."

"This CD rack was full the first time we were here," Rocky said. "Unfortunately, at the time, we thought it was music."

"Okay, so someone knew what they were looking for," Shipley said. "Question is, did they find it?"

"Depending on who they were," I said. "If it's whoever has Bonnie, my guess is no. If it's someone else, then maybe."

"There's a definitive answer."

"Sorry. It's the best I can do right now."

Shipley ran his hands through his hair. "What now?"

"Assume it's not here," Rocky said. "How many more places can we look?"

I knew he was right. I just didn't want to admit it. "Let's take one last walk-through, then call it quits. After that, I don't know what else to do."

We did, coming up empty-handed.

Shipley put his arm on my shoulder. "You tried."

"Yeah," I said, not feeling good about this. I didn't want to think what this might mean to Bonnie's and Daisy's safety and looked at my watch. It was past the hour. "Let's go."

We walked out to the front where the Tremaynes stood waiting with Zim. Mrs. Tremayne held her husband's hand and watched us file down the porch steps. "Did you find it?" she asked. "What you were looking for?"

"No," I said.

She turned her head into her husband's shoulder.

"We should go now," Tremayne said. "Lucas said he'd finish packing Eve's things for us."

"Where is he?" I said. "I'd like to ask him a few questions."

"He was in the house," Mrs. Tremayne said. "He said he'd only be a minute. You're welcome to come in."

"We'll be right there," I said.

As the Tremaynes walked into Mrs. Harrington's house, Zim said to me, "You want us to go check that dumpster?"

Somehow I doubted that anything we were looking for would be there, but I said, "It's worth a try."

"Thanks," Shipley said. "I always wanted to go dumpster diving for sex toys."

"And now you get to," Rocky said. "The perks of working Homicide. Who would've thought?"

Shipley headed to his car. "Probably a good thing they don't advertise this crap when you sign up for the Academy," he said, as he and Zim got in.

Rocky grinned as they drove off. "Was it my imagination, or did Zim look a little too excited when he offered to check the dumpster?"

"That's one of those things I try not to notice," I said.

"Hell," Rocky said, as we stepped up onto Mrs. Harrington's porch. "I left my radio in Eve's little room. I'll run up and get it."

He left just as Tremayne came to the door, holding a picture of Eve and Gran. "You want to come in? Faye's looking for Lucas right now."

"That's okay," I said, glancing over at Eve's house. I saw Rocky standing inside, looking out the picture window, staring out at the sundial in the court, his brow knitted as though concentrating. A moment later, he turned away. "I'll wait here for my partner. He left his radio next door."

A few minutes later, Faye came to the door. "That's funny," she said. "Lucas told me he was going to get some boxes and the radio, so he could finish packing Eve's things."

"Where is he?" Tremayne asked.

"I don't know. I can't find him anywhere."

"Of course he's here," Tremayne said. "He can't just disappear."

Why not? I wanted to ask. *Everyone else in this case has disappeared.* Instead I said, "Any chance he left while we were searching Eve's house?"

"I doubt it," Faye said. "His VW's in the garage."

"Maybe he's out back," Tremayne said. "I'll go look."

He wasn't gone ten seconds when I heard Shipley calling on my portable. "Got Joshua in a black BMW in front of us," he said, "heading south toward your location. I think he made us and turned off. You want us to stop him or see where he takes us?"

"Get a marked car and stop him, Code Two," I said. "I want him questioned about Daisy's daughter."

"Will do."

"I'll be there in a couple. Rocky left equipment next door."

"Ten-four."

Figuring Rocky had to have found his radio by now, I waited a second, keyed the mike, then called him. "You copy Shipley's traffic?"

I heard garbled static in return, figured it was from Rocky. But the next transmission was from Zim.

"He's taking off!" Zim cried. His voice had that unmistakable cadence of someone running. "We're . . . foot pursuit," he said, then gave the location.

Just one street over. Suddenly I wondered if Joshua hadn't made his way to Eve's property, jumped the fence. Coming to find what we were looking for? Or to make sure we didn't find it?

Dispatch came on the air. "All units, clear the air. Emergency traffic only."

"He's . . . going . . . alley! He's . . ."

"Come on, Markowski," I said, walking over to Eve's, wondering where the hell Rocky was.

I opened the front door, took a step in, then stopped, surprised to see Lucas standing just a few feet inside. Soft rock drifted from the boom box he had plugged into the wall. He was staring at something to one side of the door and I knocked on the doorframe when he didn't seem to hear me. "Lucas? Is my partner there?"

He turned, looking as if I'd startled him. "Um, I don't know," he said, not moving. "I just got here."

"From where? Your aunt and uncle were looking for you."

"Through the back door," he said. "There's a gate between the yards."

I glanced toward the stairs, wondering if Rocky was still up there—wondering *why* he was still up there, then paused. "I see you got your grandmother's stereo fixed," I said.

"Oh, it wasn't broken after all," he said. "All her other CDs work fine."

"Really?" I wasn't even sure what it was, just something that hovered at the edge of my awareness, then started to take focus. *Other CDs* . . . I glanced into the room, saw the reflection of the bay window in the large mirror over the couch. The reflection of the window Rocky had been staring out of. The church bell tower. Agent Lloyd had asked about the other CDs.

Son of a bitch. Suddenly I knew what Rocky had seen. The connection he'd made between the music, and the view from the window. Who the killer was.

Beside me the door swung open.

I took a step back.

Too late.

I saw something long and thin coming at my head. Like a cane. And then I hit the ground.

30

"Well, well, well."

The voice sounded like it was coming from a tunnel in the back of my head. Like a distant dream.

I opened my eyes, tried to focus. Saw what hit me. Someone holding it, leaning on it as he watched me.

"I thought maybe I hit you too hard," he said. "Which would be a shame. Dead bodies are such a pain."

As I moved my gaze up to see his face, everything in front of me shimmered in black and white, like pieces of a kaleidoscope. I felt sick to my stomach. I'd been hit over the head and tried to reach up to see if I was bleeding. Couldn't move my hands from behind me. Handcuffed.

I wanted to close my eyes. Rest.

But nagging at my senses was a sound I couldn't place. Something I knew I should be worried about. I struggled against the cuffs. Useless.

Stop. Breathe slow. Don't let it get to you. Breathe. And when I did, colors returned. Things started to focus.

I saw my radio about a foot from me. A lot of good that did. Just beyond it the bay window where I had a perfect view outside of the skyline beyond, where the bell tower for the church could clearly be seen, and below it, in the courtyard, the sundial surrounded by the boxwood hedge. The "sun triangle." That was what Rocky had been looking at. "You have Bonnie," I said. "You were working with Lloyd."

Agent Morley smiled. I didn't see a lot of emotion behind it. "Brilliant, Inspector. How did you figure it out?"

"You knew he had asked me about the CDs. I hadn't told anyone else."

"A slight error on my part. If only I'd known they were here the whole time."

An error on my part, I thought, *for commenting on the stereo not working.*

"Where's my partner?"

"Upstairs with the others. And to think he could have avoided all this if he hadn't forgotten his radio."

"Upstairs?" I said, thinking it didn't make sense.

"You missed the panel on the wall. There's a second room up there. Small, but useful. It made a nice place to hide a child. Eve had it built on the off chance that she might be raided. And who knows? Eve might still be alive if she hadn't been careless."

"Careless?"

"The CDs. We had a nice little business going. Imagine my surprise when the case comes across my desk alleging that Eve, of all people, is suspected of using sex to blackmail politicians."

"How convenient," I said, wishing the room would quit spinning. I was having a hard enough time trying to concentrate as it was.

"And unfortunate. Nearly a decade of business ruined, because her handyman got greedy. Tried to make a few bucks when he discovered Senator Harver leaving her little room and learned we had photographed everything. You see," he said, bending down and picking up my radio, and pulling off the battery pack, "there are some powerful people who paid us well for her private services. They would not have been happy had her photos fallen into the wrong hands. Unfortunately for Eve, it was dark out and . . ." He shrugged. "Incompetent hit, is all I can say."

"So Joshua and Daisy were supposed to have been killed?"

"It was Lloyd's idea to set it up as a murder-suicide with Joshua as the spurned lover over the affair Daisy had with Tremayne years ago. If that scenario didn't fly, then we'd set up Tremayne as the guilty party. A shame it didn't work out."

"Isn't it?" A wave of dizziness hit me and I tried to slow my breathing, but Morley moved toward me, stopping just a few inches away.

His gaze raked across me, lingered at places I didn't want to think about. "Now, what to do with you . . . I don't want any loose ends."

My brain felt fuzzy. I focused on him, saw my weapon in his waistband next to another gun. Rocky's, I assumed. "My officers are out there," I said, trying to sound confident. "They'll be coming back here to get us."

"I'll be counting on it." He shoved his foot into my side. "Now, get up. We're running out of time."

Time was all I had to work with. "How did you get my partner?"

"Same way that I took care of you and Lucas," he said, then lifted the fireplace poker. I hoped they weren't seriously injured. "Guns are not an option, so I've had to get creative since you eliminated my friends who would normally handle this side of my business."

"Agent Lloyd and his sidekick?" I asked Morley, figuring every second I kept him talking was that much closer until Shipley and Zim noticed Rocky and I hadn't come up on the radio.

"Saved me the trouble, actually. A sacrifice to the cause,

since Lloyd was bound to be upset that I'd given him up," he said, walking over to the dining room table. Still holding the poker with one hand, he picked up a brown liquor bottle and poured the contents into a teacup. "I don't suppose you have ever experimented with GHB, have you? Better known as the date rape drug? The beauty of it is that it's difficult to detect."

I stared at the cup, swallowing past a lump in my throat.

Morley smiled. "Eve used it on some of her unsuspecting girlfriends. The blackmail possibilities from those photos alone are endless." He held up the bottle. "And I used it on your partner and Lucas. And Daisy."

He took a step toward me.

I scooted back. "I don't have any problem walking on my own," I said, tucking my feet beneath me. I rose to my knees, using the wall for support. That was when I made the connection to the sound, and now the smell. Gas. I glanced at the fireplace. Saw the key in the gas valve. How long had it been on? I hadn't smelled it when I came in. Couldn't smell it on the floor. Gas rose.

I tried to remember what the arson investigator had told me. The basics. Which is why Morley said that guns weren't an option. Muzzle blast. "You blew up the Redding house?"

"That was LLoyd's second attempt at killing Daisy and Joshua," he said. "And it might have worked had you and your partner not gone in first. My plan is better. When your friends come in to rescue you. . . ." He smiled. "*If* they survive, they'll be busy looking for your bodies and I'll be well on my way with a new identity."

I looked at the fireplace. The size of the room. Less than half an hour to fill it, according to the arson investigator. Rocky and the others upstairs. I looked over, saw the door to the staircase closed. Which meant this room would fill faster. Shipley and Zim coming to look for us. Morley's comment that he was counting on their arrival . . . which meant he'd rigged the doors to set off the explosion. All it would take was one spark.

And here I stood, my hands cuffed behind me. I needed to warn them. Keep them out. Stop the explosion. How? I looked toward the bay window, wondering if I could break it.

Morley started toward me, the cup in one hand. I couldn't let him drug me. I took a step, pretended to stumble, then rushed past him with a scream. Straight to the window. I lowered my head like a battering ram. And he brought the poker crashing on my shoulder. Pain splintered down my arm. I fell to the ground. Hit my head. Tasted blood in my mouth. `

"Not very smart," he said, leaning over me, pulling me by my shirt until I sat up.

Dammit, dammit, dammit. *Why?* "Why any of this?" I said aloud, trying to keep him talking, distracted. Keep me from panicking.

Morley eyed me. "You mean besides the exquisite affliction of pain? It's a shame we're running out of time, or I'd show you myself," he said, lifting the poker to my inner thigh, caressing my leg. "Eve liked sex even more than I did, which is hard to imagine. And me? I liked money. And the people she brought in gave us both. Exquisitely painful sex, and lots and lots of money to have it with us. But the blackmail was even more lucrative, until Joshua Redding stumbled across it and tried his hand, unsuccessfully."

I barely heard. Simply nodded as though I had.

Seconds wasting. Gas building. They'd come in, try to rescue us, blow us up. Maybe kill themselves—and I couldn't even break the goddamn window.

My glance strayed to my weapon in his waistband. Muzzle blast.

I could ignite the gas.

Scolari's lighter.

He turned away, moved toward the table—and the cup with the GHB in it.

Could I get it before he could pour the drug into my mouth? Before it took effect? I sat up straighter. Worked my hands to my right, past my hips. Just reach the front pocket. I felt it. Worked it out. Turned. Hoped he wouldn't see me.

He picked up the cup. Looked in my direction. "All you need to do is swallow," he said.

The lighter fell from my pocket. Clattered to the floor.

He eyed it, then me.

My heart pounded. I strained against the cuffs and grabbed the lighter.

He froze. Ten feet away and he knew I had him.

"Are you trying to kill us both?" he asked.

I didn't answer. Just gripped the lighter.

"I'd think you'd want to know about your father," he said.

"My father?"

"How Eve lured him. What she had on him. If there are any more photos floating around . . . photos that might ruin his reputation . . . maybe yours."

God help me, but I hesitated, the lighter in my hands, my palms sweating. I know I shouldn't have, but I had to ask, "More photos?"

His smile told me he knew my weakness, my desire to preserve and protect what was left of my father's memory, if not for me, for my family.

"Photos your father would never want shown," he said, taking a step closer. "Cooperate with me and I'll destroy every last one of them."

What the hell was I thinking? What was done was done. My father was dead. "Screw you and screw the photos," I said, then scraped my thumb across the wheel of the lighter.

And nothing happened. I tried again as Morely strode toward me, his face the picture of confidence.

"You bitch," he said through gritted teeth as he dragged me to my feet. He slammed me against the wall. Knocked the breath from my lungs.

My shoulder scraped against the light switch as he brought me up. Made me face him. Jerked me around by my shirt.

The chandelier glared overhead. The lights hurt my eyes. All I could think was that methane rises.

"Do you like pain?" he whispered, putting his mouth against my ear. "I should kill you for that lighter trick, but I have a better idea," he said, grinding his hips into mine. "I'll take you with me. Share you with some friends. Make new photos. You see, it's like a game. You're the prize and I win."

"What makes you think you've won?"

"This," he said, then had to step back as he reached for the cup and held it toward my face. "Now, drink deep." And with his other hand, he grabbed me by my hair and yanked my head back.

I pressed my mouth closed. Brought my hands up behind me. Prayed I could reach high enough. The cuffs scratched the rough wall.

He stopped. Narrowed his gaze. Pulled my hair tighter. "What are you doing?" he asked.

I knew if I spoke, he'd dump the drug into my mouth. But I couldn't help it. Not when I felt the light switch behind my hands.

Not when victory was so close.

"Winning the game," I said.

He brought the cup to my lips. Tipped it. I felt the cool

liquid on my lips. My heart pounded. I closed my eyes. Prayed. Then flicked off the light.

I heard a loud *whoom!*

Felt searing heat.

Then blessed darkness.

31

"**Y**ou look like a lobster. A lobster with a fat lip."

I opened my eyes to see Shipley standing over me, beside him an EMT, and above them, blue sky.

Shipley smiled as he dangled my handcuffs. I smiled back. My face hurt. And then I remembered what happened. "The others are in the house."

"They're fine. When the place exploded, you were blown right out the bay window. Path of least resistance, according to the Fire Department. Which basically saved everyone's life. Blew open the door of the room they were in, but that was about it."

"Agent Morley tried to kill us."

"He's in custody. Well, he will be, once he's released from the hospital. Daisy and her daughter are safe. Markowski's sort of out of it. So's Lucas. Morley drug them?"

"GHB."

"You?"

"Right before the explosion. I tried not to swallow it. Don't know if I actually got any, or if I blew us up in time."

"*You* ignited that place?"

"Out of desperation," I said, recalling the moment of panic—what if it worked, what if it didn't? "He had it rigged so that whoever busted the door would set it off. Morley knew you'd be sending in a rescue team, so I hit the light switch."

"I don't get it."

"Every time you turn on or off a light, the switch sparks."

He nodded. "Not bad, Gillespie."

"What about Joshua?"

"Got Joshua as he was jumping the fence. He told us that he suspected Morley had brought Daisy and Bonnie here. Something Lucas had told him on the phone about the FBI investigating the place again tipped him off. When we didn't hear from you and Rocky, we called in SWAT and the negotiators. We were about five minutes from entry, actually surrounding the place, when it blew."

I closed my eyes, not wanting to think of the possibilities. But even that slight a movement made my face hurt. I reached up, touched it. Figured this must be what it felt like to fall asleep for about a year under a tanning lamp.

"How about we get you to the hospital, have you checked out?"

Frankly, after my week, anyplace with a bed sounded good. "Sure."

From what I was told at the ER, I was luckier than my captor. Aside from his concussion and burns, Morley's left leg was broken, and he suffered not one, but two broken wrists.

Rocky and I were given blood tests and CAT scans and were both released that same night. He came to visit me the next day at my apartment with Shipley. My aunt was in the kitchen making me casseroles and things I could just pop in the microwave whenever I was hungry. Food in the fridge and friends nearby. *A girl could get used to this stuff,* I thought as someone knocked on the door.

Aunt Molly answered it. "Oh, hello, Sam," I heard her say. "Kate's on the couch. What pretty flowers. I'll put them in some water for her."

"The flowers are for you, Molly," he said. "Kate gets the six-pack."

"Oh, well, I'll put that in the refrigerator with the other gifts. Try not to say anything about her face, though," I heard her whisper a little too loudly. "She looks a bit greasy from that stuff they made her put on it."

"Don't worry. I won't say a thing about her face."

He walked in, the newspaper tucked beneath his arm, grinning when he saw me. He made a show of looking from me to Rocky. "What is this? Keep-up-with-the-Joneses stuff? Markowski gets blown up and you gotta top him?"

"Can't let him have all the glory."

"Yeah," Rocky said. "It's tough to live in my shadow. Besides, she needs a good war story or two."

I looked at Shipley and asked, "How did you survive all these years working with these guys?"

"You just learn to play second fiddle."

Scolari tossed me the paper. "You get to read it?"

"Not yet. I woke up late."

"Couple changes on the political horizon."

I opened it up. Senator Harver's photo with the headline: HARVER TO ANNOUNCE RESIGNATION DUE TO HEALTH PROBLEMS.

"Nice," I said, as someone else knocked at the door. Pretty soon, we'd have enough for a party. The article was short and vague, with no indication of the truth behind his resignation.

I handed the paper to Shipley.

"I bet this is only the beginning," he said. "We subpoena everyone who appears in each of those CDs at Morley's trial, they're gonna have to hold a special election just to fill the vacant slots."

"Hello, Kate."

I looked up from the couch and saw Torrance standing there, his face pale, thinner.

The room around me stilled.

"Hi," I said, breaking the silence.

Scolari glanced at his watch. "Look at the time. Got an errant husband to follow, get some proof. I'll call you later." He nodded at me, shook hands with Torrance. "Good to see you up and about," he said, then left.

Rocky and Shipley both stood. "Gotta run, too," Rocky said.

Shipley nodded. "Uh, yeah. See you both around."

And they left as well.

My only saving grace was that my aunt was still here, so I wasn't *completely* alone with him, which meant I could probably avoid . . . all that stuff I wanted to avoid. "Have a seat?" I said, just as my aunt came into the room.

She was putting on her jacket, a bad sign.

"Are you going?" I asked her.

"Yes, dear. The food is wrapped, so you need only to reheat it. There's plenty in case Mike wants to stay for lunch. You'll just have to move all the beer to get to it. And I put some in the freezer for next week. Food. Not beer."

"Thanks."

"You're welcome, Kate." She kissed the top of my head. "Call if you need anything."

"I will."

She smiled at Torrance on her way out, and the kitchen door closed with a sharp and very final click.

Leaving me alone.

With Mike Torrance.

Who stood there, holding a white paper bag, looking better than a man should in nothing but old blue jeans, a black T-shirt, and a worn leather jacket.

I turned away, closed my eyes. Remembered.

"Look at me, Kate."

I did, figuring it was best if I came straight to the point. "You told Mathis—"

"You know, if you weren't so stubborn, you might have stuck around and let me explain."

"Explain? You told him your being there was a mistake."

"The *mistake* was that if I'd done my job, none of this would have happened," he said, setting the bag on the sofa table. "I wouldn't have been in Napa, because *you* wouldn't have been in Napa."

I didn't know what to say to that, primarily because I didn't know where we stood. I knew where I wanted us to be, but didn't have the courage to say anything.

"Old history aside," he asked, "how are you feeling?"

"Oh, not bad. A bit toasted. How about you?"

"There's a few things I can't do. Laugh, cough, move . . ."

"I hope you don't have a cold."

He smiled and I wanted to cry. I hated that he was hurt because of me. I wanted to take it all back, wished to God it had never happened. But since I couldn't change history, an apology was the only thing I could offer. "I'm sorry. I—"

"Kate, I'll be the first to admit we have issues. Someday we'll even work them out. But what happened is not your fault."

"Yes, it is."

"Okay. You win."

I frowned. "You're supposed to argue the point."

"The only point I want to argue is that you promised me a rain check in the hospital. Since neither of us is in any condition to collect . . ." he said, pulling out two paper coffee cups with plastic lids, "and God only knows when we might be, I figured I'd bring the next best thing." He handed me a cup. "You did say mochas were better than sex, didn't you?"

ACKNOWLEDGMENTS

I owe a number of people deep gratitude for their advice along the way. Any errors are mine. As usual, this is my fictional world of San Francisco PD, a city chosen for its diverse history. This book and the preceding books (and any that follow) are in no way a reflection of the actual department or anyone who works there. It is all a product of my imagination and meant strictly to entertain. But I could not have put it all together without the help of some friends along the way.

Way back when I was a rookie, Ernie Nies and the late Rex Hegwer, with both of whom I had the pleasure of working many graveyard shifts, were kind enough to test out a scene in this book. Little did both officers know when they walked into that house filled with gas (and that guy flicked his lighter and blew the place to smithereens), and both officers returned to work toasted like marshmallows, that it would spark something in my own imagination. (It certainly makes me wonder if that's how Ernie ended up on the County Bomb Squad.) Ernie shared with me his personal expertise about surviving a natural gas explosion.

To James A. Inman, Battalion Chief, LFD, for teaching me everything I needed to know about deflagration and other fun stuff.

To my current partner, Jeff Gardner, former Sacramento PD homicide detective, for info on homicide investigations.

To Lt. Lori Babbage, for info on DA investigators.

To Lt. Frank Grenko, for last-minute expertise in investigative matters.

To Mickey Steyaert, RN, and Dr. Thomas McNett, for hospital info.

On the technical aspect of writing, I send out the warmest thanks to Jennifer Sawyer Fisher, my editor, whose patience with and enthusiasm for my writing is beyond measure. I am truly going to miss you. Good luck.

To Jane Chelius, my agent, for being rock-solid when I need you.

To Susan Crosby, who once again came through with flying colors, seeing what I failed to see.

To my three girls, who have grown up believing that everyone has a mommy who writes books and arrests bad guys. I love you, I love you, I love you. I said it first!